COLD LOGIC

COLD LOGIC

C.J.R. CASEWIT

METROPOLIS INK

METROPOLIS INK

5629 Windstone
Cave Creek AZ 85331
USA

P.O. Box 145
Daylesford
Australia 3460

web
www.metropolisink.com

email
enquiries@metropolisink.com

I am grateful to my first encouraging editors and readers: Ron Rukujzo, Debra Moss, Anne Macdonald, Bob Newsham, David Burton, B. T. Huntley, Mary Ann Michels, Airie Dekidjiev, Margo Allmaras, Anne Wilcox, Andrew Stuart and Marsha Zinberg. *Thank you!*

My special thanks to Bill McCoy, Mike Moxcey and Alberto Squassabia for their sensitive readings of the entire novel.

This book is dedicated, with all my love, to AKR.

.

1 / Terra

"Crackers usually look for thrills, not for secrets to steal," Terra Breaux said. "Just breaking into a computer is reward enough."

Marc Elliott, the president of Silicon Silk Inc., regarded Terra with his deep-set, dark eyes. "Crackers? Why don't you call them hackers?"

"Because it's insulting to hackers. Hackers love computers and programming. Crackers break into computers."

"A cracker, then," he said, "defeated SSI's computer security, took code, and did it without leaving an electronic trace."

"That's not an easy thing to do," she said. She gazed around his office. Austere and modern, in understated gray and silver, the orderly space reminded her of the inside of a computer. Without heart, cold and calculating.

"Nonetheless, they did it," he said.

She looked back at him. "So what does your firewall administrator have to say about all this?"

"I don't know. I never discussed it with Keith."

That didn't make any sense. "Why didn't you?"

"Because I'm discussing it with you."

What was that supposed to mean?

The president and founder of SSI had invited her to Mountain View to do contract work on natural language processing. She was supposed to refine the technologies that gave people the ability to interact with computers using normal everyday language. She

1

couldn't wait to start. When would Marc Elliott finally get around to telling her about the project?

He sat in the chair across from her, silent, apparently waiting to hear her comments on the unlikely break-in. She wondered if he was testing her.

Terra shifted in her chair, uncomfortable. "I don't get it," she said. "If the intruder didn't leave a trace, how do you know that someone actually broke into SSI's machines, let alone took secrets?"

"Several weeks ago someone approached a competitor and tried to sell them a bit of our source code."

"That's your evidence for a security breach?" she asked. "Somebody *claimed* to have SSI software code?"

"Our competitor actually saw it. The code was ours."

"It sounds like your thief is a company employee."

He raised his thick eyebrows. "I don't think so. I suspect an outsider. Understand, outsiders try to penetrate SSI's computer systems a hundred times a day—or more. Our storefront on the Web invites further investigation, I suppose. Most would-be electronic trespassers just knock at the front door of the web server and run. Some twist the doorknob. A few try to kick the door in, attacking with brute force."

Terra could well imagine the cracker community being attracted to Silicon Silk. Red-hot Silicon Silk Inc. was the dominant player in the "information agent" software market. SSI's agent had the modest name of "Scout," but it was used by the biggest and the best electronic commerce companies. Amazon.com, E★TRADE, Cisco Connection Online—all used SSI's high-end, server-based information agent to collect and analyze complex data on whole groups of Web users. The company had a larger-than-life mystique. Like Apple of the early eighties, SSI was thought to be full of brilliant visionaries inventing epoch-making software products. The daredevil genius culture of SSI had tugged at her imagination, too. That was one of the reasons she was here.

"Do you think the intruder used the web server as a jumping-off point for further invasion?" she asked.

She studied Marc Elliott as he considered her question. Outsiders seemed to know very little about the man himself; he was frequently described as "private and savvy." Every picture she'd ever seen of him showed an unsmiling, fierce-looking man. Based on those photographs, she'd anticipated he would be aggressive and ruthless. A bastard. Adding to his reputation were the rumors that he was a control-freak. By force of will alone, the talk went, Marc Elliott had managed to resist the venture capital that enslaved most start-ups. A rare thing in the Valley, he and the rest of the founders still owned 100% of their company. The word was that now he refused—against the advice of the best financial minds— to take the company public because he'd have to give up a measure of dominion.

As excited as she was to come to work at SSI, she had been a little afraid of the president and CEO of Silicon Silk. His reputation had left her completely unprepared for the real man. He had offered her espresso, conversed with her about Internet security, and seemed to be intensely interested in her opinion. And she hadn't expected the real life Marc Elliott to be ruggedly handsome, either.

Maybe he just wasn't very photogenic.

"I don't know if the intruder used the web server or not," he said. "Perhaps they slipped in through another door entirely. But it's never happened before, someone successfully breaking into our network, out for profit—until now."

"Profit? Did your competitor actually pay for the stolen code, and then tell you about it?" she asked, incredulous.

"This competitor wouldn't buy secrets."

"So what's the problem, then?"

"The problem is that someone is stealing our intellectual property." His dark eyes seemed to throw off sparks, and his tight, controlled voice told her he intended to fix the breach in SSI security—personally and permanently. "Not all software firms will say no to the cracker. The thief will eventually find a company more receptive to stolen secrets. And once he finds a buyer, he'll be back to attack us again—to get more."

He leaned toward her slightly.

"And when the intruder penetrates Silicon Silk's network again," he continued, "he'll fall into your electronic traps. Then you will hunt him down."

A sour feeling curled in her stomach. "I'll do *what?*"

"Trap and hunt the electronic thief," he said. "That's why I hired you."

She stared at him, hoping she'd misunderstood his tone and implication. Hard, uncompromising eyes glittered beneath his imposing brow. He *knew*. Alarm forked through her. Had she spent six years building up her consulting business, her reputation in computational linguistics, only to be drawn here so Marc Elliott could exploit her best-forgotten cracker past?

And how the hell did he even know? *Nobody* knew.

Except maybe the FBI.

"I don't do that anymore," she said weakly, feeling ill. Her eyes dropped to her white linen trousers. Trying to appear unconcerned, she picked off a nearly-invisible strand of her white-blonde hair, and let it fall to the floor.

"I'm not asking you to break into any machines. I'm only asking you to *think* like a cracker so you can trap our intruder."

She raised her eyes to his. "I don't think like that anymore, either."

"Like riding a bicycle," he said, "I've heard it's a skill you never forget."

His flippancy about her past made her bristle. She forced down her anger; she needed brains now, not emotion, to figure out how to get out of this. The best way to deal with a corporate bully, she figured, was to bully right back. She arranged an arrogant and nasty expression on her face, mimicking all those photographs of the unsmiling Marc.

Bluff, girl, bluff.

"I expect to work on natural language interface development," she said.

"You'll work on natural language, all right," he said, apparently not reacting at all to her dirty look. "It makes a great cover for you. Develop to your heart's content, my dear, just as long as you don't get carried away and think that's why you're here."

My dear? What condescending nerve. He couldn't be more than thirty to her twenty-eight! Her resolve to stay composed collapsed.

"I didn't come all the way out to California to *pretend* to work on natural language processing," she snapped.

He crossed his arms over his chest, and leaned back into his chair. "I need you," he said, as if that statement alone was enough to settle their dispute.

She realized she couldn't bully him. He had years of practice, and she had none. She had to come up with some other way to convince him, or all her plans would go down the drain.

"Call the FBI's National Computer Crime Squad for help with your security problems," she finally said, nearly choking on the words.

"I won't be calling the FBI."

"At least let your firewall administrator know about the penetration. It's his job to make sure your network is secure."

He ran his hand irritably though his curly brown hair. "I won't discuss the attack with anyone but you. Not with *anyone.* I can't run the risk of our vulnerabilities somehow becoming public knowledge. If the company can't keep thieves out of its own computer system, how will anyone trust that we can keep the information compiled by Scout secure? I want to solve this problem internally. I want *you.*"

"My skills aren't unique. Find somebody else."

"Somebody else? I don't know 'somebody else.' But I do know you. I know your past work. And your abilities in computational linguistics give you a clever cover. No one will wonder why you're working here."

"I won't chase down computer criminals, for you or anybody else," she said.

He fixed her with a look that seemed to pin her to the back of the chair. Here was the real Marc Elliott. A man nobody ever said no to. A man nobody wanted as an enemy. Especially her. Swallowing her considerable pride, she offered him a compromise.

"Look, I'll help you set up intruder tripwires and audits," she said. "I'll explain how the traps work, and we'll figure out some good bait files. I'll be here a week. But that's it. I can't wait around SSI until the trap snaps. I won't help you hunt the intruder down if the audit trail leads to somebody. I'll only get you started. And then, unless I work on natural language, I'm out of here."

His dark eyes bored into her. "I'm not a negotiator."

"Meaning what?"

"Meaning I don't negotiate. You either agree to trap and hunt down the thief to the very ends of the electronic earth, or you don't. If you don't, you leave."

With her chance to use SSI to solidify her reputation in computational linguistics gone, she'd be damned if she would try to compromise with him any more. She stood up, and walked over to the door. Glancing over her shoulder, she took one last look out the floor-to-ceiling windows. Manicured green grass surrounded the cluster of low-slung, black glass and steel buildings that made up SSI's campus. To the west, she could see the Bayshore Freeway, to the east, the gigantic wind tunnels of Moffett Field. She was leaving the congested, freeway-bound, pale green and beige materialistic heart of Silicon Valley. And the life-blood of her career.

Terra looked away and pulled the door open. As much as she had wanted to work at Silicon Silk, she drew the line at thinking like a digital trespasser. It would be like forcing a reformed alcoholic to drink.

"Then I'm out of here," she said.

If she was lucky, she'd get back to New Orleans by tomorrow evening, and be able to put SSI completely behind her. Silicon Silk

Inc. was *not* the only software company in the universe.

So why did she feel like crying?

"I had hoped you'd enjoy the challenge of hunting down a digital crook," she heard Marc Elliott say from behind her.

She balled her hands into fists, turned and looked down at him. "What a load of crap. You could care less about what I'd enjoy."

The president and CEO of SSI silently stared up at her, his loose-fitting chambray shirt open at the neck, his legs stretched out in front of him. He looked like a bored graduate student. Only his shoulders betrayed tension.

What did *he* have to be tense about?

"Natural language processing deserves respect," she said. "And so do I. How dare you use the promise of a natural language project to try and trick me into being your cracker-for-hire."

"Re-read your consulting contract with me. That's not what I promised."

Why was he implying the contract was with him personally rather than with his company? She struggled to remember the document she'd signed. Had the consulting contract specifically mentioned computational linguistics? Maybe not. Even if she'd realized that part was missing, she wouldn't have thought it was odd. After all, why else would he hire her?

What she remembered most was what happened before she had signed the contract. How Marc had phoned her out of the blue and urged her to come to Mountain View to work on state-of-the-art computational linguistics. They had discussed her natural language work then, he had made her believe that's what she'd do at SSI.

"I take it you promised to sue the pants off me if I bolt Silicon Silk?" she asked.

"It'll never come to that," he said.

His non-threatening tone disarmed her long enough for logic to slow her accelerating anger. He was right. It *would* never come to that. She couldn't afford to be sued. Her fame in computational

7

linguistics, and her reputation as a consultant mattered more than anything else. If she ever got sued for breach of contract, especially by a major player like SSI, she'd end up with a reputation as an irresponsible flake. And that would hurt her even more than the pain of quitting cracking cold turkey all those years ago.

And she couldn't ignore the financial impact of a lawsuit. If it was just her, she might tell Marc Elliott to go to hell. She'd be happy living in poverty as long as she had a computer and her work. But she had responsibilities; she had Marina.

"I need you," he said again. "You were the best cracker around."

"Says who?" she asked, irked for being complimented for a past she had worked so hard to bury.

"I do. I've been an admirer of yours for a long time."

"You don't know me from Adam."

He chuckled. Her assertion that he didn't know her was absurd, and they both knew it. He could hardly have guessed about her past. Miserably, she wondered if he had some connection to the FBI.

She studied the brass nameplate on Marc's open door. "C. Marc Elliott III," it said. His name was pretentious and self-important. And it didn't match the sucker-punching mentality of the man that bore it.

"Yes or no?" he asked.

Was that a trace of anxiety in his voice? He rose from the chair, and his graduate student casualness was gone. He looked tough and mean.

"Yes," she said, feeling raw.

"You never would have come to SSI if you had known what I was going to be asking you to do, Terra. The only way I could get you to work for me was by letting you believe that you'd work on a computational linguistics project." He walked over to her. "I need you."

She winced.

"Your stay isn't going to be half as bad as you think it'll be." He reached out to shake her hand. "Welcome to Silicon Silk."

The callused strength of his grip shocked her. Reflexively she looked down. Scrapes, half-healed cuts, and bruises covered his large hand. What was a software company executive doing with injuries like that?

Still clasping her hand, he surveyed her silk and linen clad form. His look, in concert with his touch, made her feel trapped. She held her breath, waiting for him to let go.

"You don't look the part," he said, unclasping her hand. "You might want to dress down."

"I don't need to *look* the part," she snapped. "I *am* the part. Not all programmers are slobs."

Her eyes met his in angry challenge, but he answered back with warmth and amusement. He was teasing her. But he had no right to that kind of intimacy, especially after tricking her into working for him the way he had.

"Dr. Nancy Beck, our VP of Products, is expecting you," he said, guiding her out of his inner office, and through the outer office. "She insisted on seeing you once she found out you were coming. I got the impression you know each other."

"We've met," Terra said, not wanting to elaborate. After all, at least Nancy Beck was a decent person.

Terra had first met the pioneering Dr. Beck at an AI conference back when she was an undergraduate. She recalled Nancy's bittersweet and bizarre tales about her start as one of the first female scientists at IBM's Almaden Research Center. Still, Terra was surprised when she'd heard Nancy had left IBM for a stake in Marc's software startup. In the end, Nancy had helped mold SSI into the multi-million dollar company it now was.

"I'm sure you'll have plenty to talk about," he said.

Nancy, a tall and slender woman in her forties, greeted Terra warmly at her office door. Marc said he'd return to pick up Terra later for lunch, and left.

Terra let out a sigh, happy to have some breathing room again.

Silicon Silk's VP of Products invited Terra to sit in one of the pink-striped chairs in front of her desk. Terra sat, noting with pleasure that—in contrast to Marc's office—Nancy's space showed signs of a human occupant. She admired the still-life oil paintings on the walls and the flowered couch in one corner.

Terra updated Nancy on her career, and then they indulged in a little gossip about IBM. Nancy's sly and perceptive observations about the software industry, and the people in it, greatly amused Terra. The fact that Nancy was at SSI would make her bondage a bit more bearable.

In the middle of telling Terra one particularly juicy tidbit, Nancy cleared her throat. "Excuse me," she croaked. She sipped water from a bottle of Fiji Natural Artesian Water, rubbing her bony upper chest. The heavy gold jewelry on her wrist bounced against it. "Hmm," she said.

Nancy stopped talking, pulled her purse to her lap, and searched through it. She then dumped its contents out onto her desk. Frowning, she sifted through the debris.

"What's wrong?" Terra asked.

Nancy whispered, "I need my inhaler." She pulled out her desk drawers, one by one, rifling through them. Red blotches appeared on her neck. Her perplexed expression now changed to alarm. "Oh God, I'm having another reaction," she said. She took a gasping, rattling breath. "Need EpiPen. Epinephrine. Help me?"

Terra must have looked as confused as she felt because Nancy started to describe the drug.

"It's…" Nancy stopped and took a labored breath. "Injector…." She took another breath. "Size of pen…"

Terra could see Nancy was getting scared. Terra was afraid, too, because she knew practically nothing about medicine or injectors or reactions. Terra leapt up, and tried to think of a logical hiding place for an injector the size of a pen. She ran over to Nancy's coat rack and thrust her hands into the pockets of a blazer. Nothing. She then rooted through a briefcase stashed on the flowered couch.

Nothing. Terra heard a nasty-sounding thump and turned to look.

Nancy no longer stood. She lay on the floor, her eyes half-open, nearly unconscious. Terra didn't know CPR. Panicked, she snatched the phone and tried to call emergency. But she couldn't get an outside line. Either something was wrong with the phone or they did things differently here.

"Geeze!" she cried. She didn't want to leave Nancy alone. But either she ran to get help, or she'd have to scream loud enough for someone to come to investigate. Terra made a noise of frustration, and raced out, toward Marc's outer office. She ran inside, and told the first woman she encountered, "Nancy Beck's collapsed. Call emergency."

The woman punched the phone. "Eight," Terra said aloud, exasperated. *Eight to get an outside line?* Whoever heard of such a thing?

The woman spoke to emergency, and then addressed Terra.

"Do you know why Dr. Beck's collapsed?" the woman asked.

"She was gasping for breath," Terra replied quickly, wanting to get back to her. "Now she's lying on the *floor*."

Terra's voice must have carried. Marc and some other people came out of his office. Marc reached her in two strides.

"Nancy's having trouble?" he asked her.

"Yes! She needs some kind of drug—epi something. An injector. I couldn't find it."

He ordered someone to call the infirmary for the drug Nancy needed, and then flew out of his office toward Nancy's. Terra ran after him.

Marc took one glance at Nancy's prone form, and then sifted through the purse innards on the desk.

Terra sat down on the floor, and cradled Nancy's head and upper body in her lap. Nancy looked worse. The red splotches on her neck had now spread to her face. She stroked Nancy's hair as she watched Marc search for the drug. Her heart hammered in her throat. Should she abandon Nancy to get up to look for the drug

11

too?

"Aren't you supposed to give her mouth-to-mouth or something?" Terra asked Marc.

"No. The epinephrine is more important," he said, opening one file cabinet after the another, and then slamming them shut. "Damn!" He moved on to search the bookshelves.

"It's all right," Terra whispered, more to herself than to Nancy. "Marc's not going to let anything happen to you." Nancy's eyes were completely closed now.

Apparently not finding the injector on the shelves, Marc came over and knelt beside Terra. He slid Nancy's unmoving body off Terra's lap, and lay her down flat on the floor. Leaning over Nancy, he put his mouth to Nancy's bluish lips. He blew. Then he blew again.

"It's too late," he whispered furiously. "My breath isn't reaching Nancy's lungs."

2 / Like kicking dead whales down the beach

"**H**er throat must be swollen shut," Marc said as he bent down to try again.

It didn't seem to take long for the paramedics to arrive. Marc moved away from Nancy, and Terra let out a shuddering, relieved sigh.

Within minutes, the paramedics carried Nancy, lying still and blue, out on a stretcher. Marc started to follow them, but apparently reconsidered. He stopped, turned, and spared Terra a sympathetic glance. "I've got to go."

She heard him running down the carpeted hall.

Terra felt unsettled and afraid. Nancy wasn't going to die, was she? All in all, Terra hadn't helped her much. Medical things had always made her uncomfortable. She was ignorant about first aid, CPR, drugs. All she could do was try to comfort Nancy, speak to her, smooth her hair.

She decided right then and there to learn CPR.

Not sure what she was supposed to do next, she collected her purse and briefcase from Nancy's office. Marc had been directing her day so far, and now he was gone. Was she scheduled to see somebody else? Should she try to find out where she was supposed to work, and start doing her job? And if so, her real job or her fake one?

Damn. What she really wanted to do was fret about Nancy in private.

Suddenly Nancy's office was crowded with people asking Terra what was going on. She struggled to sound coherent. But she was no doctor. Based on her sketchy description, the assemblage concluded that the VP of Products had another reaction to kiwi. But what did that have to do with anything, Terra wondered? If Nancy knew kiwi could close up her throat like that, she would avoid eating it, wouldn't she?

She left the jammed office, nearly stumbling over the VP of Product's half-full bottle of Fiji. She picked up the square bottle and set it on the desk. A symbolic gesture, she hoped. Nancy was going to need her water because she wasn't going to die.

★

Terra decided against doing any more unpacking when she got back to the corporate condo. Yesterday she'd put away all of her clothes, and taken out some of her computer equipment and her CD player. Those were high priorities. The rest she'd worry about later. Maybe. She walked into one of the two bedrooms, the one she'd decided to use as an office. She slid a Zydeco CD into her CD player, kicked off her shoes, and lay on the bed. She hoped the ebullient, two step rhythms would lift her spirits.

It didn't work. She kept worrying about Nancy, and anguished about her job.

How had she gotten suckered so thoroughly by Marc Elliott?

When he had called her in New Orleans, he had told her that Silicon Silk was going to enter the "personal" information agent market. She was supposed to develop the interface for the new product. When she was finished, people could use computers in the same way they used a human assistant. Not by pointing and clicking, or by typing, but by speaking to the computer in their usual way. Someone might tell their agent, "Buy me a cheap blue chip stock that will diversify my portfolio. You have $2,000 to spend." The agent would already know what a blue chip was, where the person had an online brokerage account, which sectors would diversify the portfolio, and how to pick a battered stock with great fundamentals.

Yes, the SSI consulting job was supposed to be Terra's big break. She'd seal her reputation as the best in computational linguistics, and she'd have a blast doing it. After her stint at Silicon Silk, she'd have to turn down consulting jobs. Nobody would question her technical expertise just because she didn't look like someone's idea of a geek. Never again would people ask why she worked out of low-tech New Orleans, instead of out of high-tech Northern California. She'd do what she loved most, and she'd do it her way.

But now...

Jumping up, she found her consulting contract with SSI. She sat on the floor and reviewed it. Just as she feared, the contract didn't mention natural language processing at all. Marc suckered her in legally. She re-read the part about the CEO being the sole arbiter of when she fulfilled the terms of the contract. She cringed. That statement had impressed her as slightly unusual back when she'd first read the contract. But she had squelched her internal sirens; she just *had* to work at Silicon Silk. Now she was stuck here until Marc said she could go.

She groaned out loud. What if she never could trap the intruder and Marc Elliott refused to give up? Would she end up becoming some kind of well-paid technology slave to this paranoid control-freak? She slid onto the bed, and sent the contract sailing across the room.

How had Marc found out about her cracker past?

Back in her undergraduate days at the University of Texas, she had been one hell of a good cracker. Her favorite cracks were Motorola and Apple. She loved the adrenaline surge she got when she first broke into their network. She savored every triumphant minute devouring files containing information on the newest, most secret technology. Afterwards she'd carefully wipe away her electronic fingerprints. Never in a million years would she have sold or divulged the trade secrets she'd discovered. Misuse of knowledge violated her personal code of ethics. Even so, what she did was illegal, and she well knew it.

She trespassed Apple Computer's Cray one time too many. She fell right into the baited traps Apple had prepared just for her. As soon as she realized she'd been tricked, she logged off. It wasn't soon enough.

A few days later, two men, looking out of place in suits and ties, interviewed some of the computer jocks at the University UNIX lab. They never spoke to Terra. She found out later they were from the FBI. Confident that the agents would never be able to trace her, she continued doing what she loved most, night after night. She left Apple alone—for a day. Then she was back again, using different techniques, exploring different files.

She tried to satisfy her addiction by cracking Argonne's network. It got her mind off the riches at Apple, and she returned to the government lab computers again and again. After another successful night, she got a knock at her dorm room. Her stomach twisted when she opened the door to the same FBI agents. She figured she was in big trouble. The agents questioned her about her activities with computers and modems. Terrified of going to jail, she lied through her teeth. She played dumb, even going so far as to claim she hated technology. She invited them into her dorm room. See, she didn't even own a computer! She had a feeling that if she hadn't been a female, the FBI would have probed further. But she played against type—who ever heard of a beautiful female computer criminal? The agents never came back, and she assumed they dropped the investigation.

She never cracked again. But it nearly killed her.

Her thirst to explore and play, her desire for intellectual challenge, was still intact. She'd channeled all that passion into her natural language work. And now Marc had made sure she wouldn't have that outlet.

She had the skills to do what Marc had hired her for: hunt down the intruder. She was still a cracker at heart. During the last eight years, she'd kept up by reading *Phrack*. She still poked around those maddeningly vague CERT advisories. It hadn't been much of a substitute for breaking into computers, but it was safe. Now, she'd have to do more than *think* like a cracker. In order to find the weakness in SSI's computer security, she'd have to attack the network. Once she felt that incomparable thrill again, she doubted she could stop at Silicon Silk.

And this time, if she got caught cracking and tossed in jail, she'd do more than kill her career. She'd hurt Marina. The risk was too great.

Terra dialed her little sister's number. Marina was eighteen, and in her freshman year at LSU. As usual, Marina wasn't at home, so she left a message with her roommate. She wished her sister would get over her mistrust of computers and get on-line so they could save big bucks on long-distance calls.

Terra had just finished microwaving herself dinner when the phone rang.

"Hi, Honeybunch!" Terra exclaimed.

"Sorry. This is Marc Elliott. I hate to have to call you at home like this. But I thought you would…"

"Is Nancy okay?" she interrupted.

"She died a few minutes ago."

Her stomach contracted. "She died?"

"Her family chose to take her off life support. Brain damage was too great," he said stiffly.

"Why did she stop breathing like that?"

"It's called anaphylactic shock."

"What does that mean?"

"She had a severe allergic reaction."

Terra didn't understand. Allergies were hay fever. Sneezing, runny nose. Not death.

"*Allergy?*" she asked.

"Yes." He cleared his throat. "Nancy's husband asked me if I would let you know how grateful he was that you comforted Nancy."

Terra sighed. *For all the good it did her.* "Well, um, thanks for calling, Marc."

He murmured something unintelligible and then hung up.

She looked at her chicken oriental and wasn't hungry anymore. Bringing the plate to the sink, she thought about Nancy. Tough and smart—and dead. She recalled how Marc had tried to breathe air into her. How she, ignorant of CPR, had attempted to calm Nancy in the only way she knew how. Marc had apparently told Nancy's husband what she'd done. The man had some kindness in him.

She hoped Marina would call her back. Her sister never did.

Very early the next morning, Terra headed to Nancy's office. She hoped to find the peace she couldn't get by just sitting in the condo, guiltily playing the same scene over and over again in her head.

Marc was already there, wearing the same casual shirt and pants as yesterday. His face was unshaven, his dark, curly hair was uncombed. At first she thought he was looking for closure, too. But then she noticed everything from the drawers and file cabinets was stacked on the desk or on the floor. He was apparently looking for a file. Perhaps trying to solve some business problem caused by Nancy's death.

Leaning back against the wall, she watched him. He didn't seem to notice she was even there. She hoped that by being near Marc, in the room where they had both been when Nancy was dying, she could ease her terrible tension and guilt.

He hunched on the floor, pulling out the contents of a low file cabinet. Strangely, he never opened any of the files.

He spoke suddenly, startling her.

"I've torn this office apart. Nancy's EpiPen isn't here." He stared at the spot where the paramedics worked.

"You're here looking for the injector?"

He grunted assent.

She walked over to stand in front of Nancy's desk, and fiddled with the now empty Fiji bottle. What happened to the water that had been in it?

"Some of the people on this floor think kiwi killed her," she said.

"It was the only thing she knew she was allergic to."

"Why would she eat kiwi, if she knew she was allergic to it? Isn't kiwi sort of obvious?"

"Not always. Sometimes it's hidden in things like fruit tarts and fruit drinks. That's why she carried the epinephrine around with her. She had one attack before. At a company party. She drank some fruit soda that had kiwi juice in it. After that she stuck to bottled water."

"What happened to her medicine?"

"She must have forgotten the injector. Just this once. And it killed her. Extremely bad luck. Especially since the infirmary didn't have it, either."

"Was the infirmary supposed to have back-up medicine?"

"Yes," he said. His eyes now looked like black holes, absorbing all light, and all joy. Somebody in the infirmary was going to get fired.

"It's just so awful," she murmured, looking away from him, a little afraid of his expression.

"Well," he said, his tone more friendly, "I suppose that after running out on you on your first day, the least I could do is give you a personal tour now." Rubbing the back of his neck, he stood. His gaze swept over the mess he'd made, and then rested on her. "Why don't I show you around, and introduce you to Ray Iverson and some of the rest of the guys in the Applications and Commerce Group, and then get you settled?"

"Okay," she said. She supposed the sooner she got started, the sooner she could leave SSI.

He showed her Silk Cafe, the vending machine locales, and the various supply rooms of Building C. He seemed to apply the same sense of urgency to making her feel at home as he had in tricking her into coming in the first place.

As they walked to Building B in the breezy morning air, Terra finally asked him what kind of software the thief took.

"A portion of our neural network code," he replied.

"You say just a *piece* of code?"

"Yes."

"Would that piece of code work by itself?"

"No. It's not self-contained," he said.

"But even so, it's state-of-the-art?"

"No. We've pretty much used the same technology since Scout 1.0."

"So the code can't have a lot of commercial value," she said. "I don't get it. If the thieves could break into the network and take code, why didn't they steal something worth more?"

"All of our intellectual property is valuable," he said tersely. "What's important is that one of our machines was compromised."

His tone made her aware of how deep his contempt for crackers ran. Marc Elliott might need her, but he also hated her.

As the entered Building B, she felt his dark eyes fix on her like he wanted to make sure she wasn't going to scurry away. His predatory gaze made her feel more trapped than ever.

The Applications and Commerce group was housed in a cavernous, beige, warehouse-like space, subdivided into a hundred or more cubicles. Marc introduced her to some of the programmers. They all seemed surprised to see the company president and CEO on their turf. Terra was clearly getting special treatment.

Either the programmers hadn't heard about Nancy's accident, or they were unwilling to ask Marc about it. Toward Terra, they were friendly and inquisitive. She felt in her element; she already knew several of the people. She was especially glad to see the bearded, bear-like Ted Newsom off in the distance. He, like many programmers she knew, had come to Silicon Silk a couple of years ago, drawn by the brilliance of the company's founders.

One spiky-haired boy followed Terra and Marc around as they

made their way through the warren of cubes. She got the feeling the kid was worried she might touch a piece of hardware and accidentally break it. She teased her nervous shadow by stopping here and there to tap terminals and finger keyboards.

They stopped at what was apparently the boy's cubicle, where the kid took a rare opportunity to inform the CEO personally about some achievement. A cage with two rats in it sat on the boy's desk. Yuck. Biological. She pawed through the kid's *Numerical Recipes* book. As she expected, the boy suddenly stopped talking, horrified that she would touch his things. She slapped an innocent expression on her face, and looked up from the book—straight into Marc's laughing eyes.

"Mean," the CEO told her with mock severity.

She felt herself turning red, embarrassed Marc had caught on. Here she'd been teasing the kid in front of the company president, the day after Nancy had died. It seemed disrespectful. She put the book back on the boy's desk, and the kid finished his breathless exposition.

Marc walked her over to another cubicle. The occupant brought up some sudden C code on his terminal as they approached. She wondered if cubicle-dweller been indulging in some X-rated website browsing and was trying to hide it. Marc introduced the coder to her as Jack. Gangly and sandy-haired, Jack looked younger than he probably was. She disliked him right away, as he had a bad case of perfect programmer syndrome. Jack questioned her arrogantly about her credentials while he sucked on a can of Surge. She interrogated him right back, discovering he was a local boy with a degree from Stanford. As they left Jack's cubicle, she took a peek behind her. Postings from a programming newsgroup replaced the code. Jack was probably a big know-it-all, giving advice to the few people dumber than him. Or was he trying to find a buyer for stolen trade secrets?

The lax security she'd seen in A & C Group reinforced her belief that the computer criminal was a company employee, not an outsider. Most machines were left logged on, even if the user was gone. Anybody could easily walk up to any unattended computer and steal secrets. She wondered if that was C. Marc Elliott III's fatal weakness—that he assumed everyone in his organization was loyal.

SSI's Chief of Technology's office was along the outer wall of A & C. Terra knew Ray Iverson, a tall, slightly chubby fellow with thinning blond hair, from several previous encounters. As the three of them stood and talked in his office, she wondered how such a pleasant, easy-going man could have founded SSI with Marc Elliott.

"Did you give up your consulting business?" Ray asked her.

For some reason Ray's question humiliated her. Maybe it was because Marc had her over a barrel, so she didn't feel like an independent consultant anymore.

"No," she answered Ray. "I just have an extended consulting contract. I think of it as kind of a sabbatical."

Sabbatical. That is an optimistic way to look at it.

"Well, I'm glad Marc managed to convince you to come, even if it isn't permanent. Might as well start out with the best if we're about to leap into personal information agents…" Ray's voice trailed off.

She sensed that the Chief of Technology didn't think the company should be involved in personal agents at all. Disagreements between Marc and Ray about the company's products would make her cover a lot harder to pull off.

Like she needed more problems.

"Well, Terra," Ray continued, smiling. "I don't suppose you actually want a place to work?"

Ray took her and Marc over to an empty cubicle just a short wall away from Jack's cube.

"It's yours for the time being," Ray said. "I'm sorry we don't have a real office for you. We're gearing up for a launch, so we have a lot of temporary people."

Terra had noticed A & C seemed crowded.

Jack called Ray over to discuss some project, so Ray left. Terra was alone in her cube with Marc. She scanned her cube. It was perfect. Here she could easily keep an eye on Jack. He was her only suspect—mainly because she didn't like him. A C2 sat on her desk. She'd been dying to get her hands on that particular workstation ever since SGI had announced it.

"Wow," she said.

"I figured you'd like it," Marc said.

"How'd you manage to get it?"

"My guess is bribes. The SGI salesman claimed the C2 was hard to come by, and we owed him big." He glanced around her cubicle. "I do hope the crowding situation will improve here in a few weeks."

She stared at Marc's handsome, windburned face, trying to understand what made him tick. What did he care if she was happy?

"There's not a thing wrong with this cube," she told him. She didn't want a fancy office. She wanted to work on natural language processing. Which he wasn't letting her do. "Thanks for the C2 and the tour."

"You're quite welcome." He flashed her a wicked grin and sat down in front of her machine. "Let's see if that Cray symmetric multiprocessor technology lives up to its hype, shall we?"

He must need this distraction after Nancy's death, she thought. She watched him play with the workstation, intent and absorbed. After awhile, his continuing and unexpected presence suffocated her.

"I'm going to hunt down some caffeine," she told him. She doubted he even heard her.

Instead of coffee, she found the women's room. She combed out her fine, shoulder-length blonde hair in front of the mirror. How could Marc have manipulated her so heartlessly, yet now make sure she had fantastic equipment? Dabbing water on the cowlick at her forehead, she smoothed the random hair down. And why wouldn't Marc just go away?

Finished primping, she left the restroom. She paused to stare at a poster on the corridor wall. An arty image of a young man with one earring, and Perl code marching across his forehead, grinned at her. "Who is the best person you've ever worked with? How can SSI hire him or her?" the poster asked.

The best person she ever worked with was Ted. And he was already at SSI. She whirled away from the wall and smacked straight into someone hard.

"I'm sorry," she gasped, embarrassed. "I hope I didn't hurt you."

Her victim chuckled. "I'm fine. Are you?"

She took a quick, appraising look. Slick and blond and very good-looking.

"Yes. I really am sorry," she said.

"I'm Peter Donohue. I'm pleased to meet you." He shook her hand in a gentle manner.

She'd seen the name. Peter Donohue, Chief Financial Officer.

"I'm Terra Breaux," she said. "Nice to meet you, too."

He walked off, and she saw him turn his head to look back at her. His interest lingered in her memory as she walked back to her cubicle. Maybe she'd have a little fun while she was at SSI after all.

★

The next day Terra struck up a conversation with Keith, the company firewall administrator. He was delighted to discuss the network with her. Initiating conversations with people to get information about a network's security was called "social engineering" by crackers. She thought Keith's openness made him a slight risk. But he was also an expert. He wouldn't make mistakes. She knew Marc should be telling the administrator his security problems. Not her.

Keith outlined the network security of the company for her. Firewalls and proxy servers guarded the company connections to the outside world. There were apparently no internal firewalls.

Terra asked Marc to give her copies of all recent and all old files for each machine that had a connection to the outside world. Once she got the files, she started looking for obvious vulnerabilities.

She found no non-local hosts in the .rhosts file, no poorly configured FTP service, no user accounts without passwords. To be sure, Keith knew what he was doing.

Next she wrote and deployed an automatic script that compared current binaries with old binaries, looking for evidence of tampering. Day after day, she ground away, unhappy and frustrated.

Marc expected to be kept up-to-date on her search, and that made her even more miserable. He would come out of nowhere, ambushing her in a deserted hallway or machine room, and ask her what she had discovered. He was polite enough, but his sudden appearances thoroughly unnerved her. She would stammer something in response, and wish he would communicate with her by e-mail instead of in person.

Even if she disliked her cracker-hunter job, she enjoyed the crowded, hectic atmosphere of A & C Group, with its under-watered spider plants, out-of-date calendars, colorful hardware vendor posters, and blow-up baseball bats used to beat computers into submission. And after working alone as a consultant for so many years, she savored having daily conversations with other coders—even if she didn't program. Most days she'd have lunch at the Silk Cafe with Ted and Lyle. Lyle was the boy with the rats and the *Numerical Recipes* book. He was a very smart kid, even if he was young. A hacker's hacker. She thought he was the real-life model for the young man on the poster, except Lyle's expertise was in Java, not Perl. Terra, Ted, and Sherry, an older female programmer, would also go out for dinner at one of the ethnic restaurants on Castro Street a few nights a week.

True to the promise she'd made to herself after Nancy had died, Terra took a Saturday class in CPR. She wasn't very good at it, but she did manage to get certified. Having those new skills eased her residual guilt about Nancy. Except she hoped to God she'd *never* have to use her training.

She ran into Peter a few times. His mild but sexy flirting made her day. She'd almost forget how much she hated what she was doing, how upset she was that her sister didn't return her calls, and how frustrated she was at not working on computational linguistics. After weeks of gnawing tension, double and triple checking, her security investigation was complete: there were no backdoors or Trojan horse programs left by the electronic invader. Next she had to transform theory into practice, and she dreaded it. Using her understanding of the company's network security, it was time to attempt an attack on SSI's computers from the outside. The invasion would be best launched from her condo, late at night.

With a nice homey cup of herb tea resting next to her computer, she started.

Like a bank robber who uses a series of getaway cars, she electronically hopped from one hijacked computer to the next, finally using a French Silicon Graphics workstation to launch her attacks against the Silicon Silk network. The first time she knocked at the door of an SSI proxy, and the computer responded, she got chills up and down her back. God, how she had missed doing this. Yes.

She decided to pay Apple's network a visit using the same techniques. *Just out of curiosity,* she told herself, only as a little check to see what kind of security Apple had nowadays. And then after that, she'd get right back to invading SSI. But she did more than knock at Apple's door. She twisted the knob—as only she knew how to do—and pressed on. Suddenly horrified by the progress she'd made invading Apple's network, she closed the connection, and logged off her computer.

Her misery returned full force. She held her face in shaking hands. Asking Terra Breaux to think like a digital criminal was like handing a loaded machine gun to a crazed sniper.

There was no way she wouldn't get into trouble.

3 / The launch dinner

After taking that unplanned digital detour of Apple's network, Terra reasoned that she didn't have the discipline to control her cracker heart. She couldn't confine herself to cracking Silicon Silk. That was just the excuse she needed to abandon the electronic invasion of SSI, and begin work on natural language processing instead. Doing computational linguistics was the only way she'd survive her stay. And, besides, what she did after hours was her own affair. From eight to five she worked for Marc and his criminal trapping, doing everything she could think of to avoid attacking SSI's network from the outside. In the evening hours she worked on natural language, listening to Lyle's rats running in their wheel. Doing two jobs wore her out, but she felt more fulfilled.

Her search for suspects who might have stolen the code was unproductive. Just one suspect, and that was the Surge-sucking Jack. And she still had no real reason to suspect him. Only that he was a jerk.

One Friday night, she stayed late to do some real natural language work. The warehouse space of A & C was more active than usual, and the tension was higher, as the push to finish Scout 4.0 was on. After a few good hours, she walked through the landscaped grounds of SSI over to Building C, where the best company vending machine room was. Deep in thought and happily pondering her next programming moves, she didn't recognize the figure waiting on the path. Until he spoke to her.

Marc.

"Anything new?" he asked.

Startled, she blinked at him. Rather than his usual casual long-sleeved shirt and loose-fitting pants, he wore a tuxedo.

"What have you found out?" he prodded.

Why did he always have to get his updates from her like this? By surprise?

"That I'm extremely good at computational linguistics," she tossed back. "Couldn't you try to e-mail me instead of pouncing on me in the middle of the night? We're not secret agents."

"You're working on interface design?"

She nodded.

"Why?" he asked.

"What do you mean, *why*? That's what I'm supposed to do here, remember? At least that's what everyone in the Application and Commerce group thinks." She started walking towards Building C again, hoping that he would give up his third degree once they got near people.

"You're responsible to me, not to A & C," he said.

"And like Ray isn't going to figure out that I'm not doing my job? My cover job?"

"Like—it doesn't matter what Ray thinks."

She didn't appreciate his mimicking her.

"Maybe it doesn't matter to you. But it matters to me," she said. "Mediocre references from the Chief of Technology can hurt me and my reputation."

"By the time Ray figures out you aren't doing anything on natural language, you will have nailed our thief, and then I can explain it to him."

"And are you willing to tell everyone in the Group about me hunting your cracker down? My cube-mates will be wondering what I'm doing with my time, too. I have to produce. My reputation in computational linguistics means a lot to me."

"You know I won't tell everyone in A & C what you really worked on."

"So," she said. "There you have it."

They had reached Building C. He opened the door for her, and she walked through the hall and into the vending machine room as fast as she could. There were about a dozen people there, many of them probably contract workers making that last push to get the latest version of Scout out on time. He would surely stop harassing her now that they were in a public place.

She bought herself a bag of microwave popcorn and nuked it. He stood behind her the whole time. She found an empty table and sat down.

He followed her, planted his hands on her table, and leaned over. "You can't do both jobs, Terra. You can't do both well."

"Oh, yes I can," she said, ripping the bag open.

"I won't let you burn out. I need your expertise," he said. He walked off.

And how the hell are you going to stop me?

"Geeze," she huffed through her teeth.

Peter Donohue slid into the chair next to hers. "Mind if I join you?" he asked.

"Oh. Hi. Yeah, sure."

He winked at her. "So, what kind of expertise is the company about to lose out on?" He grabbed some of her popcorn, and tossed it into his mouth.

She took in Peter's sparkling blue eyes, his sexy, dark blond sideburns. Her eyes moved lower. He wore a smooth cotton shirt, cut close to his body. The pair of suspenders stretching down his chest intrigued her. He smelled inviting. The CFO of Silicon Silk had just about everything she liked in a man: superficiality, confident charm, and just a pinch of sleaze.

"I model human language so a computer can understand it," she said.

"Sort of a translator, huh?"

"That's pretty much it. It's called computational linguistics," she said.

He gave her an appraising look. "So what is it that you enjoy most about computational linguistics?"

"I suppose I find the end result—a friendly interface—the most satisfying. It's a way to make computers more like people. But then again, I do really adore the actual mechanics of translating a human being's casual communications into the formal and cryptic language of the machine. I'm working on a voice-based interface for a personal version of Scout."

"You obviously love what you do," Peter said. "And I suspect if Marc wants to point the company in the direction of a personal agent, it'll probably be the next killer app. He's got extraordinary instincts."

"Yeah," she said.

Sadness surged through her. Personal Scout was such a neat idea. Bridging speech recognition and SSI's agent technology with a natural language interface would have been incredible. Even if she didn't get to do the work herself. But Nancy had been the driving force behind the agent. And she was dead.

What if there never was a Personal Scout? Tuxedoed Marc was still in the cafeteria, talking with some guy from the Platforms Group. Terra gestured in Marc's direction.

"Why is he hanging around here, when he obviously has better things to do?"

"Unlike you and me, huh?" Peter replied, laughing. "My guess is Marc craves the superior ambiance of the vending machine room."

When she didn't smile at his joke and she didn't stop staring at Marc, Peter continued in a more serious tone, "Good heavens, Terragirl, quit working here if you can't stand Marc. He *is* the company."

If it had been anyone other than Peter who had called her "Terragirl" she might have been annoyed. But his smooth delivery charmed her. She sighed loudly and considered what he'd said. If only she *could* quit.

"I've had a tough week," she said.

"Don't let Marc get you down. That's just the way he is." Peter waved his hand in the CEO's direction. "See, now he's busy overwhelming someone else. The firewall guy, I think."

Poor Keith looked like a deer caught in headlights. "Keith will probably be here all night reconfiguring," she commented. "Teach *him* to get a snack."

Peter smiled. "I'm no expert on computer security, but sometimes I have to wonder if all this protection isn't just paranoid overkill. Anyway, back to Marc. He's like a brand-new father. The company is his baby. He thinks his child won't grow big and strong unless he's always there, worrying, managing, prodding, stimulating, feeding, scolding."

Did a compassionate understanding of human nature lie behind Peter's slick facade? That made him doubly—no, *triply*—appealing. She felt herself smiling at him. Oh, but she *liked* Peter's slick facade. Especially the suspenders.

"So, Terragirl who's had a bad week, would you like go out to dinner with me on Wednesday night?" he asked.

"Wednesday? Sure."

"Great. Version 4.0 of Scout is going to be launched on Thursday. The shareholders always get together for dinner the night before a launch. It's a tradition Nancy started. We decided to continue the dinners. In her honor, I guess you could say. I think you'd enjoy it."

"Oh," she said. "A business dinner."

"More celebration. Or at least it used to be. Or will be again, I hope. Just the shareholders and their spouses or dates. Drinking and whatnot. Not much software talk. Although maybe you'd like the software talk even more." He winked at her again. "So we're on?"

"On," she replied.

"Pick you up at seven, then. Corporate condos, right?"

She watched him walk out of the cafeteria, and admired the way he moved. His smooth, effortless stride struck her hard. That and his suspenders.

After finishing her popcorn, Terra went home. She realized gloomily that Marc would never let her get away with half-baked attempts to catch the trespasser. He'd hound her and hound her until she did it right. Eventually he'd realize she hadn't tried to attack SSI's network from the outside, and make her do it. On edge, and admitting that his bullying had worked, she tried once again to break into SSI from the outside. This time she controlled herself well enough not to get diverted into investigating Apple's systems. Leaving Apple alone took so much effort she could barely breathe. The experience was torture, and she quit before she had made any progress.

During the next few days she continued looking for unusual and hidden files, perhaps left by the cracker, without success. She couldn't find any evidence of tampering. To prepare for another attack by the thief, she made exciting-sounding bait files for the A & C servers. She installed audit programs to log every connection to the machines, and packet sniffers to monitor any potential intruder. But she didn't try to invade the network from the outside again.

On the personal front, Terra couldn't manage to wrest any information from Marina's roommate, even though Terra had been downright hostile. After awhile, Marina's roommate stopped answering the phone altogether.

When Terra got home on Wednesday evening, the night she was supposed to go out with Peter, she moved about eight boxes from her bedroom to the spare bedroom, singing to an old Linda Ronstadt song.

"I've been cheated," she cried, moving now to straighten up the living room and kitchen. "Been mistreated..."

She slipped into her lavender shantung silk pantsuit, and put on pearl earrings. "When will I, I be loved?"

Smirking at her reflection in the mirror she answered herself. "Maybe tonight."

Peter arrived at her condo at seven. He wore a deep blue double-breasted suit, and a thin indigo tie, looking every inch a CFO. She tried to get a glimpse of suspenders to engage her erotic imagination during dinner. No go.

He helped her into his little black Porsche, and they drove off to Los Altos. Peter ran his car hard; he seemed to like hearing the engine scream.

The restaurant reminded her of a French country house with its fresh-cut flowers and burgundy-patterned wallpaper. Comfortable and cultured, she felt at home here.

The party had already been seated, and Peter introduced Terra to Marc's date, and to two other SSI founders. Terra recognized David Houle as the vice-president of the Platforms group, and the other man, Steve Myatt, as SSI Chief Counsel. She slipped in to sit next to David, the platforms head, so she wouldn't have to sit next to the lawyer. The last thing she wanted was to make small talk with the very man Marc might ask to sue her ass off. Lawyers were as bad as the FBI.

Marc looked edgy and downtown in a black striped suit worn with a simple black shirt open at the neck. His date, a pale and beautiful woman with the improbable name of Velvet, exuded a helpless air, like sleeping beauty waiting for her prince. Large, hammered gold earrings set at her delicate jaw made her look even more frail. A few dark tendrils curled down from Velvet's upswept hair, brushing her bare shoulders.

A tall blonde woman arrived, and Steve introduced her to Terra as his wife, Kathy. Though no beauty, Kathy was an imposing creature. Tanned and toned, fiftyish, she wore a pale silver turtleneck and slim pants; Diamonds sparkled coldly at her ears and wrist. She gave Steve a little peck on the cheek and sat down next to him, immediately settling into a bored expression.

"We might as well order drinks now that we're all here," David said. "You know Carolina and Ray'll be late as usual." The small and wiry VP of Platforms pulled out a cigarette from a Winston package and then, as if remembering he wasn't supposed to smoke, slid it back in.

They ordered drinks, and Carolina and Ray Iverson arrived not long after. Carolina was a lovely Hispanic woman with a round face and pixie haircut. Terra liked her right away.

"Sorry we're late," Carolina said. "Ray nearly didn't make it back. He got fogged in at SEA-TAC. Of course, after busting my behind to look presentable, I would've come without him. And almost did."

Ray raised his eyebrows at his wife. "*I* made us late?"

Carolina giggled, and they both sat down.

"What were you doing in Washington state, Ray? Defecting to Microsoft?" Peter asked.

"They wish," the Chief of Technology replied. "I went to talk to Doering Group, a little startup."

"Hey, Peter! Long time, no see," Carolina said. "What's new in your life? Have you bought that Ferrari yet?"

"I thought we both agreed you'd give crap to Marc," Peter said, laughing, "not to me. I'm the nice shareholder. And by the way, the answer is no."

Carolina smiled and gave her husband a little snuggle. "Ray's the nice shareholder."

"So how's the mothering life, Carolina?" Peter asked.

"Good," she replied, her black eyes dancing. "Hard, though."

The waiter came, prompting them to look at their menus. They all ordered seafood, the restaurant's specialty.

"Your little Emily is as cute as a button," Marc said to Carolina. "David and I got to see her last week when Ray brought her in."

"Cute until she decided she wouldn't drink from a bottle," David grumbled. "Ray had to leave in one hell of a big hurry to search you out, Carolina."

"That's still a problem," Carolina said. "But I promised Ray I wouldn't regale you all with tales of my breast-feeding adventures— even if *you* did bring it up, David."

"Well, if you insist," David replied, reaching for his cigarettes again.

Carolina giggled. "Babies are a good thing, David."

Terra enjoyed listening to the good-natured bantering between Carolina and the men. Even Steve seemed to be drawn to Carolina's lively warmth, apparently abandoning thoughts of suing people's asses off. Kathy still looked stiff and bored, smiling quickly at anything amusing, like she was trying to get the humor over with. Marc's girlfriend seemed to be lost in Velvet-land waiting for prince Marc to wake her up.

With the arrival of their drinks, the party toasted the launch of the new version of Scout. Terra sipped her bourbon and watched the company founders raise their glasses one by one.

Marc started the toasts. "To progress."

"To growth," said Peter, ever the CFO, "and opportunity."

"To 4.0," SSI's Chief of Technology said.

"To long life," said lawyer Steve. "Ours and SSI's."

"To the Internet," offered David.

The food arrived. Carolina grimaced when she saw her plate. It was garnished with a brilliant green slice of kiwifruit. "They should use pickles," she grumbled, pushing the very poison that had killed Nancy around with her fork. She finally folded it into her cloth napkin.

"What is it that you do at the company?" Velvet asked Terra.

Not knowing how much Velvet understood about the industry, Terra made her answer simple. "I'm working on enhancements for the next version of Scout." It wasn't too far from the official lie.

Velvet turned to Marc. "And what does Scout do again?"

"It's an agent, Sweetheart." He gazed at her. He seemed to be there only for her now. "It collects information for sites on the Web."

Velvet smiled, basking in his sweet devotion. "I forgot what the Web is, Marc."

Terra was intrigued by Marc's ability to make Velvet, apparently an ignorant woman, feel important.

"The Web is the friendliest part of the Internet," he said. He captured a long tendril of her hair, and tugged playfully. Marc and

Velvet now engaged in silent sexual communion, excluding everyone at the table.

"The Web isn't all that friendly," Carolina countered. "In fact, it can be downright cruel and disgusting. Marc's obviously never seen the Silicon Silk hate sites, or he wouldn't say that. Hey Peter, I'll bet you and Terra both that I've seen the *most* gross thing on the Web."

"I can top you easily," Peter said.

"Fine," Carolina said. "Let's compare grossness. We'll have a contest to see if you really *can* top me."

"You're on," Peter replied.

"You're doing this during dinner?" David asked, appalled.

"We're almost done eating, David," Carolina pointed out.

"So now what's the bet?" Terra asked, pulling her eyes away from Marc and Velvet. "Grossest or unfriendliest?"

Carolina and Peter grinned at each other. "Grossest," they said at the same time.

"Who decides who wins?" Terra asked.

"I say Marc should," Carolina said. "It'll teach him to say the Web is friendly."

"No. He's too busy being friendly in RL," Peter said, "David? How about you?"

David swirled the swizzle stick in his drink and raised his eyes to the ceiling.

"It's an enthusiastic yes!" Carolina cried. "Thanks, David."

Terra started the contest. "Well, once I saw this disgusting bug website. Cockroach world, I think it was called. Thoroughly awful. Lots of pictures. Big. Bigger. Biggest. Yuck."

"That's not gross!" Carolina said. "It's just bugs."

Terra mock shuddered. "It's gross if you don't like cockroaches."

Ray laughed. "I agree with Terra."

"I know of a site that's not only gross but it's funny too," Carolina said. "Anyhow, it's called 'Microsoft bought our balls.' There's this disclaimer that says they don't know what Microsoft *does* with the balls. However, they do speculate…"

"How's *that* funny?" Terra interrupted. "It's just *balls*."

"I haven't finished telling you! So anyway, this site has this doctored-up picture of Bill Gates stuffing himself with balls, followed up with a photo of him grinning stupidly!"

"Just exactly what kind of balls are we talking about?" Steve, the lawyer, asked.

"*Men's* balls," Carolina said. "Hairy ones." She cracked up.

David, the contest judge, grimaced. So did Terra.

Now both Steve and Ray began to laugh. Marc and Velvet still gazed at each other, while Steve's wife stared off into space.

"Well, I don't get the connection between Microsoft and emasculation," Terra murmured.

"That's because you don't have *balls*," Steve said.

Now Peter made an even more disgusting offering, describing a site devoted to shrinking heads.

"Either you are both lying," Terra chided at the end of the first round, her stomach churning, "or you have too much time on your hands!"

Both Carolina and Peter got guilty looks on their faces, and denied making anything up.

Terra began the second round of gross-out. But once Carolina and Peter were finished she realized she couldn't compete. Like pool sharks, Carolina and Peter had started out slow and easy in order to lure her into thinking she had a chance. Good thing it wasn't a real bet. Terra withdrew before the third round.

Carolina cackled, rubbed her hands gleefully and then launched into a description of some weird devil-worship website.

Peter countered with a report on a newsgroup called soc.subculture.bdsm, a forum for the Internet community devoted to the discussion of kinky sex. He detailed an ongoing thread about corporal punishment. Apparently whips left marks that lasted for hours: were there any good alternatives? Yes. Peter described a few of the ways to cause the most pain with the least marking.

Terra was shocked. Was there actually a group of people that embraced the dominant/submissive lifestyle and shared torture tips over the Internet? Even worse, why would the suave Peter ever venture into that newsgroup? It didn't seem like the sort of thing he could have just stumbled into—unlike a website devoted to cockroaches. For one long minute, even the talkative Carolina was cowed into silence. She stared at Peter, her black eyes wide, her mouth open.

And then Carolina finally spoke—and it wasn't to admit defeat. "But that's cheating, Peter! That's not a website. It's a newsgroup. David, we were supposed to describe the grossest website, not the grossest newsgroup. That means I won."

Peter chuckled good-naturedly, and David declared both Carolina and Peter the winners before they had a gross-off round. Trying to recover his appetite, no doubt.

"And I'd appreciate it if you'd leave me out of this contest from now on," David added. "I now know rather more about the psycho-side of the Internet than I ever wanted to."

"Oh, it's so easy to find road kill on the information superhighway, David," Peter pontificated.

Velvet picked this moment to emerge from her reverie with Marc. "I'm in real estate," she said to Terra. "If you ever need help with anything in that area, give me a call. I'm with Coldwell Banker."

The unintentional juxtaposition of road kill and real estate agents set both Peter and Carolina laughing.

When hell freezes over I'll buy a house here. "I'll keep that in mind, Velvet," Terra said.

"Speaking of real estate, Marc, how's that house of yours on the coast side coming?" Carolina asked.

"They're doing the finish work now."

"How much longer?" Carolina asked.

"Three months, maybe."

"Are you putting in a climbing wall?" Steve asked.

"It's already built."

Velvet bit her lower lip. "I was hoping you'd give up free climbing, Marc."

"No," Marc said, his sleepy eyes resting on Velvet's delicate face. "I'm not giving up climbing, Sweetheart." He absently placed his worn and wounded hands out flat on the table in front of him. Velvet lay a conciliatory hand on his.

Terra suddenly felt bad for Velvet. For all of Marc's devastatingly attractive devotion to Velvet, he apparently didn't care that his sport worried her.

Carolina stood up and announced, "I hate going to the bathroom by myself."

Terra got up to go with her.

"I don't blame Velvet for being upset," Carolina said to Terra on the way to the women's room. "If Ray ever hung a hundred feet off the ground with his hand jammed up in rock crevice, like Marc does, and the *sport* didn't kill him, *I* would."

"I was wondering why Marc's hands were so beat up," Terra said. "What's the appeal in jamming your hand into rock, anyway?" She took a look at her hair in the ornate gilt-edged mirror. The cowlick was back in full force. "It's got to hurt."

"I would think so." Carolina echoed from the stall. "So how long have you been working at SSI?"

Carolina pronounced SSI as "sigh." Terra thought "sigh" sounded prettier than SSI—less like a Nazi organization. "A few weeks."

"Seems like a lifetime, huh? I'm on maternity leave for another month, so I'm out of the loop. I'm a technical writer." She emerged from the stall. "How're the boys in A & C been treating you so far?"

"Pretty good. Well, one programmer is kind of a jerk. I suppose I'd get more respect from him if I wore a codpiece."

"Skinny, snotty kid? Has to be Jack. For *him* you'd need a whole entire cod!" Carolina said, laughing. "I take it you knew Peter from before?"

"No."

"No kidding? I'll bet you knew Marc from before."

"Why would you think that?"

"Well you and Ray know each other. Don't all you software folk know each other from somewhere?"

"I only knew Marc by reputation before I came to work here."

"So, what do you think of His Marcness in the flesh?" Carolina asked, her black eyes wickedly alight.

Terra wondered if Carolina disliked him too. "He's okay."

Carolina raised her brows, and a soft smile played on her lips. "Your response is rare. Usually people love him or hate him. Nothing in between, like 'okay.' I'm in the love camp. I absolutely adore him, because he's someone you can really count on." She washed her hands, suddenly somber. "That's right. You were there."

Terra didn't have a clue what she was talking about. "Where?"

"You were there when Nancy Beck died. You would know that Marc's good in the clinch."

"Oh," Terra said. The memory of those minutes suddenly rushed back, startling her. She recalled Nancy's stillness, her own panic, Marc's fierce search for the injector, his attempt to breath air into Nancy's lungs. Terra began to wash her hands too.

"It must have been awful," Carolina said.

"It's even worse remembering it now than it was living it. Because back then, you know, when it was actually happening, I didn't realize that she'd end up dead. Now I know."

Carolina nodded, and lay a gentle hand on Terra's arm.

They left the posh environment of the women's room, and went back into the restaurant. When the waiter came to take away their plates, Carolina hurriedly put her napkin with the kiwi folded up in it on her dirty plate. She looked happier once the slice of death fruit was gone. Carolina and Peter ordered dessert. Terra had another bourbon.

The little celebration broke up, and Terra felt rising anticipation at being alone with Peter again. He was so easy to be with. So perceptive. So incredibly good looking.

She tilted her seat back for the short drive back to the condo, and turned to look at Peter. She enjoyed being confined in the little car with him. She liked his long strong fingers, the way he smelled. He glanced over at her, and patted her on the knee, sending thrills up her thighs.

They arrived at her condo complex. He helped her out of his car. Holding hands, they started walking on the path to her condo. He pulled her close in sight of her door. They fit together well. He kissed her; the kiss was playful and fun, and a bit aloof.

"Would you like to come in?" she asked him.

"Not tonight, Buck," someone answered from behind.

4 / Late

Terra swung around in the direction of the voice.

A beautiful young woman with pale, waist-length hair stood on the lighted walk. A backpack was thrown over one shoulder.

"Marina!" cried Terra.

"Where have you been?" Marina asked. She looked Peter up and down.

Now that was a question *Marina* was going to have to answer. Torn between relief and annoyance, Terra introduced Peter and her sister.

"Hello, Marina," he said from behind Terra.

"Hello." Marina's eyes still flicked over him like he was some kind of repulsive insect she considered squishing.

He folded his arms around Terra's waist, and whispered into her ear. "I guess you've got company."

She liked the way his arms felt. If Marina was going to show up out of the blue, why couldn't she have come tomorrow? "Yuh," Terra murmured to him.

He gave her a quick peck on the cheek, and unwrapped himself. "See ya, Terragirl." It took him a minute to hop into his car, and he was off, roaring down the road. Terra followed the taillights with her eyes, the promises of his kisses still only promises.

"He's kinda old, isn't he?" Marina said.

Terra turned to her sister. "What's going on, Marina? I've been calling your apartment all week trying to reach you. I've really been worried."

The girl shrugged.

Marina's routine of "I'm in big trouble, but you're gonna have to drag it out of me," always irritated Terra. For the millionth time she felt inadequate. She knew she was a crappy guardian. Why else would there be more conflict than love in their relationship? She thought once Marina went off to LSU, things would go more smoothly. But seeing her sneering sister at her doorstep made her realize maybe they never would. She walked back to her door and the girl followed. She led her sister inside, and flicked on the lights.

Marina cast a glance about the room. "Nasty," she said.

"It belongs to the company I work for," she said, trying not to show her exasperation. "So, what are you doing here?"

Marina dropped her backpack onto the floor, and sank into the couch. "I hate LSU."

She had played Marina's game so many times before, she knew it was a false lead, but one her sister expected her to follow.

"Okay," she replied, "you hate college." She sat down next to Marina. "Why?"

"I hate the work."

"Homework?"

"*All* the work. It's boring. I'm flunking all my classes."

"So, how did you get here?" Terra asked.

"I rode the bus for twenty-eight hours, and then took a taxi."

"Are you hungry?"

"No," Marina said. She seemed to slouch even more, like she was digging herself into the couch to escape something.

The rest of the evening Marina watched MTV, and Terra sat next to her, thinking about Peter and feel of his body. She tried going to bed. She tossed and turned, kept awake by the flickering in the living room and the awful music. When would her sister tell her what was wrong?

Around midnight she gave up, and went to her spare-bedroom office. She had to get the hell away from SSI, and that meant she'd have to solve Marc's cracker problem. Although she hadn't made any progress in attacking SSI's network—especially since she reasoned that the thief was an insider and wouldn't need elaborate methods to get into the network anyway—that excuse was getting her nowhere. Whether the digital invader was an insider or outsider was irrelevant. She had to seek him out—not wait until he came to her.

She paced the spare room. Crackers sometimes bragged. And where might he, or she, brag about those brilliant cracking exploits? One possibility was on the electronic grapevine—Internet Relay Chat, or IRC. Unlike modern chat rooms, rife with avatars, and sounds, and color, and motion, IRC was old-school. Command line interface, nerdy UNIX at its core.

She sat down at her computer, and joined channel Crack. #Crack was one of thousands of channels on IRC, each with its own distinctive culture. Channel Crack was a meeting place for both real and wannabe crackers.

She had given herself a nickname of u4ea. She snorted at her wry humor. u4ea. Euphoria. Of which she had none.

Back in her cracker days, Terra wouldn't have been caught dead on channel Crack. Even though her, and her computer's, identity could be faked, why take the risk of letting something personal slip? Cracking was a solitary joy—kind of like masturbation. She didn't want to share it.

Which was why nobody knew she'd been a cracker. Except for Marc. And whoever had told him.

There were about forty people on channel Crack. Five of them were channel operators. Terra took special note of the operators. These were the people most likely to have real knowledge, and they also had the power to kick her off of the channel.

It seemed to be amateur night on Crack. One after another, a parade of idiots joined the channel, made their demands, and got kicked out for their efforts.

"I want to buy America Online passwords and accounts," offered SuprCrkr.

Kick. No more SuprCrkr.

"Looking for revenge big time. I need a real cracker for hire," stated e-me.

Kick. No more e-me.

Terra snickered.

"Has anyone here heard about that bug in sudo?" asked LordUnix.

She sat up straight, curious how the operators would respond to LordUnix. Sudo was a real program, and a bug in it might indeed offer a good crack.

"What's sudo?" asked an operator named Fuxor.

"Y34h, wh4t d03s 1t d0?" added another operator with a nick of t3ss.

"You know what sudo is. Anyway, the bug lets you exploit a race condition to gain root," LordUnix explained.

"What does "gain root" mean?" Fuxor asked.

Terra burst out laughing. Fuxor was pulling LordUnix's leg by pretending ignorance. To gain root was a digital invader's stock-in-trade. That was how someone with a low-level account could become the super-user and control the computer. Gaining root was kind of like tricking the janitor into exchanging a closet key for a master key.

The teasing and playing dumb went on until the operators got bored with earnest LordUnix. Fuxor kicked him off. The #Crack operator must have assumed that LordUnix was a Fed trying to "get in good with the guys" by showing off how much he knew about cracking.

"I saw RogueKnight last week," announced someone named Sylvie.

Saw him in prison, no doubt. Terra recalled the first time she encountered the cracker known as RogueKnight. Years ago, she had heard about a group that gathered regularly in a public place in New Orleans to share break-in techniques. RogueKnight was said to be the mentor of the group. Terra went to one of the meets, curious about anyone that bold.

RogueKnight was a forceful and passionate twenty-year-old. He

45

considered himself a liberator—freeing knowledge from corporate computer prisons. He called computer executives knowledge-hoarders, and he hated them for it. Unhampered dissemination of data was RogueKnight's credo. Indeed, he lived that way, sharing cracker methods with anyone who asked. Terra had never been attracted to RogueKnight's rough-cut, reckless charisma, but the then eleven-year-old Marina had. Terra's sister idolized RogueKnight as an electronic Robin Hood, though she had no real understanding of what he did. The then twenty-year-old cracker had merely been amused by the girl's eager devotion.

But that could easily change, and Terra had feared that her sister's adoration of this reckless man was bound to lead to pain. Soon after, RogueKnight was arrested, charged with computer fraud. He'd been caught slicing salami: digitally stealing small amounts of money from a large pool. He got out after about a year, only to end up in prison again for the same thing soon after. During those years Marina had grown up.

"He's skinnier," Sylvie continued on the channel.

"I heard some inmate broke his face. True?" new arrival ksh asked.

"No. That's crap," Sylvie replied.

Without warning, the channel was subject to a "mass-kick." Terra, along with everyone else the operators didn't recognize, got kicked out of Crack. Now, if there was any *real* knowledge, the sharing of information would begin. Terra suspected that some legitimate crackers actually did hang out on channel Crack. She installed a sniffer program on one of the chat servers to record the "secret" conversations. Later she would search the collected data for the word SSI and so on, to determine if anyone on Crack had bragged about attacking Silicon Silk.

She turned off her computer, sat in the now-dark room, rubbed her eyes, and wondered if RogueKnight could be involved in the penetration of SSI's network. Certainly he'd always despised companies like Silicon Silk. But he was in prison.

Terra got up, feeling better than when she'd started. At least she'd done something. The living room was now quiet. Marina had turned off the TV, and was asleep in Terra's bed.

★

The next morning Marina seemed to be in a better mood. "So what are we going to do today?" she asked.

"I have to go to work, Honeybunch," Terra said.

"What about me?"

"You could hang and watch TV. You could swim at the pool outside. I've got some swimsuits in a box around here somewhere."

"We should go do something really California. Like shop on Rodeo Drive or go see the Hollywood stars or go to Chinatown."

Terra laughed. "Rodeo Drive and Hollywood are in a completely different part of California than Chinatown. I'm sure we'd have a blast together in San Francisco, Marina, but I can't take any time off today. I'm in uh… an unstable position at work."

"Gee, Terra, what are you? A slave? Call in sick."

How could Terra explain adult realities to an eighteen-year-old?

"I *can't* entertain you today," Terra said. She dug through her purse and gave Marina an extra set of condo keys. "Look, we'll do something fun on Saturday. Maybe go up to the city. And I'll be home at a reasonable hour tonight, too. Okay? I'll write down my work number; you can call me anytime." She looked over at the stove clock. "I need to be out of here in a half an hour. What do you want for breakfast?"

"Maybe I'll fix something for myself later."

Terra studied Marina's face. She seemed a bit pale. "Are you feeling okay?"

"Yeah. Fine. Hey, Terra, why don't I drop you off at work, and that way I'll have the car and I can show myself the sights? I'll come pick you up at work whenever you say."

Terra agreed to Marina's plan. When they reached the SSI gatehouse, Terra pulled out the area maps from the glove

47

compartment and put them on the dashboard. "Don't drive into San Francisco, Marina. Don't go into Berkeley, either. Meet me here, exactly at six. If you can't come for some reason, just give me a call here. Okay? Do you need any money?"

"How about a credit card?"

"Ha, ha." Terra handed her two twenties.

Marina crumpled the bills up into her jeans pocket. "Thanks." She slid into the driver's seat of the blue Saturn, waved, and went down the street.

"Oh, boy," Terra said under her breath. "There goes trouble."

★

Terra spent the day as she usually did, searching for—and failing to find—security holes in the computer network. She told herself she'd have to attempt to crack SSI from the outside again. But not yet. Some other day.

A & C seemed abnormally quiet, now that the latest version of Scout was finished, and most of the contract workers were gone.

Late afternoon, she heard Jack whining from over the half-wall, presumably speaking to someone on the phone.

"How is this my problem?" Jack asked. "And what am I supposed to do?"

This conversation of denial went on for a while, and Jack got more and more irritated. Finally he left his cube in a hurried huff.

Around five-thirty, she heard a knock on the outside of her cubicle. She thought it might be Marc, coming to check up on her again. Whipping her head around, she saw it was Peter, wearing his I-know-you'll-be-thrilled-to-see-me grin. That man didn't lack confidence, that's for sure, she thought. She couldn't help but smile back.

"Hey," he said.

"Hey." She scooted her chair back to get a less neck-crunching view of him.

"Your sister all right?" he asked.

"Probably not. She's supposed to be in college. She hasn't told me what's wrong, though."

He asked her a few more questions. She answered them. Small talk. Her mind drifted toward suspenders. They were hidden under his jacket. She pondered reaching inside, and snapping his suspenders. She wanted to see the finance chief jump. She wanted him to feel excited and breathless, as off-kilter and unsettled as she did when he was around.

By the time she took in a long breath, and exhaled, Peter was gone. She could still smell his aftershave.

Terra logged off her computer, and headed outside to meet Marina. As she walked through the parking lot, she noticed Peter's Porsche took up two spots. She ambled past the gatehouse, feeling conspicuous. The guard studied her: *who in California walks, anyway?* She hoped her sister would be waiting. She wasn't. Terra stood outside the SSI campus, in the grass, pacing. Several people stopped their cars and asked her if she needed a lift. She hadn't given up on Marina yet, and so she said no. Besides, she didn't know them all that well.

By six-thirty, Terra was pissed off. She thought about going back inside the building and calling her sister, or a taxi. But then she'd have to walk by that gatehouse again and that guard would look at her funny. So she stood out in the grass, peering down the street, trying to decide what to do. She was getting angrier by the second; her professional appearance meant everything, and here she was looking like a damn hitchhiker.

A light brown Range Rover pulled up next to her. Another Good Samaritan. The window rolled down. "Need a ride?"

By now she'd given up on Marina. And this person she knew. She sighed. "Yeah. Thanks, Marc." She opened the door and climbed in. Maybe Marina would finally arrive after she left, and wait and wait for *her.*

"Where to?" he asked.

"The condo. Thanks."

He nodded and drove. She got the feeling he wasn't going to make small talk, that he didn't care why she was standing around SSI looking like an idiot. Gazing at his imposing brow, his stiff jaw, she realized he looked mad. If she'd taken a better look at him before she hopped into his car, she probably would've told him "no thanks."

She hoped that whatever angered the president and CEO of SSI wasn't going to end up changing her life for the worse.

Whatever. There was no help for that now. She looked around the car. The masculinity of the wood and leather interior put to mind a mobile men's club. A Mac laptop and some papers rested on the floor near her feet. An incongruous metallic sparkle on the dash caught her eye. Velvet's earrings?

She examined Marc's profile again. He stared straight ahead, his jaw clenched like he was wrestling with something in his mind— and losing. Strangely, whatever was bothering him didn't affect his driving. He seemed to interact kindly with the Rover, one wounded hand lying gently on the steering wheel, the other shifting smoothly. She recalled how differently Peter had treated his Porsche—with near-violence, like he was trying to force his car to submit to his will.

When they arrived at her condo complex, she leapt out of the Rover, springing from the tension. Marc got out fast, too, and met her halfway around his car.

"Thanks for the ride," she said.

"No problem. There's something I'd like to show you, Terra. The sooner the better. Is there any way you can come into work sometime this weekend?"

If what he wanted to show her had anything to do with his grim mood, then her life was going to go downhill for sure.

"If you need a lift," he continued, "I'd be happy to pick you up and take you back. It'll only take about a half an hour."

And what about Marina? She'd promised Marina they'd go into San Francisco. "Um, my little sister is visiting me this weekend," she said.

"Why not bring her along? It shouldn't take more than an hour. Just say when."

She noticed how he'd raised the estimated time from a half an hour to an hour. It probably would end up being an all-day thing. Her silence seemed to make him uncomfortable.

"Look, I realize I'm not being fair," he continued, "especially since I ragged on you about burning yourself out…"

"What do you want to show me?" she asked.

"The company's been attacked again."

Her life did just get worse.

"I could probably come in Sunday night at around eight," she said.

"Perfect. Do you want me to pick you up?"

"No," she replied. "I don't think I'll need a lift."

She resented having to come in on a weekend to do cracker-chick chores. Now if he had wanted to discuss natural languages with her, that would have been a different matter. Did he want a midnight conference on syntax with her in the worst part of town? Gladly. How about an underwater meeting to discuss knowledge systems? Absolutely.

She'd been tempted to lie to him, and tell him she needed a ride. That way he'd have to chauffeur them around. The Breaux sisters could sit in the back of his car and say, "Home, James." But of course that would mean that she'd actually have to be in a confined space with Marc.

"Thanks, Terra. I appreciate this." He got back into his car and drove off.

Terra found Marina lying on a lounge chair by the pool.

"You forgot to pick me up," Terra accused.

"Yeah, I must've lost track of the time. I'm sorry." She smiled her best rueful, eighteen-year-old smile. "So how'd you get back?"

"Some guy from work. He happened to see me standing outside SSI looking lost and lonely, and took pity."

"The old guy?"

"No. This one's a bastard."

Marina pretended shock, but laughed, ruining the effect. "Why would you take a ride from a bastard? I thought you knew better than that!"

"Yeah, well, I just happen to know he's a very good driver, despite being a bastard. He wears a seatbelt and everything. I'm going to change my clothes, Marina. I'll be right back."

Terra got into her swimsuit, and pulled up a lounge chair next to her sister's, scraping the cement loudly. "So, what did you do today? And more importantly, is my car in one piece?"

She listened to Marina describe her excursions around town in her exuberant, teenage way. Maybe Marina did just need a little time away from school. Sure, her baby sister was simply discouraged, and a little poolside chatter would be enough to revive her and she'd go back to Alexandria, all better. Terra wondered when she herself would be all better. Marc was right; she was burning out. Watching Nancy die had eaten away at some of her natural resiliency.

With the waning spring sun warming her eyelids, Terra could feel the SSI personalities that had crowded her dreams and actions sliding away, their voices and demands muffled by Marina's lighthearted banter. She was nearly asleep when she sensed a change in Marina's tone.

"What did you say?" Terra asked, yawning.

"I'm late."

"Tell me about it. I waited almost an hour for you today."

"I'm *late*, Terra," she said.

Terra opened one eye and looked at her sister. Marina's pale gray eyes fixed on her, unblinking. The girl now sat at the side of her lounge chair, her arms wrapped around herself.

Terra opened both eyes. "What are you saying?"

"I'm saying the stick is blue."

The stick is blue? I'm late? Why couldn't Marina just say she was pregnant? Terra had never been pregnant; she'd never even had a false alarm. Because she made sure she'd never get pregnant. She was terrified of having to make decisions about another life. It had been hard enough when their parents had died and she'd become her sister's guardian. Terra was an inadequate guardian. But at least Marina had been thirteen, not a fetus or a child.

Terra just wasn't the mothering type; she knew she was supposed to help and comfort Marina, but instead she felt angry. How could the girl ruin her life when pregnancy was so easy to prevent?

"How could you let that happen?" Terra asked.

Marina flinched and she regretted the question. Tears rolled out of Marina's pale, pleading eyes.

She moved to sit on the edge of her lounge chair, and face her sister.

"I'm sorry, Marina. I know I'm screwing this up bad. I'm really, really sorry I'm not doing it right. What do you want to do about the pregnancy?"

Marina sobbed. Terra figured that meant she hadn't made up her mind yet. She knelt on the cement and held her sister tightly, wondering if she should eventually ask her about the father. Did the girl love him? But Terra didn't actually give a damn about him. Marina was the one that would have to make all the tough decisions. Whether she kept the baby or not, it'd be her sister's body, mind and soul that would endure the changes, not his.

5 / The shareware

On Saturday Terra and Marina took Caltrain to the city. After checking into the Hotel Monaco, they squeezed onto a packed cable car and rode it the few blocks into Chinatown. They both enjoyed the walking tour of the streets lined with temples and tearooms, shops and grocery stores. They did more giggling than walking.

In the afternoon they decided to take a boat tour of the harbor. Terra gazed out at the water, and fretted over Marina's future. She knew just exactly what she would do if she were in Marina's shoes. Get an abortion. There was no way Terra would have a baby—out of wedlock or any other time. But Marina? Terra glanced affectionately at her sister. Marina was a different animal. A little bit softer, a little more sensitive. Maybe mothering would be more natural to her.

Sunday they took a stroll on North Beach, and both agreed it was the best part of San Francisco. After an obligatory stop to buy a few trinkets at the Cannery, they went back to Mountain View.

Marina didn't seem to mind dropping by SSI. They had bought a new *People* magazine for Marina to read. But Terra hated having to go to meet Marc. A lot. She wondered why he couldn't have waited until a workday to show her whatever was bugging him. They arrived at the gatehouse around eight, where the guard obviously expected them; he gave Marina a temporary ID. Through the black glass of Building A, Terra could discern Marc waiting in the lobby. He didn't want to waste any time.

Terra introduced Marc and Marina.

He smiled fondly. Terra was used to that gentle, sentimental expression when people first saw Marina and Terra together. It was usually followed by an exclamation about how much the sisters looked alike. But she hadn't expected to see that look on his face.

"Are you the reason Terra was stranded on Friday?" he asked the girl.

"Yeah, I'm the reason," Marina said. A wicked glint of recognition grew in her eyes. "So *you're* the um…" Marina looked over to Terra.

She hoped her sister wasn't going to repeat what she'd called him.

Marina giggled, and finished, "…good driver."

He raised his thick brows at that, but didn't ask why she'd say such a thing. Terra thought she'd better stop calling him a bastard out loud.

They took the elevator to the second floor. Marina plopped herself onto a chair by the cleanest-looking desk in Marc's outer office. She put her feet up on the desk, next to the computer, and started reading her *People,* starting from the last page.

He went inside his office.

"I hope this doesn't take too long," Terra said to Marina.

"Have fun," the girl said, laughing.

She felt a little sick when she got inside his office. She hadn't been here since he told her she would be his private electronic thief hunter. In contrast to her unease, he seemed in good spirits, despite the attack on his company. His new attitude mystified her.

"Should I be worried?" he asked her. His dark eyes were liquid and jovial.

"About the attack?"

"No," he chuckled. "About Marina."

"Why should you be worried about my sister?"

"She doesn't have any electronic hobbies does she?"

"You mean, does she break into computers? Of course not. It's not genetic. She hates computers."

"Now I'm really worried," he said. Laughing, he raced to his door and peered out into the outer office. "We're safe. She's reading a magazine."

"She's not going to even use that computer, Marc, much less wreck it accidentally."

"I wasn't worried about her *accidentally* wrecking anything. I thought I'd invited some super-cracker to sit in my outer office and rifle through my files."

A feeling of déjà vu crept over her. The back of her arms prickled; she just knew he was preparing to screw her over.

"My sister doesn't deserve that."

"She doesn't. But you do." He shut his office door, and turned toward her. Inexplicably, he had a grin on his face. "Oh, Terra, I'm teasing you. It just struck me as funny that you once made that very same claim—of hating computers—after you nearly got bagged for computer crimes by the FBI."

"I said I hated technology," she said, flooded by helpless anger, "not computers. And how do you know what I said, anyway? Were you FBI, or what?"

"Or what."

"Is this why you hired me? Revenge? You couldn't manage to get me arrested me eight years ago, so now you've fixed it so you can torture me whenever you're in a bad mood?"

"I've pissed you off," he said. He sounded surprised.

"No shit, Sherlock. And from now on you're going to have to torture me during the work week," she said, her voice cracking. "I'm not coming in special for it." She walked over to the closed door and stopped when she felt his hand on her shoulder.

"You won't take a look at what the attacker did?" he asked.

She turned around slowly, and faced him. He removed his hand.

"There really was an attacker?" she asked. She thought he'd made the whole thing up just to lure her in over the weekend.

"Yes." He exhaled. "Let's get this straight, Terra. I need you. Not to hurt you, but to save my company. If you bail out on me, Silicon Silk will be destroyed piece-by-piece, bit-by-bit. You have a rare skill. And what's even more unusual is that your expertise is combined with utter integrity and honesty. You're the one who holds all the cards here."

"Do I? I don't know how you found out about my past, or if most of it is bluff, but you know enough to hurt me and my future in consulting."

He frowned, and bent over so his eyes were level with hers. "Are you accusing me of blackmail? Are you really working for me because you think I'm going to tell the world you used to be a computer criminal if you don't?"

"I'm working for you because I signed your contract."

"Good. That's what the contract was intended to do."

"But I don't doubt for one second that you'd tell the world I used be a computer criminal if it suited your purposes," she said bitterly.

He straightened and appraised her. "So that's the way it is with you."

"That's the way it is."

Why couldn't he understand how desperately she wanted to work on natural languages, and how dangerous it was for her crack again?

He walked over to his desk and picked up a small padded envelope. "I got this in the mail." He held it out, expecting her to take it.

Still feeling manipulated, she retrieved the envelope from him. There was a disk inside.

"What's on it?" she asked, pulling out the disk.

"It's a Windows program."

"Okay," she said, waiting for him to explain what the disk had to do with an electronic attack.

"The program uses one of our agent adapters. We had originally wanted to use the adapter in Scout 5.0 for Internet Communications."

"And now you're not?"

"No. Most of the code on that disk was stolen from SSI."

"So what does this program do?"

"Apparently it's a spider that goes out on the Internet and collects the IP addresses of X-rated servers."

"Pretty lowbrow application," she sniffed.

Yet again, someone had stolen a nearly worthless section of software code from Silicon Silk, except this time they had gone to great pains to let Marc know about it. This attack seemed personal. Again she thought about RogueKnight. He used to get his kicks out of tormenting certain software executives. If he weren't in prison, RogueKnight would be the perfect suspect.

"That's not the worst of it," Marc said. "What you have in your hand is shareware."

"*Shareware?*" she repeated, astounded.

You couldn't buy a shareware program from a store. You generally downloaded shareware off the Internet, and then if you liked the program, and were honest, you'd send the shareware author fifteen bucks or so. Shareware was a tough way to make money.

She shook her head, waving the disk around. "Are you telling me someone would steal this code from SSI, risking big jail time for industrial espionage, and then practically give the software away as shareware?"

"Mr. Shareware claims he didn't steal it," he said.

"I'll bet your lawyers believed that," she said sarcastically.

"Lawyers didn't talk to him. I did." He leaned back against his desk, and folded his arms across his chest.

Of course. Micromanaging Marc wouldn't be relying on lawyers to solve his problems.

"So what did the developer do when he found out it was the CEO of Silicon Silk calling him about stealing code? Besides pee his pants, I mean."

"I wouldn't go so far as to call him a developer," he said. His eyelid twitched. "I didn't accuse him of stealing. I flattered him. I told him he was obviously a gifted programmer, and was interested in having him come work here. He was thrilled. And then I questioned him until it was clear he barely knew AUTOEXEC.BAT from a baseball bat."

She shook her head, both amused and appalled by the way Marc had manipulated the shareware guy. She'd been jerked around by the head of SSI in much the same way.

"Mr. Shareware finally admitted to finding the source code posted in some programming newsgroup," he continued. "He'd taken it, slapped on a shitty GUI, and then expected the bucks to come rolling in."

"Was the code really posted like he claimed?"

"Yes. It's still there for anybody in the world to look at."

"So who posted it?"

"My guess is the person who stole the code from us."

"Well," she said, "What was his e-mail address?"

"A Finnish anonymous remailer."

That meant dead end. It would be nearly impossible to trace the real e-mail address if the thief had used a remailer. Terra put the disk back in the envelope, and then lay the envelope on Marc's desk.

"So now what?" she asked. "How are you going to stop the shareware guy from giving away your software?"

"We won't stop them."

"Them? There's more than one shareware guy?"

"There will be. The code's out there on the Internet for anyone to grab. This guy just happened to be the first—that I know about, anyway. Even if it was just one person, we can't sue him for copyright infringement without the world knowing we've been victimized. We'll have to start over and write clean code, or we can't re-copyright the Internet Communications module."

"That's not good," she said.

"There's something else I want you to see," he said. "The disk had a sticky note attached to it."

He pulled a yellow piece of paper off his desk, and handed it to her. "I'd like you to tell me what you think it means."

The note said:

</SSI>?

The tiny piece of computer code was in HTML, a programming language used to publish documents on the Web.

She looked up at Marc, and felt an unexpected rush of empathy for him. "I suppose the note could be interpreted as, 'is this the end of SSI?' I'd take it as a threat."

"That was my reading of it, too. But why use an HTML tag? Why couldn't they just write 'Is this the end of SSI?' or better yet, 'this *is* the end of SSI.'"

In any case, the note gave her the creeps. "I don't know. Maybe it's supposed to be more sinister in HTML. I've told you this before, Marc; you really need to talk to your firewall administrator."

"And I do. Just not about this. Keith quite faithfully informs me about anything suspicious. Lately he's just observed the usual break-in attempts, mainly late weekend-night attacks by the dot-ee-dee-you crowd. Except Keith did mention an interesting set of tries, that after a little tracing, turned out to be someone using an SGI workstation in France. I assume that was you."

"Why would you think that?" she asked, amused. He was, of course, correct.

"You like SGI machines," he said. "And the first attacks were strictly old-school. Then they got increasingly more sophisticated. Have you succeeded in getting into the company?"

"Um, no," she said. She swallowed, half guilty, half afraid. She hadn't tried to break into SSI's network again, because the first attempts had been so unpleasant. "Not yet."

"That's a relief," he said. "I appreciate your coming in this weekend. If you have time, I'd like to discuss something else with you."

"Okay." *What now?* she wondered.

"Down the hall," he said, opening his door.

As they passed through his outer office, Terra saw that Marina and her magazine were getting along just fine. He stopped at an office door halfway down the hall. He opened it and turned on the light.

"It's yours," he said. "I can have all your stuff moved over here by tomorrow morning."

The office was large, and had a window.

"I'm fine where I am, Marc," she said.

He strode into the space, and made a big show of slowly lowering his body into a strange-looking black chair sitting in front of the desk. "Mmm. Comfortable." He then grunted happily and got up. He patted the metal mesh fabric seat. "Try it."

She couldn't help but submit to his silly invitation. The chair was indeed comfortable, but she didn't care about status symbols like offices with windows, or high-tech chairs. More importantly, she needed to stay in her cube at A & C because she still suspected an insider, like Jack, of the electronic thefts.

"I'm fine where I am. But if it will make you happy, you can move this chair over to my cubicle," she said, laughing.

He put his hands on the armrests of the chair, and leaned over her. "I would have preferred to have you close when you first arrived. But we had a big space problem, and I couldn't see kicking someone out of their office." He rotated the chair to the left and then to the right, and then back to the middle.

Moving her like that struck Terra as being a shade too intimate.

"I'd like to stay in Applications and Commerce Group," she said. "In the thick of things." Maybe her declaration would have more impact if she said it standing up, instead of sitting there melting in the chair. Except she couldn't get up, because Marc was looming over her.

"You still think it's someone from A & C who's stealing our intellectual property," he said.

She shrugged. "Maybe. It would be easier for an insider, anyway."

But this new code theft had put a different spin on things. For someone to steal company secrets and give them away as shareware made no sense. Insider *or* outsider. Unless, of course, the theft was intended to be an act of computer terrorism or torment.

He let go of the armrests and unbent himself. Looking around the little office, he cajoled: "There's enough room in here to pace when you're thinking. The carpet's so soft you could even think barefoot. See, there's a coat rack. There are lots of bookshelves. You could store reference manuals for fourteen flavors of UNIX!"

None of it mattered. She was in a different world when she worked; beyond the basics, her environment just wasn't important.

"And best of all," he continued, "The guys in A & C won't be breathing down your neck wondering what you're doing with all your time." He planted his palms on the armrests again. "Which you said bothered you."

But the last thing she wanted was to work in an office a few doors down from the president of SSI, and have *him* breathing down her neck. Or breathing down her front. His closeness disturbed her. She didn't think he'd be leaning over her like that if she were a man.

"At this point it would be a whole lot more suspicious if all of a sudden I rate a cushy office," she said. "That would really start A & C gossiping."

He pulled away. He gazed at her silently, as if he were trying to decide if he should just force her to move.

"I suppose you're right," he finally said.

"So we're done here?" she asked.

"We're done," he said.

She felt the charge of exhilaration. She had just swayed C. Marc Elliott, the man who claimed he wasn't a negotiator.

6 / The hate site

Once the sisters got back to the condo they decided they needed a snack. Terra still felt giddy about getting Marc to back down about the office. She was now a combatant, not merely a prisoner. They stood in the kitchen, sneering at each other's poor taste in brand of microwave popcorn.

Marina announced, "I'm going back." She didn't look at Terra when she said it.

Did that mean the girl was going to get an abortion? She waited for the other shoe to drop, but her sister didn't elaborate. She started the microwave. "Do you want to fly back to school instead of taking the bus?"

"And I'm keeping the baby," Marina said.

Bad choice, Marina.

Terra suppressed an anxious sigh. "Okay," she said.

"I really am." Marina leaned back against the counter, and put her hands on her hips.

"I believe you. Why not stay here with me then? I could keep an eye on you so that you'd eat right and stuff."

Not that she actually knew anything about taking care of a pregnant woman, but the idea of her sister being all alone, so far away, made her apprehensive.

"And do what? Sit around and eat right? I don't like it here at all."

"*We* could go back to New Orleans," Terra said recklessly, hopefully.

How could she let Marina deal with pregnancy alone? Besides, Marc wouldn't hold her to her contract. She'd tell him that she had some serious family problems, and of course, he'd release her. When it came right down to it, he was a decent man. Right?

Maybe. Maybe not. But even if he weren't decent, she'd have to risk leaving. She couldn't fail her sister.

"Terra, your popcorn's burning," Marina said.

"Oh." Terra stopped the microwave. "It would be fun. Just like old times. Really."

Marina shook her head slowly. "You wouldn't leave here."

"Of course I would, Honeybunch. And I will. I don't like Silicon Valley any more than you do."

"You say that, but you don't really mean it. Everybody here is like you, living and breathing computers. I mean, you work all the time. And then when you don't work, you come *home* to live and breathe computers."

"That's not true."

Marina smiled. "Look at you now. You're in a great mood because you had to go into work this weekend and live and breathe computers."

"I'm in a good mood because I managed to stop that bastard Marc from dictating my life."

Oops. She called him a bastard out loud again.

"Marc seemed nice to me," Marina said. "I swear, Terra, you get so used to computers doing what you want without any back talk or argument, you think if a human being disagrees with you, you have the right to hate them. "

Computers always argued with her, thought Terra. *It's called debugging.* She got the bag out of the microwave and tore it open. The stink of burnt popcorn assaulted her. "Oh boy," she said, groaning.

Marina laughed at her. "Redenbacher never burns. Especially when I bother to pay attention to how long I cook it."

Terra could feel her mouth turning up in a smile.

"You can't take care of me forever, you know," Marina said. "I need to work this out myself. And before I figure out how I'm going to do it, I've got to get some things straightened out. Maybe

I can get a flight out tonight. Can you take me to the airport?"

"Sure."

Marina went from room to room picking up her belongings and stuffing them into her backpack. Terra opened the windows, and put the bag of popcorn outside her door.

By the time they got to the San Jose airport, Terra was overwhelmed by frustration. The girl was about to needlessly wreck her life. But what could Terra do about it? *Make* her sister get an abortion?

"So what do you need to straighten out at school?" Terra asked. "Tell the jerk with the sperm?"

"I don't sleep with jerks."

"I shouldn't have said that, Honeybunch. It's just that *I've* slept with a lot of jerks." Terra said. She sighed loudly. "Of course I didn't think they were jerks at the time." She patted her sister's knee. "I hope you know you can always come live with me, whenever you want, for as long as you want. I'll do my best to take care of you and, um, the baby."

"I think he'll do what's right."

Terra kept quiet, even though she bet she knew exactly what Marina's lover would say when confronted by the news.

Marina got on a flight at about ten-thirty. The sisters hugged, and Marina headed off to go tell the jerk with the sperm, who Terra feared would break the girl's heart.

Terra's own heart hurt, like it had been squeezed dry, and the organ couldn't figure out how to beat anymore. "Damn," she said.

She didn't know how to deal with parental anxiety.

★

When Terra got to work on Monday she discovered Marc had to have the last word. The weird, high-tech chair was in her cube. At first she giggled. The chair looked out of place in her cramped workspace, so chic and futuristic. But then, after more thought, the chair bothered her. He seemed to be intent on demonstrating his power: he could make her life pleasant or unpleasant, depending on whim. But in the end, Terra kept the chair; it *was* comfortable. She draped a sweater over the back, hoping to camouflage it.

Jack spotted the chair almost immediately. "Is that one of those thousand-dollar, zero-gravity chairs I read about?" he asked.

"No. It's a knockoff," she said, hoping it *was* a knockoff. *A thousand dollars for a chair?*

Jack wanted to test it out, so she got up and let him sit in it.

"Nice," he said, as he drank his can of Surge. "Even if it is ugly."

Ted came by and sat in her chair, too. "Cool," he said. "Where'd you get it?"

"Um," she hesitated. "I found it in one of the machine rooms and snarfed it."

"How come *I* don't ever find anything this good?" Ted asked, swiveling the chair around.

"Just lucky, I guess."

Had she known the chair would create such a stir, she would have rolled it out into the hall and abandoned it. Marc probably knew everyone would ask her about that chair, and loved the idea of putting her on the spot.

Finally Jack and Ted left her and her chair alone. And just in time. Her heart was hammering hard. The strain of being under Marc's controlling thumb was getting to her.

She had to get away. But that meant solving the cracker problem.

Forcing herself to calm down, she reviewed what she knew about the break-ins. First attack: The attacker got Silicon Silk code somehow, showed a competitor that code, and the competitor warned Marc about it. Second attack: The attacker got more SSI code, posted it on the Internet, and Marc got an anonymous note informing him about the danger to his company.

Now Sherry came by the cube to examine the chair. Terra tried to be patient and gracious. This was *Marc's* fault, not Sherry's.

Once Sherry left, Terra called her sister. Marina's roommate—the one so sketchy with information—answered. She told Terra that Marina had arrived in Alexandria, but was now out at a party, which didn't reassure Terra much. She left a message for her sister to call back. She then returned to her analysis, determined to wrestle the facts into submission.

Fact One: Neither piece of stolen intellectual property was especially valuable. The thefts seemed to be about demonstration rather than inflicting damage: "Look what I can do to you," the cracker appeared to be saying. That made the thefts more consistent with extortion than with industrial espionage.

Fact Two: The invader seemed to go to great lengths to let Marc know about SSI vulnerabilities. Also consistent with extortion. But then again, maybe the cracker broke into SSI solely to torment the CEO. Perhaps the attacks were purely personal.

RogueKnight used to pull pranks on high-tech personages he didn't like. She recalled RogueKnight's preferred target had once been Michael Dell. The cracker would telnet to a low-numbered port on a machine with a Dell domain name, and then create and send e-mails, pretending to be Michael Dell. These hilarious fakemail messages would end up as posts on newsgroups discussing cures for premature balding, or extolling the wonders of the Macintosh computer. Michael Dell, a man who, in reality, had hair down to his eyebrows and was a well-known Macintosh-hater, presumably didn't appreciate RogueKnight's humor, but he never could shut the practical joker down. RogueKnight's fun with Dell ended abruptly when the cracker went to prison for something else.

Back to Marc. OK, so someone hated him enough to mess with the thing he loved most—his company. But who? The HTML message on the sticky note just didn't fit RogueKnight. HTML was a Web language, and the cracker viewed the Web as cartoon—kid stuff, best left to the drooling masses. Her analysis gave her a potential motivation—hurting Marc—but not a suspect. He had to have a lot of enemies—even though sometimes she thought nobody could possibly hate Marc more than *she* did.

Hate. Terra remembered Carolina had once mentioned the existence of SSI hate sites. Maybe the attacker would use the forum of an "anti" website to boast about cracking the despised SSI? Or perhaps the site would merely give her a lead. It was a long shot.

She fired up her favorite data-fetching program, the Google search engine, and asked it to comb the Web for SSI hate sites. All told, Google listed eleven anti-Silicon Silk sites—rather more than she expected. Once a software company became successful it also became the object of ridicule. Terra linked to a promising-looking SSI hate site in Sweden.

As the site appeared on her screen, her mouth dropped open. Scrawled in vivid, snot green was "Welcome to SSIck."

"Sick is right," she murmured, staring at the chaotic feast of images vying for her attention. The author of this site didn't just hate SSI—he hated Marc.

A retouched graphic of Marc with red eyes, horns, and vampire teeth glared at her from the top left of the screen.

In small print, on the bottom of the screen, also in snot green, blinked an acknowledgment:

Greets go out to Alberto, *Bill*, cassie, Deb_M, Davis, fmg, hObbiTt, ksh, LordLuke, macht, Otter, Phat, RogueKnight, sbin, Voy, zap and Zenna.

Ranger

"Interesting," she said.

She had no idea who Ranger—the supposed author of the site—was. But she recalled the nickname "ksh" from channel Crack. And of course, she knew RogueKnight. The name zap was also familiar; the red-haired young woman had been part of RogueKnight's New Orleans cracker group. She wondered if zap or RogueKnight had been involved in the site, or merely knew Ranger.

She clicked on the devil graphic of Marc, and a diatribe against the company and the man appeared: "Hello there!" the page read. "I'm Marc Elliott. I'm the genius behind SSIck. My company works day and night, exploiting anyone with innovations and ideas. Like bloodthirsty little leeches, we suck at their souls until nothing is left but empty husks." On and on it went.

She returned to the on the SSIck home page, where a link led her to a full-screen graphic of Marc's head glued onto Arnold Swarzenegger's body. The Marc-Arnold hybrid was the bully at the beach; his Java cartoon foot kicked sand into his competitors' faces. She laughed out loud. Mean, but funny anyway.

Another page offered the chance to "punch Marc Elliott." A black and white photograph of Marc glowered in the center. She clicked on a button that said, "SSIck it to him!" A fist shot out across Marc's picture, leaving him with a missing tooth and a black eye. Even funnier and meaner.

She then viewed parodies of SSI logos and trademarks. These graphics bordered on true wit, rather than mere vulgarity. Another page contained RealAudio clips of Marc Elliott speaking. Taken out of context, he appeared to be a true megalomaniac. As much as she disliked Marc, she thought the speech collection was unfair. Nonetheless, exploring the hate site was turning out to be a enjoyable excursion.

A humor page listed SSI and Marc Elliott jokes. She'd already heard most of them from Ted, but one of them was new, and made her chuckle:

Q: How many Marc Elliotts does it take to change a light bulb?
A: One. He puts the bulb in the socket and waits for the world to revolve around him.

Another page offered a dictionary of euphemisms for the word "bug." The hate site claimed that the Silicon Silk phone support people had been ordered by Marc never to use the word "bug" in connection with SSI software. Because of that, the support staff had to invent new words. Terms defined on the page included "insect," "design side effect," "challenge," and various forms of "issue." Even though Terra didn't know if the support people were allowed to use "bug" or not, she got a big kick out of the dictionary.

She returned to the home page of SSIck. The Marc-devil glared at her while she contemplated how best to learn more about Ranger. One option was to crack the Swedish hate site; the other was to seek out someone who knew Ranger. She still feared to let the horse out of the barn by cracking even the hate site computer in earnest. She just wasn't ready yet.

So that left RogueKnight, who was in prison, or zap. She preferred to contact zap. Perhaps she still went to the regular Wednesday mall meetings. Speaking to zap would be the perfect excuse to go back home. Terra dialed Sally, a neighbor who was looking after her apartment, to let her know she was returning for a short visit.

"Terra, is that you, darlin'?" asked the whispery voice on the other end.

"Yeah," Terra replied. Unexpected homesickness flooded her when she heard her neighbor's distinctive voice. "I wanted to let you know that I'm coming back for a visit as soon as I can arrange it."

"Good. The apartmen' fine. I seen your sister aroun' here."

"Marina's staying at the apartment?" Terra's stomach constricted apprehensively. Had Marina changed her mind and gotten an abortion—alone?

"Terra darlin', she not stayin' at the apartmen'. Fact is, she don' get close ta me at all. Marina hopin' I don' see her, I thin'."

7 / Family

"Marina's trying to hide from you?" Terra asked.

"Seem like it. An' I worry 'bout her. She don' look too good."

"What do you mean Marina doesn't look too good?"

"She look pale, Terra Darlin'," Sally said in her barely-there voice. "Upset."

"Marina's supposed to be at school in Alexandria, Sally."

"Not no more. Deidre tol' me she see Marina workin' at Jackson Square someplace," Sally said.

"Thanks, Sally. I'll be back as soon as I can."

Terra caught the first flight out.

★

Terra fidgeted most of the flight. If her sister was back in New Orleans, why wasn't she staying at the apartment? What had Marina done about her pregnancy? And why hadn't she asked Terra for help?

Terra felt certain that Marina's difficulties were soon going to force her to leave Silicon Silk. If she hadn't substantially solved the cracker problem by then, she would have to have an unpleasant confrontation with Marc. Her whole body tensed at the prospect. She hoped the author of the hate site was the SSI attacker, and that zap would help her find him.

Poor Marina. What had that college bastard done to make her return to New Orleans in such a hurry?

★

Terra arrived in New Orleans in the early afternoon on Tuesday. She threw open every window in her upstairs apartment. She loved everything about the Quarter: the intoxicating cooking smells, the dark, crooked alleyways, and memories of old scandals lingering in every colorful doorway. But she didn't spend much time at her apartment, heading now to Jackson Square to find Marina. Her sister was working in a fancy art store, just as Sally said. Terra stood outside the glass windows of the shop watching Marina move around inside, wondering why her sister had come back home. What had happened when Marina told her boyfriend about the baby? Terra couldn't decide if she should pretend that she'd just happened to come upon Marina, in town on other business, or that she'd actually been searching for her. Just then her sister glanced Terra's way, and their eyes met.

Marina smiled and waved her in.

"Hey, you're back home, I see," Marina said cheerfully.

Terra's eyes scoured her sister's face for signs of distress. She didn't see any. "Yeah," she said. "I've missed it a lot."

"So did I," Marina said. "So, are you home for good, or just here to buy some fresh beignets to take to California?"

Terra plunged in, hoping her sister wouldn't get mad at her. "Actually, Marina, I'm here to talk to you."

Marina just laughed. "I'm fine, Terra."

"I can see that. Are you due for a break?"

"In fact, I am. Just a sec," Marina said. She disappeared into a back room, and an older woman emerged to take over.

The sisters bought take-out pastries and chicory coffee from a bakery nearby, and sat on a bench in the gardens of the Square.

"I was worried about you," Terra said. "Your roommate said you were out partying. And then yesterday I spoke to Sally and…. So you're doing okay, huh?"

"I told my roommate to tell everybody I was out, because I wasn't sure what I'd end up doing. I did mean to call you, you know, when I got settled."

It almost hurt not to ask Marina outright what happened when she told her boyfriend about the baby. But what *could* have happened? Marina was in New Orleans. And he was in Alexandria.

"Are you settled?" Terra asked. It was as close as she dared get to asking her sister outright what her plans were.

"Yeah! I got this great apartment on Bienville and Royal, you know in that bright blue colored house with all that iron scrollwork out front? I have a job. And I'm home. What more could I want?"

You could want family. An irrational emotional pain flooded Terra. Marina was happy, proud of her independence. And she should be. For the first time the girl was behaving maturely. So why did Terra feel like Marina was supposed to still need her? Especially when she was such an inadequate parent substitute?

"You are *set*," Terra said, forcing herself to sound positive. "So are you feeling all right?"

"I'm not feeling sick, if that's what you mean. Maybe I won't." She leaned closer to her and lowered her voice. "Supposedly your boobs get bigger when you're pregnant. Did you know that?"

"No. I didn't." Terra dug into the white sack for a pastry, hoping that the conversation wouldn't drift to the more intimate physical aspects of pregnancy.

The girl sank back into the bench again. "Oh, well," she sighed. "Maybe that won't happen either." She pulled out a pastry, and picked at it. "You know I went to Metairie Cemetery a few months ago, the last time I came for a visit."

"Everything okay?"

"Yeah. I straightened things up a little."

Terra looked at the ground. "I should go, too." She didn't want to go, not at all. She'd put it off for months now, because she knew the old anger would come back with full force once she saw his grave. But it wasn't fair to her mother to stay away.

Marina gave up picking and took a bite of the pastry. She winced.

"Something hard in there?" asked Terra.

Marina rubbed her jaw with a disappointed look on her face.

"No."

"Wisdom tooth coming in?"

"It's nothing. My jaw's just sore." Marina stopped rubbing.

Terra stared at her face. The girl had tears in her eyes. Was she in that much pain? Marina's jaw was a bit darker right where she had just rubbed off a little makeup.

"What's that on your jaw?" asked Terra.

"The medical term for it is *bruise*."

Marina's snotty tone told her they were in for another fight. *Fine*. "Sally told me she thought you looked upset. What's going on?"

"Look, Terra, I fell into the side of a door when I first got into town, okay? I'm pissed that it's taking so long to get better. Okay?"

"You fell?" Terra asked anxiously. She wondered if her sister had fainted. "Did you see a doctor?"

"Relax. I have an appointment next Monday with Dr. Dread." Marina smiled a little, and her tears seemed to recede.

"*Our* Dr. Dread?"

"The one and only."

Their old family doctor had a real name, of course, but his gaunt skeletal look had earned him the nickname Dr. Dread. His appearance was terrifying to them as children, except the good doctor was competent, had warm hands, and had known the girls since they were born.

"Is Dr. Dread going to follow your pregnancy?" Terra asked.

"Sure thing."

She felt a whole lot better knowing Dr. Dread would be caring for Marina. Here again her sister had shown her maturity by making an appointment with their old family doctor. Terra decided she'd been unfair to her sister by jumping all over her about the bruise. She had to let the girl go and stop worrying.

Marina put her uneaten pastry back in the sack. "I've got to get back to work now, Terra. I'm glad you came by to see me."

"Do you need any money or anything, Honeybunch?"

Marina smiled, her face now pain-free, and alight with optimism and pride. "No. I'm fine. You go back to Silicon Valley. I'll call you soon, okay?"

Terra gave her sister a hug in front of the art store. "You know how to get aholda me," Terra said. She watched Marina slip into the art store, and then turned away to fulfill her other familial obligation.

★

The family tomb always gave Terra the creeps, and today was no exception. The air around her was hot and humid, but she shivered anyway. Her mother's inscription said "Viveca Le Monnier Breaux." She tried to visualize Mama, hoping to remember the exact sound of her laughter, or maybe the hue of her eyes, or perhaps recall the smell of her skin. But she couldn't; it had been too long.

Terra knelt down and pulled out a few weeds. She wasn't one to stand there and tell her dead mother about her problems. Or even think about them at her tomb site. She didn't want Mama's soul to catch a whiff of her concerns. Mama should enjoy heaven; she deserved it.

But she showed no such restraint toward her father.

"You piece of crap," she hissed, eyeing his inscription: "Judd Arnaud Breaux." "You coward." She stood up, and said what she always came to say. "Why in the hell weren't Marina and me enough to keep you here?"

Absolute silence. It was the same answer she'd gotten for the last six years. "We should have been enough."

She refused to forgive her father for killing himself less than a year after Mama died. His suicide left Marina and Terra alone, orphaned. Grieving and angry, Terra had to be the parent, taking care of Marina, a job she was so unprepared for.

A short and intense vision of Mama—the way her brow furrowed when she inspected a scrape on Terra's knee, and how she told Terra it would be all right—surged through her mind. She got goose bumps. She had the strong feeling Mama's peace was disturbed. That right now in heaven Mama was upset.

She spoke to her dead mother nervously, quickly—afraid of contact, but even more afraid she might be crazy. "We're okay, Mama. Marina's pregnant. But she came back to New Orleans, and she got herself a job. She's seeing Dr. Dread. I'll keep an eye on her, but you know, I think she's growing up, Mama."

And then her feeling of unease was gone. She knew her mother was satisfied. She was too. Marina *was* growing up. She and Marina weren't orphans anymore. They were simply women who didn't have parents.

A warm breeze touched her bare arms and she took a step away from the tomb. It was time for her to grow up, too, and let go of some of her anger. She stepped back even more, distancing herself from the tomb, and from the events that put her parents there.

"Goodbye, Mama," she said. "Goodbye Papa."

Terra left Metairie Cemetery and returned to the Quarter in the evening, feeling drained. A horse-drawn carriage with a newly married couple passed by her, and the groom tossed her a silk flower. Terra caught it with one hand. It was a yellow rose and it revived her.

She stopped by Jackson Square, and was delighted to catch another glimpse of Marina still working in the shop. Her sister really would be okay. The shop lights turned off, and Marina walked out into the street, and into the waiting arms of a man.

The sight of Marina with a man hit Terra full force. Who was he? She got as close as she could without being seen, and discovered he wasn't a man at all.

He was Jared Grant—also known as RogueKnight.

8 / RogueKnight

Jared wasn't in prison. All this time Terra had assumed her sister's lover was some college kid. She'd never even considered that the father of Marina's baby might be Jared. Now, far too late, she realized that her sister's girlhood infatuation with RogueKnight had matured into something more.

She turned away from the departing couple, and walked back to her apartment. When Jared, aka RogueKnight, ended up in prison again for salami slicing, as was sure to happen, Marina and her baby would need her to help pick up the pieces. To do that, Terra had to be free of Silicon Silk. She needed RogueKnight's help to fulfill her contract with Marc—and she had no guarantee the cracker would. The irony of the situation made her sick and anxious.

★

The cracker gathering was supposed to take place at two in the Food Court at Riverwalk, a waterfront mall. Terra arrived at about two-fifteen. She spotted RogueKnight slouched at a table over by the Taco Bell. Several other young men sat with him. Zap wasn't there. No one acknowledged her as she pulled up a chair. Apparently, if you wanted to lurk, and just listen in, that was okay. If you wanted to share, that was okay, too. She listened, intrigued that these face-to-face discussions were far more open than the #Crack chatter had been.

A dark-haired, heavy-set boy began to ask RogueKnight to explain some technical detail about IP spoofing code. Breaking into a computer using an IP spoofer was not unlike someone from a banned country gaining entry into the US by forging a passport with a friendly and harmless country of origin.

Another participant, a young man with short, white-bleached hair, kept shaking his Taco Bell drink, making the ice smash into the sides of his paper cup. He called himself Daemon.

Terra now studied RogueKnight, trying to discern any physical impact of his time in prison. His forehead held a few new creases, but his dirty blonde thatch was still uncombed. A tuft of reddish-yellow hair now skulked beneath his lower lip. He seemed thinner. His faded flannel and denim clothing, along with his solemn demeanor, wrapped him in an air of a wronged Robin Hood—drama that would play all too well to an eighteen-year-old girl like Marina.

Daemon peeled the lid off the cup and shook some ice into his mouth. Still crunching, he asked the dark-haired boy, "Hey, jdr, did you see that the Department of Justice website got hacked again last night?" He put the lid back on and shook his cup.

"Ugh-ugh," the heavy-set jdr said.

"Course I only saw the archive, not the real thing."

"So was it good?" jdr asked.

"Yeah. Pussy, and more pussy."

"Those that can," said RogueKnight, "crack. Those that can't, make web pages." The salami slicer's tone was dismissive.

The playfulness and mischievousness that had once distinguished RogueKnight was gone. Tormenting Michael Dell with e-mail tricks just wasn't in the cracker anymore. She wondered what *was*.

The electronic underground continued their relaxed conversations, alternating between security vulnerabilities, movies, encryption, music, and obscene remarks by the white-haired Daemon.

Terra wished she could speak to RogueKnight alone, but the others didn't seem inclined to leave anytime soon.

"Have any of you ever heard of someone who calls himself Ranger?" she finally asked the group.

"Ranger. Sure. The Swedish guy," RogueKnight replied.

"What name *you* goin' by?" Daemon asked her.

She thought aliases were childish. She had never bragged about her exploits, and she hadn't learned her skills at anyone's knee, so she hadn't needed a nickname. Not having been a social cracker, she'd had few interactions with her peer group. The notable exception being the period in her life when she had associated with RogueKnight's group—and look at the misery *that* contact would end up causing her sister.

Realizing she had to play by the group's rules if she wanted RogueKnight's information, she said, "Um. I'm Euphoria. So where do you know Ranger from, RogueKnight?"

"A BBS," he said.

BBSs, or electronic bulletin boards, were yet another way a cracker could learn break-in tricks. She knew better than to ask the salami slicer which BBS, until he began to trust her.

"What else do you know about Ranger?" she asked.

"Feds are welcome to come listen and learn," RogueKnight said, "not ask questions."

"I'm not a Fed," she said, laughing.

"Yeah, you *are*," RogueKnight insisted.

The others stopped their talking and ice sloshing, paying full attention to Terra and RogueKnight. Fantastic! A confrontation between the forces of good and evil!

"Oh come on, RogueKnight," she said, thinking the whole scene was funny. "What happened to those wonderful ideals of free flow of information? What was that you used to say? Something like, 'the sharing of information is the noblest cause; hoarding data is beneath contempt'? I don't need info about IP spoofers. I need info about Ranger."

"Like what *kind* of information?" jdr asked suspiciously.

"I want to know what RogueKnight thinks about him. Does he respect Ranger's skills?"

For starters anyway.

RogueKnight shook his head no. "Ranger gets where he needs to go. But it's through persistence, not through understanding or plan."

Daemon shook his cup, and conversations restarted. No fight between good and evil today.

Terra wondered how someone with poor skills could invade SSI. Even *she* couldn't break into SSI's network—not that she'd tried that hard. But she couldn't abandon Ranger as a suspect. He was the best lead she had. Ranger could still be viable as the SSI attacker if RogueKnight's standards were too lofty, or Ranger's persistence had paid off.

"What makes you think that Ranger doesn't understand what he's doing?" she asked the salami slicer.

RogueKnight scratched his scrawny chest. "Well, let me give you an example. This was a couple of years ago. Ranger broke into this computer at...." the cracker stopped abruptly, and studied her. "Now I get it. You're a *corporate* Fed."

He waited for her to deny it. But she wouldn't. Thanks to that bastard Marc Elliott, that's exactly what she was. A corporate Fed. And as much as crackers tricked and deceived computers and networks, they didn't lie to each other. Honor among thieves.

The group went silent around her. Maybe there'd be a fight after all.

"This is a really good story," RogueKnight said suddenly, resolving the tension. He gazed around at his buddies. They seemed eager to hear it. He turned back to Terra. "I'm going to say—just for grins—that this machine Ranger broke into was at Silicon Silk. Ranger had targeted SSI because that company is one of the premier profiteers of data hoarding. Anyway, Ranger gained root. He made himself a new account with superuser privileges. He even changed the root password. That computer was hijacked solid. Even if SSI discovered the break-in, they wouldn't be able kick Ranger off the computer and ruin his little operation."

Using a real-life metaphor, Ranger had traded a stolen shack for a stolen mansion. He'd also changed the locks on the doors of the mansion, so the real owner of the mansion couldn't get back in.

"What was his operation?" jdr asked.

"He'd set up a warez FTP site," said RogueKnight.

Terra snorted derisively. "Warez." So, the SSI computer had been set up as an electronic warehouse to deliver pirated software over the Internet. Using the house analogy again, the stolen, re-keyed mansion was being used to distribute hot merchandise. Ranger had to be a pimple-faced loser.

"His warez site worked for months," RogueKnight continued. "Anyway, one day Ranger's hijacked FTP site is gone. He can't get on the machine at all. He's scared, thinking he's left so much evidence that they're going to come get him. He tells me this, and I say, 'You're in *Sweden*, you're safe. Nobody's gonna come get you.' But he wants to know how come he got kicked off, and asks me to check it out." RogueKnight now broke into a smile. "This is the good part. So I get on this SSI machine, no trouble, and take a look at the backups to find out what happened. You know what that Swedish fucker had forgotten to do?" RogueKnight now paused for effect, and gazed around at his peers. "He'd forgotten to give his own account a password!"

The group laughed and snickered. Terra shook her head: Ranger *was* stupid. Even though Ranger had changed the locks on the mansion, he'd forgotten to lock the door to his own little shack. And there, in plain sight, lying on the dresser in that shack, was the key to the mansion. He was a luser all right.

"So did you help him get his warez site up and running again?" asked Daemon.

"No," RogueKnight said. "I could give a fuck about warez or Silicon Silk. That was Ranger's deal. I just deleted some of the logs."

"You say Ranger did that a few years ago?" Terra asked.

"Yeah."

So then the penetration of SSI had happened before Keith. "You think Ranger's back to invading SSI machines?" she asked.

"Not that I'd tell you if he was, Euphoria, but last I heard, the dumbfuck was in love with HTML," RogueKnight replied in a sneering tone. "Gonna set up some website against Silicon Silk."

HTML. Terra recalled the sticky note with the HTML tag. A million people knew HTML. But not everyone was in love with it. Ranger could still be a suspect, even if he was a sloppy cracker.

A chubby, sweet-faced girl drifted in and pulled up a chair next to RogueKnight. She smiled at the older cracker. "Hey, I heard you were back!" Then she addressed the assembled group. "Anybody around here know Windows NT?"

Stocky jdr was apparently the expert on NT security weaknesses, so he offered her a slew of tips. After thanking jdr, she turned to RogueKnight again.

"So, you allowed access to computers anymore?" the girl asked.

"No," the salami slicer replied. "I'm lucky I can use the phone, Lucy. I'm not even supposed to use an ATM machine. But I got innocent friends. And *they* can have as many computers as they want."

And one of those innocent friends was undoubtedly Marina.

Terra stayed until the bitter end, to deliver a warning to RogueKnight.

"Don't mess with Marina, Jared," Terra told him. "Or I'll mess with you."

He stared at Terra, unconcerned. Her threat obviously meant nothing. Not to someone who'd spent as many years in prison as he had.

★

Terra returned to work Friday morning, feeling worn down. First thing, she headed over to the coffee station for a caffeine jolt. Some of the guys were standing around chattering about a hot software company called Calypso Inc.

Calypso had just filed for an initial public offering. Once the

Security and Exchange Commission approved the IPO, Calypso could throw open ownership of the company to the public by selling stock for the first time. The violent ups and downs of technology stocks had always kept Terra from getting too involved in investment gossip. She never bought stock, as "the street's" regard for a technology company never seemed to mesh with her insider's understanding. But she knew that the market for initial public offerings—especially of Internet-related companies like Calypso— was no longer crazed. Gone were the days when an Internet company losing tons of money could raise tons more of it from the public.

Ted's bear-frame lumbered over to the coffee station. The news about Calypso was on his mind too.

"The IPO is going to make everybody at Calypso rich," he grumbled.

Terra knew Ted wished Silicon Silk would go public—so he could be rich, too.

Ray arrived at the coffee station, looking more harried than usual. He drummed his fat fingers on the table. "Listen guys," he said, "now that this rollout of Scout 4.0 is done, we need to get some order around here."

The Chief of Technology looked straight at Terra. Like he was wondering what she was doing with her time, and he was going to find out.

"The contract employees have gone," Ray continued, "and so now we're going to get back to having senior programmers' meetings again. Monday afternoon at one, starting the week after next. Spread the word."

"Crack that whip, Ray," one of the younger female programmers chirped.

Terra went back to her cube, feeling even more exhausted. The honeymoon was over; now Ray would be expecting progress from her, just as Marc did. Why couldn't Personal Scout have been a real project rather than just her cover? She rubbed her eyes and sighed.

Maybe if she worked really hard, she could impress Ray. If she could convince the Chief of Technology that Personal Scout was a good idea, maybe he'd press Marc to move forward on Personal Scout. Once she solved the digital theft mystery, Marc would let her work on what she was good at.

"Marc's been looking for you all week, Terra," Jack yelled over from his space. "And you haven't been working here long enough to know this, but he doesn't come over here unless he's really mad."

"Oh shut up, Jack," she huffed, wondering if Marc was planning to hound her. She hoped not; she didn't feel up to a fight with him.

In fact, the only thing she did feel like doing was throwing up. She ran to restroom, and did just that. She went home, sick and disgusted. Why'd she have to get the stomach flu just when she needed to do the most work?

On Monday, after a weekend in bed, Terra felt well enough to return to work. She called doctor Dread's office in New Orleans, to ask his receptionist, a woman she'd known since she was a teen, if she would send her Marina's bills. Terra wanted to make sure that Marina didn't skimp on her medical care because she thought she couldn't afford it.

"If she needs a specialist or something, I'll take care of those bills, too," Terra said.

Dr. Dread's receptionist laughed good-naturedly. "She came in this morning, Terra. Her pregnancy is progressing nicely. We prescribed vitamins—that's it. You really should believe her when she tells you she's okay. Because she is. If Marina has problems I'm sure she'll let you know."

"Yeah," she said. *And I'm betting she won't.*

"I know you're far away, and that makes it tough, but we'll take care of her. I want you to know that little wrist sprain of hers wasn't serious either."

What wrist sprain?

"That's good to know. Thanks." Terra hung up, more worried than ever.

She tried unsuccessfully to get some work done. But a strange marriage of anxiety and exhaustion made it nearly impossible. Her personal life was clearly getting in the way of her job.

So she sat there in that fancy chair, staring at a SYSLOG file for at least an hour.

My job is also getting in the way of my personal life.

Carolina stopped by to ask her to an early lunch. It was the young mother's first day back from maternity leave. Even though Terra had little appetite, she looked forward to sitting across from a female face at Silk Cafe for a change.

The two women sat down at a table near tall windows. Terra noticed Carolina's tray was crowded with food. She looked like she was eating for an army.

"Nursing takes a *lot* of calories," Carolina explained.

"Do you like being a mom?"

"Yeah! I do! And it sure beats being pregnant." Carolina started on her dessert calories first.

"You didn't like pregnancy?"

"Not much. Now my only complaint is that I have to wake up at night to feed Emily. That and the fact that I'll probably never again fit into pants without elastic."

"When do babies start to sleep at night?"

"Oh, they sleep at night right away. For three-hour stretches."

How will Marina ever be able to raise a baby alone once RogueKnight is carted off to prison for computer fraud again?

Terra gazed at Carolina, so beautiful with her flawless brown skin, her glistening black hair. She looked happy. "So how come you look so good?"

The young mother beamed. "Thanks for saying that, Terra. Ray usually brings Emily to me when she wakes up, and I sleep while the baby nurses."

Terra blanched. She didn't even want to think about bringing a little sucking thing to Marina in the middle of the night. It was so... biological.

"Are you coming over next Saturday?" Carolina asked.

"Over where?"

"To our house. I'm having a birthday dinner."

"Birthday, huh?" Terra said. "How old are you going to be?"

"Twenty-eight."

"That means I'm older than you," Terra said. "I'm already twenty-eight."

"Except I'm going to be twenty-eight for the third year in a row. I like that age."

Terra calculated Carolina's real age, and mock gasped. "You're going to be *thirty*?"

"Keep that a secret, huh? So Peter hasn't asked you to come to my party yet?"

"No." Terra shrugged. "I haven't seen Peter in awhile. Maybe he's asked somebody else."

"Not likely."

"Why do you say that?"

"He's never brought a date to a company party but you." Finished with her cake, Carolina moved onto her roast chicken and baby potatoes.

"So Peter comes alone?"

"Or doesn't come at all. Anyway, I was hoping he'd invite you again. But it doesn't matter. *I'm* inviting you. Come without him, and meet him there." Carolina raised her brows and smirked.

"Are you setting us up?"

"Yeah. Time to marry Peter off! Actually…" Carolina stopped to look around the cafeteria. Satisfied, she continued. "Actually, I'm setting up David Houle."

"I take it David doesn't know you're setting him up."

Carolina giggled, and then said, "Neither does the friend I'm setting him up with. Anyway, back to Peter. I've never been able to figure him out. You know, someone that good looking, that smooth, without a woman. Until you, at that launch dinner. I was hoping you were a sign of good changes for him. I always wondered if he was into biker chicks or something. Or maybe he's actually part of that kinkoid sex he told us about. Remember that bondage newsgroup he was so familiar with?" She laughed. "Wasn't that just disgusting? Whips and dildos and leather and suction cups? Anyway, I guess I've always assumed that he never felt comfortable bringing his type of woman—whatever that is—to a company function, so he came alone."

"Well, has it ever occurred to you that maybe he'd rather bring a man?"

"Peter's gay?"

"I'm *kidding*, Carolina," Terra said, annoyed at Carolina's thoughtful expression. Peter couldn't be homosexual. Not as powerfully attracted as she was to him. No way.

9 / The party

Just as Carolina had hoped, Peter invited Terra to the birthday party. She accepted the invitation, and decided not to leave anything to chance. Instead of working Saturday morning, which she should have done, she went shopping at the Stanford Shopping Center. Bargain hunting was one of her passions, but it was a joy she hadn't indulged in since she'd gotten to California. She purchased a perfect white dress. She also hunted for a gag gift to give to Carolina for her birthday, but couldn't bring herself to go through with it. Not after she saw the gold drop earrings at Nordstrom's. She bought them, knowing Carolina would look gorgeous in them: gold and brown skin just went together.

In the afternoon she put the dress on, and took a good look at herself in the mirror. Short and tight, the sleeveless cotton sheath showed her curves to advantage.

"Laissez les bons temps rouler," she said, laughing at her reflection.

The dress would tell Peter, without words, what she wanted from him. But it would have to tell him after the dinner party. She slipped on a long, lean jacket of the same material, covering up the dress. After fixing small amethyst earrings into her ears and brushing her white-blonde hair, she examined herself in the mirror again. She now looked refined; her appearance yielded no clue as to her internal hormonal state.

Peter was late picking her up.

"Wow," he said when he saw her. He seemed distracted.

Terra swore that the next time he said "Wow," there would be a catch in his voice. He'd *mean* it.

"Wow, yourself," she said, appreciating his close-cut white pants and sweater. Of course it didn't matter what he wore; he was one of those men that looked good in anything.

Her tight dress made it hard to get into his sports car. As she inched in, she wondered if biker chicks did appeal to him. Playing a biker chick sounded like fun; she was always up for a bit of fantasy sex. Who was she fooling, she laughed to herself; she would be up for any kind of sex with Peter.

Carolina and Ray lived in the town of Atherton, an exclusive enclave of acre-plus estates north of Stanford. Peter parked in a circular drive shaded by old oak trees. A maid greeted them at the door of the large, stucco one-story. She led Peter and Terra through a formal, wood-paneled hall and living room, outside to the backyard pool.

Carolina's hostess instincts were in overdrive. She effusively greeted Terra, apparently delighted to see her with Peter. Carolina then introduced Peter and Terra to a woman as quiet as Carolina was lively.

"This is my good friend and neighbor, Annie MacDougal," Carolina said.

Terra suspected this was the woman Carolina wanted David to meet. Looking around at the twenty or thirty people already there, she couldn't spot David. Steve, the lawyer, and his wife Kathy came over to talk to Terra and Peter. The lawyer's wife went on and on about her children's achievements in ballet and soccer, and her own important Junior League charity work. Nothing made Terra more grateful for her own life than contact with a person with a pretentious one.

Because Terra could only take so much gratefulness without wanting a drink, she left the group, and headed over to the bar. Only wine and beer were offered. She would've preferred hard liquor.

"What do you recommend?" she asked the young man behind the bar.

"Pyramid's good," he said. "They make it over in Berkeley."

"Okay, give me Pyramid, then," she said, even though she had no idea what Pyramid was. It turned out to be a fine-tasting beer.

Marc arrived, looking darkly handsome in his usual grad student attire. He asked the bartender for two white wines. He made small talk with Terra as the bartender poured the wine. Peter came over, and draped his arm across her shoulders—a faintly possessive move that heartened her. She'd hear that catch in Peter's voice yet.

Terra, Peter, and Marc rejoined the group, which now included Carolina, and a beautiful woman who took one of the glasses of wine from Marc. She wasn't Velvet. Marc introduced her to Terra as Sunny; the others in the group seemed to know her. She had perfect cheekbones, long, black, wavy hair, and a softly musical voice. Sunny was apparently a local radio host.

Ray joined the group. He held baby Emily. "You've got to get yourself one of these," he teased Peter.

Terra took a good look. The baby's eyes were closed, and it seemed sort of unformed. A tuft of black hair poked up out of its mostly-bald head.

"Emily's real pretty," Terra said.

Carolina punched Terra in the arm. "For heaven's sake, Terra, stop grimacing when you say she's pretty! You'll scare Emily!"

Terra's jaw dropped open. She didn't think she had been grimacing—just studying. "Her eyes aren't even open," she complained, "so she can't see what kind of expression I have."

Carolina and Ray laughed, and took Emily over to more appreciative eyes. Marc seemed genuinely interested in the infant, reaching out to cradle her in his arms. Emily's eyes opened, and Marc talked to the baby. Emily made sounds in response that didn't seem to alarm the parents. Sunny now joined in the dialogue. She seemed determined to enchant the infant. Terra got the feeling that Sunny was auditioning for Marc: *See what a great mother I'd make?*

Kathy looked on coldly, apparently not approving of Sunny's membership in the Silicon Valley Wives' Club. *Like Kathy's opinion would ever matter to Marc,* thought Terra.

A young woman came out of the house, took the baby from Marc, and carried her back inside.

"David hasn't shown up yet, has he?" Carolina asked from beside Terra.

"I haven't seen him," Terra said. She noticed that Carolina's girlfriend—the one that was supposed to be matched up with David—looked perfectly happy chatting with a group of people.

"This isn't like David," Carolina said. "He's always early. Too early, usually. I'll see if I can delay dinner."

Finally Carolina couldn't stall anymore, and announced that dinner was ready. Everyone wandered around, looking at the many round tables set up on the patio, trying to find a place card with their name on it. Terra found hers. She was disappointed she wouldn't be sitting with Peter. Kathy was on one side of her, and Marc on the other. Not her favorite two people. Ray, one of his neighbors, and a coworker of Carolina's, rounded out the group. Sunny's place card was at an adjacent table, and she didn't look too happy about being split from her date either. Peter sat at a table that included Carolina, Annie, and the missing David.

The first course, an endive salad, was brought out. Terra amused herself with the thought that dessert should have been served first, since it was Carolina's birthday party. Kathy questioned Terra delicately about her family background and education; she got the feeling Kathy was probing for her suitability for the Club. Terra wondered how Kathy would react if she told her straight out, "I want to *fuck* Peter, not marry him." Terra kept glancing over in Peter's direction, wondering when they'd finally get to be alone.

The main course of thinly sliced rare beef and asparagus tips arrived. One of the servers brought a phone out to Ray. Ray put the phone to his ear, and then passed it over to Marc without a word.

Marc spoke to the person on the other end, and a look of stunned distress fell over his face.

★

David Houle was dead. The phone call was from David's ex-wife. David had killed himself, but his ex hadn't gone into the specifics.

Carolina's birthday party broke up in a hurry. Terra felt horribly sorry for Carolina, who seemed to be so close to David. After all, she was trying to set him up with her girlfriend.

"I'll drop you off, Terra, but then I have to go back to the office," Peter told her as they got into his car. He had to help Marc pull the company together during the crisis.

Remembering how distraught Marc was when he got the news about David, she wondered if he and David were good friends. Whatever the reason for Marc's reaction, Terra had strong feelings of empathy for him. And she wished she didn't; it was easier to hate Marc when she thought he wasn't altogether human.

"What's going to happen to the company now?" she asked Peter.

"David's death will put a big dent into our development timetable," Peter admitted. "And into the corporation. We just went through this with Nancy."

In contrast to Marc's devastation, Peter's concern about David's death seemed to stem only from his position as corporate bean counter. David's suicide hurt the company, but not him.

Once Peter got her to her door, he gave her a peck on the cheek. But his hand lingered on her hip, and she thought she might be able to convince him to stay for a little bit.

"Come on in, Peter," she said.

Patting her hip absently, he said, "Can't, Terragirl." He smiled his lazy, confident smile and left.

She watched him roar off, and realized she didn't want Peter to stay because she was horny. No, as much as she wanted to get that man naked, sex wasn't the reason. It was because she was scared to be alone.

She opened the door to her condo, slipped inside, and quickly locked it. Nancy had died—practically in her arms—not all that long ago. And now David was dead, too. She made herself a cup of herb tea, hoping to shake her feeling of unease. But she couldn't relax. The urge to flee was stronger than ever.

Her fear that something was wrong at SSI, and that she might get caught up in it too, was just the push she needed. Steeling herself with two extra-strength Tylenol, she set about cracking Ranger's SSIck hate site. She had to solve this problem once and for all, so she could get the hell out of Silicon Valley.

Before she could crack Ranger's computer, she needed a series of machines to obscure her tracks. She electronically jumped from a hijacked IBM machine in the US, to an HP in Brazil, to another IBM in Japan, to a Sun in Greece. Finally, from Greece she penetrated one of her favorites, a brand-new and vulnerable Silicon Graphics web server in Korea. The Korean SGI was the computer she would use to launch her attack against the hate site. SSIck's Web address was *www.darkside.se/SSIck*, corresponding to a computer with an IP address of 257.82.75.12.

She rammed 257.82.75.12 with full force: every bit of her knowledge, experience, and fear went into the digital attack. And she needed that intensity. Either Ranger was a better technician than RogueKnight believed, or Ranger had gotten help from someone who had superior defensive skills.

Terra wiped the sweat off her upper lip. *Try again.*

Forty-five minutes later she was in.

257.82.75.12 belonged to her now. Her entire body and mind seemed to shiver with orgasmic delight. *I love it. I love knowing I've tricked a trickster.* It had been years since she'd felt that kind of rush. She could do what she wanted to this cracker's computer. Anything. Even if her trail wasn't as obscure as she thought, what could Ranger do to her? Call the FBI? His machine was in *Sweden.*

Languidly, like a lover exhausted after an explosive encounter, she probed the machine called darkside. Knowing cracker thought processes, she first examined files in the directories with boring names. In a directory called temp, she found a large file called

Scout_5.Z. The file had been created only days ago.

Scout_5.Z could be shorthand for Scout 5.0, the SSI program in early alpha testing. If it was, Ranger had something that nobody outside of the company was supposed to have.

Was it possible that she'd finally found evidence that Ranger was the cracker that had been plaguing SSI?

The Z suffix on the filename normally meant that the file was compressed. Compressing was a way of sucking the extra white spaces out of the program to make it smaller. But the program had to be *un*compressed, or white spaces pumped back in, before it could actually run.

Further searching didn't reveal any uncompressed copies of Scout_5.

"Weird," she said aloud.

Why hadn't Ranger bothered to uncompress the file? Why would a thief steal a bunch of gift-wrapped presents and never open them up? That's what crackers were *about*: finding out what was *inside* stolen presents.

Using her elaborate, international chain of hijacked computers, she eventually got Scout_5.Z transferred to her own machine. She made herself a trap door to get into darkside later, logged off Ranger's computer, and then uncompressed the program on her own machine. She ran the program. It *was* Scout 5.0: buggy, and containing the usual programmer's horseplay, like menus liberally sprinkled with four-letter words.

Ranger had intellectual property belonging to SSI. The fact that he hadn't bothered to examine his booty didn't sit right with Terra, but maybe he didn't have the time. Perhaps right after Ranger had stolen the compressed program, an asteroid had plunged down to earth, striking Sweden. Shards of that asteroid had penetrated Ranger's forehead, forcing him onto the floor. So Ranger lay there next to darkside, dying. And with his very last thought and breath, he wished that he could reach his computer to pump the white spaces back into Scout_5.Z.

Weird. And unlikely.

She shrugged. It wasn't her job to explain every anomaly. Her job was to investigate that one final detail, and then she'd be able to wrap up this whole stinking mess, and get the hell out of Silicon Valley.

She stretched, trying to get a kink out of the center of her back. The clock said 4:25 am. She brewed herself strong coffee, anticipating the job ahead; she'd have to figure out how Ranger had penetrated the SSI network, and then plug up the hole. Gulping the caffeine down, she started to attack Silicon Silk's proxy servers using the French SGI.

She got nowhere.

Another two hours went by. And another three. Another forty-five minutes. She finally managed to penetrate one single, pathetic Silicon Silk machine. It didn't take long for her activities to trigger the automatic security; each time she typed in a command, the computer's response was slower. She slogged on, only to find that this computer didn't seem to have any useful information on it, nor did it appear to have any exploitable connections to any other part of the Silicon Silk network. Eventually the computer was so slow in responding she might as well not have been connected at all.

Suddenly a message appeared on her screen.

Get out and don't come back.

Her connection to the Silicon Silk computer then was severed. She'd been kicked off—probably by Keith, the firewall administrator, who'd been roused out of bed on a Sunday morning to defend the network.

Damn.

How in the hell had Ranger broken in? Until she found out, she wasn't going to be able to leave Silicon Valley.

10 / Hot buttons

Ray canceled the programmers' meeting on Monday because of David's death. He wasn't around at all. Slowly, over the next few days, everyone in A & C Group began to learn the awful truth. David Houle hadn't simply fallen dead of a heart attack or something. He'd killed himself. Nobody knew how, though. Terra's irrational feeling of being in peril had worn off. David's death was awful, but it didn't endanger her.

After a week, normal life in A & C resumed. Ray was back. There were new posters on the walls at work. Gone was the grinning Perl kid. Now a pale, pixelated woman, with chips for eyes, replaced him. She still asked, "Who is the best person you've ever worked with? How can SSI hire him or her?" The scary chip eyes generated a lot of snide commentary, especially since the company didn't even design chips. Sherry started calling her the "chip witch," and soon everyone else followed suit.

Calypso was also a topic of conversation at the coffee station. The day of the Calypso IPO was here.

"Have you heard?" Ted asked Terra. "Calypso's gone up like 125 percent since this morning. It's eighty-six and five-eighths now."

"Do you own some Calypso stock?" asked Terra.

"I wish," Ted said, stroking his beard. "You have to be really connected to get part of a hot IPO. And now that Calypso's hit the aftermarket, it's too expensive."

Jack sneered. "Calypso is losing money hand over fist. They're like 23 million in debt. How can people ever buy stock in a company that loses money like that? I thought the public had wised up after the dot com trainwreck."

"The future," Ted said. "Calypso is supposed to be the next Netscape."

"That's not saying much," Jack said between swallows of his ever-present Surge.

"Yeah, yeah, Jack," Ted said. "The next Microsoft, then."

Sherry laughed. Everyone knew Jack was a big Microsoft lover.

"When those guys left SSI to form Calypso last year, they asked me to become a partner with them," Lyle said. "For five thousand bucks I could have been a partner. I said no. I mean, all they had was an idea. I wish I'd known." He shook his head. "Eighty-six dollars a share."

"An idea is *still* all Calypso has," someone quipped. "More video game than business, I heard."

"Ideas are better than a product," Sherry said.

"Then let's think of something idiotic to do on the Internet, and sell stock in it, eh? A high concept Internet company," Ted said.

"Too bad the Internet gold rush is over," Sherry said. "Remember when a company could go public when all it had was a name that ended with "dot com." Or had an exclamation point. Hey, let's call our company 'Thrill!'"

"Or 'Debt dot com,'" Terra said.

"Greed dot com, with an exclamation point," Lyle offered. "Hey, guys, I've got a direct real-time feed from NASDAQ to my computer. Come see my stock ticker, and watch me cry over Calypso."

The group crowded around Lyle's machine. A stream of numbers and symbols marched from the left side of the screen to the right. Lyle's rats—which she'd since learned were named Bells and Whistles, and were not rats at all but mice—slept in their cage.

"What's Calypso up to now?" Terra asked.

"The symbol is CLPS. It's going up—way up," Ted said.

CLPS was up to 104. Terra began to suspect Lyle's ticker was a fake, especially when she saw the symbol MSFT was worth only a few dollars.

Terra knocked on the screen. "What's going on with that MSFT one?" she asked, pretending ignorance. "It's falling like a rock."

"Nearly worthless," Sherry confirmed, winking at Terra.

"Poor Microsoft," Ted said. "Gonna get de-listed from NASDAQ."

"These numbers aren't real, Lyle," Jack said.

"Oh, yes they are," Lyle insisted. "Haven't you heard? Microsoft is a penny stock now; they are going to have to reverse split."

Everyone, except for Jack, burst out laughing.

"Too bad you don't really have a real-time NASDAQ feed," Ted said.

"You saw through me," Lyle admitted, turning around and grinning at the group. "It's a peek into the future." He looked back at his little dynamic lie. "I did it with Java."

"Stupid Java tricks," said Jack, turning away, unamused.

"It just goes to show that no rational person should invest in stocks," Terra said. "So what's SLCN and SLCNpr?" Those stocks were in the three figures.

"It's us," Lyle answered.

"SLCN preferred? That's a creative touch," said a familiar voice from behind them.

They all turned to look. "Hey, Marc," said Lyle.

"Working hard?" Marc asked the assembled group.

"Extremely hard. Got to monitor that fake stock market," Lyle cracked.

Marc chuckled, and Terra was again struck by how much better looking he was in person than in his photographs. Especially with a friendly expression on his face.

"Terra, you're just the person I was looking for," Marc said. "Ray's out. Let's use his office."

"Okay," she said, following him. The walk to Ray's office gave her more time than usual to formulate her progress report. She decided not to tell him about Ranger. Especially since the more she thought about it, the more she again came to the conclusion that someone on the inside must have delivered Ranger the Scout program.

Once they got there, Marc closed the door behind them. "Do you have any news?"

"Well, I tried to break into Silicon Silk again. It took every resource I had, and I finally broke into one computer. But my attack triggered some kind of countermeasure, which made it impossible to get anywhere. Then I got booted off. So, anyway, I'm finished with the basic security analysis. The SSI network appears to be secure from the outside. *I* certainly can't get into any machine that's useful. I also laid the tripwires on the A & C servers weeks ago. Not one of the traps has sprung."

"I see," he said. "Thanks for the update, Terra."

He started toward the door.

"Marc?" she said.

He stopped and turned.

"I'm still having trouble accepting that someone is breaking in to steal proprietary information, only to practically give the secrets away as shareware," she said. "I wonder if this isn't computer terrorism, and if you aren't about to get extorted. Maybe you'll get a letter that says, 'I'll ruin your company if you don't pay me a million bucks. And see, I can steal whatever and whenever I want.' Have you gotten a letter like that?"

"No," he said, staring at her, as if he was waiting for her to continue.

There was something attractive about the way he could let her know just with his body language that an atom bomb could go off around him, but all he cared about was what she was going to say next.

"So do you know somebody in this company that needs a million bucks?" she asked. "Say somebody with a big gambling problem?"

"No."

"Well, can you think of anyone at the company who has some

other reason to need a lot of money?"

"Hmm," he said. He stroked his chin silently. She thought he was just pretending to consider her question because he didn't look very thoughtful. Instead he seemed to be studying her face with singular attention.

"Look, I'm serious about this," she warned, wondering why he was looking at her like that.

His eyes were warm beneath his thick brows. "I know you're serious. But that needing a million dollars angle isn't going to help much. Just about everyone at the company has an unusual need for money. Have you seen how much it costs to buy even a two-bedroom house in Mountain View?"

"Not really," she said. "I suppose having a Realtor girlfriend gives you a leg up on that kind of information."

She suddenly wondered if Velvet was actually his girlfriend anymore, or if Sunny had taken her place. Or maybe he just had a lot of women. Probably the latter.

In his dark, intense way, he was a strikingly handsome man. In fact, if he hadn't suckered her into becoming his private cracker-hunter, she might have responded to his vigorous physicality, barely hidden underneath that loose clothing of his, too. And he seemed to have money, which was important to some women. What attracted her, though, was his crackling intelligence and his ability to listen.

But she didn't trust him, so that was that.

A spark of an idea came to life in her mind, and before it was fully aflame, she blurted it out.

"Marc," she asked, "what if David Houle was the inside man? The thief? What if he took the software code, and intended to extort you? Except he couldn't go through with the final part, the part where he demands money from you. Full of remorse, he kills himself."

"But that's not logical. Nobody fingered David as the thief, so why would he need to be remorseful?"

"Well maybe someone did find out he was stealing code and you just don't know it. He seemed nervous and depressed to me."

"That's the way David was all the time. And it's part of the job as VP of Platforms. Porting is depressing because it never ends, and the software business is nerve-wracking anyway. But it's not worth committing suicide over."

"Well then why do *you* think he killed himself?"

"I don't think he committed suicide at all." Marc absently picked up a pile of CD-ROMs from Ray's desk, and put them down in a different spot.

"What do you mean, he didn't kill himself?"

"He died of carbon monoxide poisoning," he replied. "He had his car engine running in a closed garage."

"Oh." This was the first she'd heard about the method David had used. "But how can you say he didn't kill himself?"

"Because that's just not the way a man commits suicide."

His pained expression told her that he couldn't yet accept the suicide. She knew that feeling too well: grief mixed with anger and disbelief and betrayal.

She stepped closer to him.

"You think David should have shot himself," she said. Her own father had bowed out of life that way.

"Yeah. Short and violent. Bloody. That's what a man does. Carbon monoxide is too slow, too much like sleep."

She reached out and touched his upper arm.

"I know it's hard for you to imagine that David might have been in such a miserable state of mind that he'd want to end his life," she said, "but obviously, he was very unhappy. And as long as you refuse to believe he actually killed himself, you won't have to decide whether or not you're going to forgive him for doing it."

He put his hands on her shoulders, and looked at her with a kind of teasing intimacy.

"You're full of it, Terra. But thanks for caring."

"I know how it feels, Marc," she said earnestly. "My father killed

101

himself. Not long after my mother died. That's why I'm Marina's guardian."

She wasn't sure why she told Marc so much about herself, especially since she didn't trust him. Maybe she did care about him.

His eyes trailed over her face. Lowering his head, he gave her a kiss. And another one. Her arms reached out to encircle his waist, pulling the hard warmth of Marc's body closer to hers. His gentle, sweet kisses now became more exploratory, questioning, and she responded with her own inquiries. They played and parried. And her rational brain did not understand what her body did, because her brain remembered she didn't trust him.

He stopped kissing her, and smiled down at her. "I love the way your mind works."

At that, her rational brain took control. "Next time, do me the courtesy of asking first," she said hoarsely.

"You want me to ask before I kiss you?"

"Yes." She moved her hands away from his waist, so they hung at her sides. She thought he'd do the same. But he didn't. She still felt one of his callused hands splayed around her ear, and the other flat on her back.

"I did ask you," he said. "You kissed me yes."

The arrogant bastard was right, of course. But that didn't mean he was supposed to actually say she had responded to him. It was not gentlemanly. And besides he never should have started it.

"I'm involved with someone."

"Are you married?" he asked pointedly.

His hand slid from her ear down her jaw. One of his fingers trailed down her neck, traced her collarbone. His touch took her breath away, and her rational mind hated him for it.

"No. I didn't think you were married," he said. "You're a beautiful, prickly woman, Terra. I can feel those sharp spines of yours all the way down your back." He slowly trailed his other hand down her spine to her tailbone, giving her the shivers.

"Peter's your friend," she said. "Don't you men have a code of honor or something?"

"No," he replied. "We men don't."

Now holding her head in both hands, he kissed her lightly on the cheek and nose, and then on the chin, and then her eyelids, her forehead. The seductive, patronizing little kisses promised he would be a creative lover.

"Marc," she said, "stop it."

Infinitely slowly, he slid his hands off her. He still stood close. When she was finally free of him, she moved backward. "You touch me again and I'll file sexual harassment charges."

He had the good grace not to laugh at her, yet his black eyes glittered with sure and self-satisfied understanding. He knew he could get to her sexually.

"Next time," he drawled, "I'll ask."

The door to Ray's office suddenly opened. Terra jumped. It was Carolina. Carolina took a step inside, hesitated, and looked at Terra and Marc. And then, as if remembering the office belonged to her husband, Carolina pushed the door open wider and said, "Um. I need to use the office."

Terra ran out the door, past her friend. She flew to her cubicle, sat down, and put her hands to her roaring ears. She didn't know which was worse, the surprise of Marc's kiss, or her response. Or maybe it was Carolina walking in on them right afterwards.

Damn. It was unnatural for her to respond to Marc. It violated every feminist principle to be attracted to someone who'd mistreated her. With shaking hands, she logged onto her computer. A network diagram glimmered in front of her nearly unseeing eyes.

Who am I fooling? I wasn't just attracted to Marc. If I had listened to my body, I might have had sex with him right then and there.

And she knew that if she ever did make love to him, she'd be in the worst trouble of her life.

11 / David's equity

Carolina's head poked into Terra's cubicle. "You all right?"
"Sure," said Terra, trying to compose herself.

"I didn't mean to kick you out of Ray's office like that, but, um, my breast pump is in there."

"You don't need to explain."

"I nearly turned around and walked back out of the office when I saw you two." Carolina cocked her head, her black eyes soft with concern. "What happened?"

"We had an argument."

"What on earth about?"

"It wasn't that bad. He just knows how to push my hot buttons, that's all." She recalled how Marc had slid his hand down her back, pressing every single one of her hot buttons.

"Well it looked pretty bad to me." Carolina reached out and patted her hand. "You looked really upset. Your face was beet red. And Marc, he actually had the nerve to look smug. What has gotten into that man? Just because a good friend of his kills himself doesn't mean that he can take his frustration or whatever out on you."

"His attitude doesn't have a lot to do with David Houle. It's a respect thing, I think," Terra murmured. "And besides, he doesn't think David killed himself."

"What?"

"According to him, carbon monoxide isn't manly enough."

"What a dumb reason," Carolina said, pulling up a chair in Terra's cube. "*How* David did himself in doesn't bother me. What is totally illogical is that he killed himself at all. His timing is really weird, Terra. David bought out his part of Nancy's shares right before he died. And he had a lot of trouble getting the money to do it. David's credit wasn't too good, so he needed cash to buy Nancy out. Why go through all that hell of scraping together the money to own more of the company if you're going to end it all?"

Terra didn't think buying more company ownership was odd. "Well, maybe he wanted to provide for his family after he died, and he figured more equity in the company would ensure that."

"David's ex-wife and kids won't be getting any part of SSI."

"That doesn't seem very fair," Terra said.

Carolina blinked, and then smiled at Terra. "Of course. How could you know? The remaining shareholders have to pay David's family for David's equity in the company. The shareholders don't just steal it. It's just that the corporation was set up from the very beginning so that if a shareholder dies, the other shareholders have first crack at buying back the shares, in proportion to their current ownership. With Nancy, that meant that her heirs didn't end up owning any of the company, and the surviving shareholders ended up owning more. The same thing will happen to David's equity in the company."

Carolina then launched into a detailed explanation of classes of shares and determination of value that Terra didn't understand. But it was clear that David had needed money to buy out Nancy, and he'd had a hard time drumming up the cash. He could have resorted to extortion to get it.

"Where do you suppose David finally got the funds to buy out Nancy?" Terra asked.

"David borrowed it from someone who wasn't concerned about his creditworthiness."

"Really," said Terra. The pieces began to fit. David had probably gotten loans from an SSI competitor, perhaps even before Nancy died. He might not have even known it was a competitor at first. But soon enough, as a gesture of good faith, or because of threats, David had to start delivering Silicon Silk intellectual property to his benefactor, using Ranger as a middleman.

"Yeah," Carolina confirmed. "And you'd think that the person who lent David the money would be the first one to wonder about David's timing. But no—what *he's* annoyed about is that David did himself in in such an un-macho way." Carolina shook her head.

"Are you telling me *Marc* lent David the money?"

"Yeah," Carolina said. "None other. And now we have to go through it all again with David's shares. The shareholders'll have to divide up David's part of the company. And this time there's more company, and a lot more money involved." She gave Terra's hand a squeeze. "Look kiddo, I've got to get back to work. I spend enough time over here as it is, making this whole working/nursing/mother thing possible."

"Bye, Carolina. Thanks."

Terra chewed her lower lip, and stared at the cube wall in front of her. She tried her shore up her logic construct. Just because David had gotten a loan from Marc, didn't mean David hadn't been involved with competitors and industrial espionage. Right? Maybe David had been double dipping. David could have extorted Marc into giving him the loan. In some deep, instinctive way, she was positive that David was behind the electronic attacks. Could Marc be protecting David? Himself? She had to get more information from him.

But the very thought of confronting Marc face to face about lending the money to David made her nearly jump out of her skin. She imagined the way he'd smirk, thinking she was back for more of his kisses and touches. But she needed to know if he was being extorted by David. Not even having the guts to initiate a phone conversation with him either, she decided to leave him a voice mail. A voice message would *seem* more personal than e-mail, but she wouldn't have to actually talk to him. She formulated some questions, and called Marc's office. Identifying herself to Marc's secretary, she asked for his voice mail.

"Marc Elliott here," his voice mail answered. Except it wasn't the man's voice mail, but the man.

"Oh," Terra said. She cleared her throat. E-mail would have been a better move. "Um, this is Terra. I thought of a few more questions about David Houle that I'd like to ask you."

"Drop it, Terra," Marc said. He sounded tired. "David is not germane to SSI's computer security."

She didn't expect him to say David was none of her business. Worse, she didn't anticipate that anything he said to her could *hurt* her, either. How could she have been so stupid to have revealed such personal information to him, and allow him to kiss her? Her eyes stung. She covered up her hurt the best way she knew how—with anger.

"Oh that's right, I forgot," she snapped. "Me and my entire life is germane to SSI computer security. If that means digging up my secrets, exploiting me, micro-managing my life—no big deal. Thanks for setting me straight on who's entitled to the privacy around here."

"Micro-manage your life?" He seemed to shake the words off, like a dog shaking off water. "It's not my privacy I'm protecting; it's David's."

"Oh, that makes me feel better," she said sarcastically. "David was extorting you, but it's none of my business because he was such a nice guy?"

"My financial relationship with David was not a corporate matter. *That's* what makes it none of your business."

"So he *was* extorting you," she pressed.

"Of course not." He didn't sound defensive, just worn out.

"Why did you give David the money to buy out Nancy's shares, then?"

The line was silent. She got the distinct impression Marc was counting to ten.

"Because he asked me for a loan," he finally said.

She believed him. "Oh. Well, I guess that pretty well answers my questions. Thanks, Marc."

She hung up, feeling embarrassed and rotten for having insulted

107

him. There was no dirt here: David had simply asked Marc for a loan, and as a friend, Marc had given it to him. She'd obviously never even considered that possibility, telling Marc in so many words that he was such a nasty piece of work that he'd have to be threatened before he'd do something nice for a friend.

The hollow and guilty feeling stayed with her as she checked the A & C servers for signs of unauthorized use. She admitted to herself that she'd been unfair to Marc. His kiss had shaken her up in more ways than one, making her too easily hurt. So she'd lashed out at him. But then again, she also figured that one good deed didn't make Marc a good man.

Later that day, Terra got a surprise call from Marina.

"Hi, Terra!" Marina said.

"Hey! How nice of you to call!"

"How's life in Silicon Valley?" Marina asked.

"Oh, not worth talking about. How are you, Honeybunch?"

"I'm doing great. I got a raise at work! And I have a computer at home now. It's got a modem and everything."

"Welcome to the digital age, girl," Terra said, trying to sound happy about the computer. Of course she knew who needed that "modem and everything," but Marina was still trying to keep her relationship with Jared—aka RogueKnight—a secret. So Terra, afraid her sister would withdraw completely, did not press the issue.

"How are things with you, Terra?" Marina asked.

Terra sighed. "Oh, I've sort of jumped from the frying pan into the fire."

"You? The one who's always in control? What happened?"

"Um. I kissed someone I shouldn't have."

Marina chuckled. "That's a problem? Maybe you need a *life*, Terra!"

Terra had to admit that the newly mature Marina was right. How could being kissed by someone she didn't trust compare to being eighteen, in love with a felon, and pregnant?

"Yeah, well," Terra sputtered. "It's just that the kiss is

complicating what little life I do have."

Marina mock-gasped. "Did his wife and kids catch you in the act?"

"It's complicated—not dramatic. It's mainly a professional problem."

"Huh?"

"The kiss was with my boss," Terra explained.

"Your boss. Is that the guy I met? The one you kept calling a bastard?"

"Uh…. Yeah."

"*You* kissed *him*?"

"Well, not exactly," Terra hedged, now unwilling to admit she'd kissed somebody she kept calling a bastard. "He kissed me, and I sort of let him. I shouldn't have."

Marina chuckled again. "Don't you just hate it when those really good looking, rich guys kiss you?"

"Yeah, well."

Marina hooted. "So, was he any good?"

★

All the rest of the day, she recalled the warmth and solidity of his body pressed against hers, how his kisses made her want more. The memory set off an internal alarm that shrieked: *get away from SSI as fast as you can. The longer you stay, the more likely you'll end up going to bed with Marc.*

And that, she knew with fatalistic certainty, would lead to disaster. Look how complicated her life was already, and she just *worked* for Marc.

The best way to avoid having sex with Marc was to have sex with someone else. Like Peter. Peter should be humping her for all he was worth. Which he wasn't.

Restless and irritated, she brought up a network diagram.

The best substitute for sex was staring her right in the face. No orgasms, but cracking did offer her a kind of completion, satisfaction. After a bit of searching, she found what she was looking for. The financial computers, named appropriately enough, Finance, Finance2, and so on. One of the Finances would probably lead her to Peter's private computer. If Peter wasn't going to give her orgasms, he'd at least supply her with intellectual thrills. Finance was easy to invade. She examined the list of other hosts that Finance trusted. The machines were Crux, Sysadmin, Finance2, and Porsche. Crux was Marc's computer.

She itched to investigate Crux. What would Marc's machine tell her about him? A little thrill of delight and fear ran through her body, just thinking about the risk.

Suddenly the memory of the way Marc had slid his hand slowly down the center of her back came alive. She'd have to leave Crux be. The real danger of exploring Marc digital domain was that it was an acknowledgment of how fascinating he was. And she refused to admit she was attracted to him.

That's right. I hate the bastard.

She returned to the task of exploring Peter's machine. Of the list, Porsche had to be Peter's.

Licking her lips, she whispered, "Now I've got you, Peter." She'd see just what kind of man he was. Trying to login remotely into Porsche from Finance didn't work. Obviously Finance's trust of Porsche was not mutual. She tried another protocol.

Porsche still wouldn't connect with her. Just like the man who owned the computer. She wondered if Porsche was down. The computer didn't reply to an electronic ping signal she sent to Porsche. Likely it meant Porsche was behind a firewall, the electronic analog of a barbed wire fence. Odd. Keith had told her the company didn't have any internal firewalls.

After a half an hour of fun, she had made no headway in breaking through to Porsche. Judging by his protection, Peter was a private man, and not easily tricked.

"OOOoooh, you're going to give me a run for my money, aren't you?" she said, feeling herself smile. She wondered why Peter thought his private stuff was so important.

She'd find out—eventually.

★

The Monday programmers' meeting wasn't canceled this time. She had abandoned her plan to impress Ray with the usefulness and excitement of Personal Scout. Marc's kiss had thrown those particular dreams out the window. She had to leave SSI, not be the advocate for a doomed project. Still, she didn't want Ray to think she was an idiot.

A group of about twenty settled around the long table in the large A & C conference room, everyone grumbling that the meetings were a stupid waste of time. But she looked forward to it, because as an outside consultant she'd never been invited to one. How bad could the meeting be? She took a chair next to Ted.

Marc walked in the conference room, and sat down directly across from her. His proximity made her edgy, but she'd be damned if she'd let him think he had affected her by his kiss. She made it a point to look at him squarely. His face held no expression at all, which worried her. The most dangerous enemies were those that didn't telegraph their intentions. What was he going to do, and why did he have to sit right across from her?

Jack arrived after Marc, scowling and clutching his can of Surge. Ray walked in next, and sat at the head of the long table. "Hi guys," Ray said. Then he noticed Marc. "Hello, Marc."

Ray's greeting sounded like a question. She got the impression the CEO didn't come to programmers' meetings very often.

Ray started the meeting. It didn't take long for her to figure out why everybody hated the meetings so much. They were boring. Who could get excited about someone else's work, especially when they were barely able or willing to talk about it? But poor Ray worked at making it a social experience, drawing out some of the really quiet people. He would encourage the group as a whole to coordinate the various programming problems. Marc just observed

111

silently.

She rubbed her eyes, and then glanced over at Marc. His poker face was still intact. He didn't seem to be there to give her trouble. She suppressed an outright yawn. The group working on the next Scout release finished reporting to Ray.

"What do you think, a couple of months to beta?" Marc asked Ray.

"Six months would be more realistic," Ray replied.

"Yeah, okay," Marc said.

She figured that Marc would leave now that he'd gotten a first hand account on the progress of his baby. But he sat through more programmer's reports. Jack talked, managing to steal some of the credit for Lyle's work. Ray then asked Terra to tell the group about what she was working on.

She saw Marc's poker face slip, and a small, expectant smile curl his lips. She got the bad feeling he was about to ambush her. But there was no help for that. Now she had to convince Ray that she was doing a good job so she could leave the SSI assignment with her computational linguistics reputation in one piece—once Marc finally let her leave.

She explained how her natural language interface project fit in with the company's future product line. Ray seemed satisfied with her progress and future plans.

That wasn't so bad.

And then Marc spoke: "So how are you addressing linguistic quantifiers and hedges, Terra?"

Taken off guard by his question, she was about to take a defensive stance. But then she realized what he wanted to know was perfectly reasonable.

"You mean how do I handle words like 'several' or 'most'?"

"Yes," Marc said.

"With fuzzy logic," she said.

"Aren't you missing the whole point of creating artificial languages by doing that?" he asked.

"What do you mean?"

"Well, isn't modeling the vagueness of natural language by appeal to quantification in some fuzzy sense, cheating?"

"It's not cheating!" she replied, laughing. "Vagueness is represented exactly and crisply as a vagueness by fuzzy logic!"

He then asked her a question about another aspect of natural language processing. She answered, whereupon he firmly disputed her claim, arguing the other side. She countered with more facts. He attempted to convince her she was wrong.

Glancing about the conference room, she tried to see if anybody seemed irked that their debate was taking so much time. But those around her looked uncomfortable rather than annoyed. She shrugged it off. Intellectual fights never cowed her. Why should they? She was an expert. Right now she was having a blast: cerebral confrontations about computational linguistics excited her. Too bad they were so few and far between.

She looked back at Marc, and sent him a smile. She liked the way *his* mind worked.

"Thanks, Terra," Ray intervened. "Ted, how about you tell us about your work?"

She was disappointed by the abrupt end to her and Marc's discussion. Marc's poker face descended again, so she had no idea how he felt.

"Sure," Ted said. He shifted in his chair, and started describing his project. He kept an uneasy eye on the CEO the whole time. But Marc never said another word.

"The meetings aren't usually that rough, Terra," Ted told her afterwards. "Marc doesn't normally come, you know. Anyway, it will all blow over."

"What will blow over?"

"Uhm," Ted said, "that inquisition of his."

She realized Ted must have misinterpreted what happened at the programmer's meeting. "What inquisition? I enjoyed myself."

"You're more man than I am," Ted said, looking at a wall, avoiding her eyes.

"What does this have to do with manhood?" she asked, confused.

"God, Terra, if the CEO raked *me* over the coals," Ted said, now looking straight at her, "I'd be thinking about getting another job, not about how much fun I had."

12 / #Cybersex

"Wait a second, Ted," Terra said. "You thought Marc was criticizing me?"

"That's what it sounded like to me."

Understanding hit her with unhappy force. Because Ted didn't know much about natural language, he had read Marc's questions as faultfinding. Maybe Ted's interpretation was unique. She walked back to her cubicle. Some of the guys seemed to be afraid to look at her.

They all think I'm dead meat, a loser, and about to get fired!

Fury surged through her. Damn Marc; he probably knew that was going to happen. Why was he demeaning her in public like that? Was it because she had ultimately rejected his kiss?

She intended to find out. It would serve Marc right if she marched to his office right now, without preamble, and demanded to know what his problem was. But causing a scene or acting uncivilized wouldn't help her reputation. She called Marc's secretary to make an appointment to see him, vowing to take the high road, even if it killed her.

"He can squeeze you in at three," his secretary responded. "Can you run on over then?"

"Yes, thank you," Terra said, hanging up quickly, before any curses spilled out.

★

At three, she walked into Marc's office, still simmering with anger. He sat at his desk, gazing at his computer screen, typing.

She cleared her throat.

"Hello," he said, looking up at her. "You have something to report?"

"No. I don't have anything to report. I'm here to find out if you have a problem with my natural language processing work."

Marc's secretary came into the office, smiled at Terra, and walked back out, closing the door behind her. The last thing Terra wanted was to be alone with Marc. The last time... she lost her concentration. When she regained her emotional balance, she saw he was staring at her, seemingly waiting for her to return to the real world.

"Your interface design work is superior," he said.

"But?"

"But I want you to stop doing it so intently," he said. "You have other obligations." He turned his attention back to the computer screen.

That was her cue to leave. But she didn't.

"So that's what this is about. You're trying to manipulate me into working harder on your cracker problem. Well, I've got news for you: your plan is going to backfire. The harder you try to make the guys in A & C think I don't know anything about computational linguistics, the harder I'll try to prove you wrong. And that means working more on my interface design."

"That's ridiculous. Why would anyone in A & C think you don't know computational linguistics?"

"Are you kidding? When they watched you grill me they immediately assumed you were confronting my ineptness. Right now they're sitting around speculating how long I'm going to have a job here."

His eyes drifted up from his screen to meet hers. "You thought I was grilling you?"

The idea that *she* might think he was harassing her seemed to disturb him.

"Of course not. But the guys don't know a linguistic hedge from a hedgehog." She approached his desk and noticed several monographs and papers on natural language lying there. Had he been doing homework to be able to harass her? "You knew how bad it would look if you started asking me questions like that. They think I'm dead meat now."

"I'm not nearly as manipulative as you seem to think," he said, his black eyes boring into her. "I just wanted to see for myself whether your reputation in linguistics is justified. It is."

"Then you have to understand why I can't stay here, Marc!" she said breathlessly, jumping into the unexpected opening. "It's obvious our arrangement isn't working out. Release me from my contract. Let me leave and go do what I'm good at."

"I won't let you go," he said. "You *will* find the thief. And not just because of your knowledge. Because you're clever—and relentless. And most importantly, you're an outsider. You can see what I can't."

"I already told you that David Houle is your man. He needed money to buy out Nancy's shares, and he had intended to extort you to get that money if you didn't give him a loan."

"The first code was stolen weeks before Nancy died, Terra. Can you fit that fact into your theory?"

"Sure," she replied. "Who knows what David's financial state was before Nancy died. Well, you probably do. He might have needed money, period. Nancy's death might just have made his money problems worse. Right?"

He gazed at her thoughtfully, but didn't reply. He wasn't going to tell her anything about his friend's money problems.

"Listen Marc," Terra continued, "if David was the cracker, even if he was in league with outside people, SSI probably won't have any more theft problems. Because he's dead. Okay? Suppose that's true? How long am I supposed to stay here—waiting around for another break-in that never happens—before I've finally convinced you David the culprit?"

"You can't convince me just by waiting it out. If you think David was the electronic thief, you'll need to prove it."

She sighed, dispirited. Her arguments hadn't moved Marc at all; she was right back where she started—having to solve his cracker problem.

"I have every faith you'll uncover the identity of the cracker," he continued. "And once you do, I'll ask you to stay on, this time to do what you're so good at. Personal Scout is an idea that should be pursued."

"I can't stay here afterwards," she choked out, distressed.

She'd once dreamed of inducing Marc to get behind Personal Scout as a real project, not just as a cover for her. But not anymore. Now she knew she had to get away from SSI once her contract was fulfilled, even if that meant Personal Scout would never see the light of day.

"We'll talk about this again, Terra. You might change your mind."

"I won't," she said. She couldn't continue to work for a man who knew her deepest secrets and was willing to exploit them, especially when she was attracted to him. "I have to know who else knows about me and what I did eight years ago. Like, who told you? I can't let this happen to me again."

He got up from his chair, moved around his desk, and closed the distance between them. She hoped he wouldn't get too near.

"No one told me," he said, stopping at a polite distance.

"Please, Marc. I need to know. Is the FBI investigating me again?"

"What's the point? No matter what I say, you'll just assume I'm lying to you, trying to manipulate you."

"No, I won't," she promised.

"Then I'll tell you once more, Sweetheart. No one *told* me. The FBI doesn't suspect you. In fact, they never did. Probably because you don't fit their vaunted computer crime adversarial matrix." His voice was harder now. "But I don't buy into stereotypes. When the FBI gave up, I just got started. My little electronic booby-traps would have informed you, up close and personal, that I'd pegged you. Except you never came back."

"You were at Apple Computer?" she asked in a whisper.

"Yes."

"That was eight years ago," she cried, dismayed. "How can you still be so pissed off?"

"Breaking into Apple's Cray was an intellectual joyride for you. But as far as I was concerned, you took information that belonged to Apple."

She suddenly felt like she had to explain. "I *read* those files; I didn't sell anything."

"And that's why you're here now, working for me. You had the experience I needed, along with the white hat ethics I required."

"Lucky me," she said.

If he could hold a grudge against her for simple electronic trespass against a computer at a company he worked for, how would he feel about someone attacking computers at Silicon Silk, a company he owned, with the intention to harm? Her mind sparked with new comprehension. She finally understood the fierce territoriality that had motivated Marc to trick her into finding the thief. As much as she hated his deception, she couldn't dismiss the reason for it: he loved his company, and thought she could save it.

"You'll do almost anything to protect your company, won't you?" She'd wanted to sound bitter and contemptuous, but it came out a lot nicer.

"*Almost* anything? I could do without the qualifier." He went back to sit behind his desk. "Or should I say quantifier?"

He fixed his full attention on her. His body was now still, his dark eyes intent. Gone was the disdainful disinterest he'd shown when she'd first entered his office. His almost worshipful manner had a powerful effect on her. And she wished it didn't. Her distress must have shown on her face.

"Are you going to be all right?" he asked.

Of course I'm not going to be all right! I can't stand it when you're kind to me! I don't want to see that you have good qualities!

"Sure," she said, trying to at least *sound* sure. "Did you ever get any letters or demands from computer terrorists? And please don't

119

hold out on me."

"I would've told you if I had, Terra. The answer is no."

"Hmmm," she murmured.

If David had been behind the extortion scheme, then there never would be a demand—because he was dead. She sighed. All she had to do was prove that the Paltforms VP had been in contact with Ranger, and the case would be closed. But she needed help to do that. She hoped Marc would give it to her.

"Marc," she said. "I might have a lead."

"Who?" he asked.

"A kid in Sweden. But I don't think he could have been working alone. He needed someone on the inside. Anyway, I should probably find out if anyone in the company has been communicating with this boy's computer."

"What makes you think this kid is the cracker?"

She was afraid to tell him about the incriminating alpha Scout on Ranger's computer. If Marc knew, he'd likely go after the kid in person.

"Um, mainly because he's got a grudge against SSI," she said.

"Interesting. A few years ago someone from Sweden set up a pirated software site here." He leaned back into his chair. "I wonder if this is the same person."

"It is."

"Keith told you about it, huh?" Marc's face took on a wry expression. "That penetration was way before Keith's time, but that pirate site was legend around here."

"Your firewall administrator didn't tell me."

Marc chuckled. "All right. I won't probe. How can I help? Do you want me to ask Keith to start searching the backup logs for any SSI communications with the Swede's computer? He could probably automate the entire thing."

"That would help me a lot. But I need Keith to search the last two months of backups at least. And *everyone's* computer, not just the SSI proxies."

"You got it," he said.

"It's not going to be that easy. There are internal firewalls in this organization that Keith doesn't know about."

"Where?"

"I found a firewall in front of one of the financial computers," she said.

"Suspecting Peter, are you?" His eyes sparkled with curiosity. A small smile touched his lips.

Terra was uncomfortably reminded of how she'd tried to make Marc feel guilty about kissing her by claiming she was involved with Peter. He had outright dismissed Peter as a rival. Marc's arrogance was clear now too; he seemed amused, but hardly triumphant, about the fact that she might suspect Peter of being the attacker. Marc still didn't consider the sexy CFO a rival.

"No," she replied testily. "But Peter's firewall seems to point out some potential security holes. I mean, your firewall administrator is supposed to know everything that goes on here computer security-wise. And he doesn't. How did Peter's firewall get installed if Keith didn't do it, anyway?"

"Are you asking me where Peter could find help to install and configure firewall software? Around here? At a software company teeming with software people?"

"Yeah, I guess you're right," she said. "It wouldn't be that hard."

"And don't underestimate Peter's abilities. He could have installed it himself."

She recalled how Peter had once claimed he didn't know anything about computer security issues, and thought it was overkill. Odd. Maybe the CFO had just recently decided he needed the firewall. Or maybe he was just being modest. Sure. Like a guy who drives a black Porsche could be modest. She wondered if she should suspect Peter of being the inside man at SSI. No. Protecting the information in his computer with a firewall didn't necessarily mean he was guilty of industrial espionage.

Late that afternoon, the owner of the secret firewall stopped by her cube.

"How would you like to come along with me for a business meeting the weekend after next?" Peter asked. "It's at Vail."

"Tell me more," she replied. She imagined stripping him after hours and then seducing him beside a roaring cabin fire. "Like, is there a fireplace?"

He chuckled. "Marc's lodge has everything. We're meeting with the principals of the Doering Group, a small software operation. Steve and I will be hammering out the acquisition terms with them then. Marc will play host. But it won't be all business. It never is." He winked at her. "So is it a yes?"

Marc's lodge was legend among the techno-elite. She'd heard it was a strange mix of Spartan simplicity and utter luxury, and that the CEO had forbidden the use of computers and phones there. How could they hammer out deals without machines?

"It's a yes," she said.

"Wonderful," said Peter.

"So what kind of a host is Marc?" she asked.

"You'll see. He cooks for everybody. He worries that you have enough blankets. He's quite disarming."

She recalled how Marc had made her espresso her first day at SSI, and she'd felt so comfortable… and then he'd ambushed her. Those poor principals of that small software operation. Doering Group was about to get screwed.

Which reminded her. She'd have all weekend to work on getting Peter into bed.

He bent over and took her face in his hands. "I'm glad you're coming."

Desire swept through her. "Me, too," she whispered. He let go, and she felt her control slowly return. The next time he touched her he had better deliver the goods.

★

Terra's spirits were high when she got home that night, despite the aftermath of the programmer's meeting. She looked forward to going to Vail with Peter. Those few times she'd been skiing in Vermont had been fabulous, and Colorado skiing was supposed to be even better. After fixing herself some tea, she checked the log generated by her IRC sniffer. A search for Silicon Silk and related words turned up nothing. Nobody seemed to be bragging about SSI on #Crack.

Finished with her cracker-chick chores, she drank her tea, and daydreamed about the ski trip. Maybe now she'd be finally be able to enjoy some quality physical time with the aloof and sexy Peter. She imagined Peter's long fingers stroking her entire body. His irregular, barely controlled breath would tell her how excited he was. She would then pull him close. Suddenly her fantasy involved Marc—and the two men now began to work on her together. Marc was such a good kisser, so he was responsible for her upper body, while Peter would be down below. Her threesome fantasy went on long enough for her to realize she was in an advanced state of arousal.

"Ughh," she said aloud, laughing. That little imaginary escapade had better be as close as she ever got to having sex with Marc.

Still sitting at her computer, lighthearted and happy, she decided if she couldn't have real sex, she'd get it virtually on IRC. IRC offered more than channel Crack. She always felt excited and a little naughty when she joined channel Cybersex. Her chosen chat nickname was HOT_N_TITE.

Cybersex was hopping: a constant flux of people moved in and out of the channel. She watched the conversations scroll by on her screen, scanning for a good target. A private message from Big_Dick appeared on a small part of her screen.

"Easy to *say*," she said, laughing.

Within a few minutes she got another five or six private messages, most asking if she was male or female.

"Like 'Hot and Tight' doesn't give you a hint as to what sex I am?" she asked aloud.

But of course, most of the people on the channel were actually men, and she could well be a man masquerading as a woman. She disabled private messages, so all of her conversations would be public.

She monitored the conversations, still waiting for someone who interested her.

"I'm masturbating," announced 12INCH.

Not him.

"Is anyone there?" asked Newbie.

Not him.

"Come play with my boy pussy," Mustang offered.

Not him.

"Join me in my kinky IRC fantasy," wrote Mulder.

Terra was interested enough to find out his Internet address. Unless Mulder had the technical expertise to fake it, he was chatting from Australia. Her address was fake, of course. As far as anyone could tell, she was sitting in front of a computer at Caesar's Palace in Las Vegas.

"Sure Mulder. But we do it public," Terra typed.

She figured if Mulder knew he had an IRC audience, even though it was a virtual one, he'd perform better.

"Are you female, HOT_N_TITE?" wrote Mulder.

"All female, Mulder" she typed. "But I'm a netsex virgin." That was a lie; she was no netsex virgin.

Several people in the channel announced their interest in deflowering her. Some in extremely crude ways.

"Wouldn't you rather do this privately?" Mulder wrote.

"No," she typed.

"What are you wearing, HOT?"

"You tell me, Mulder."

"Nothing but your husband's shirt."

"It's a very big shirt, Mulder. Are you my husband?"

"Maybe."

"My husband is a very jealous man."

"Is he?" Mulder asked.

"He knocked a bartender's teeth out once because he looked at my breasts."

"Good."

"He's a very big man, too." Terra typed.

"You're waiting for your husband, HOT. He's promised to come home early. You want him. You're looking out the window for him."

She could almost feel a man's shirt chafing against her bare breasts. Imagining her hands resting on the window frame, her eyes scoured for her big man. She felt a virtual breeze caress her face from the open window. Anticipation pooled in her body, waiting for her cyber husband to fuck her silly. She felt her breath quicken.

"You still there, HOT?" Mulder inquired.

"Yes. I'm looking out the window waiting."

"You hear footsteps," Mulder wrote.

"It's my husband. I can't wait."

"I'm in the room with you now. I slide my big hands underneath your shirt."

"OOOhh," she typed. This was getting fun. Her body reacted to the cyber touch.

"I trace figure eights on your breasts."

"Figure eights? Why not Monet?"

"Figure nines, then," Mulder typed. "You moan."

"I moan. I turn around. I want you to kiss me."

"No. You're afraid. Because I'm not your husband."

"Do I scream?"

"No. But you wonder what I'm going to do to you. Especially since I'm not wearing any clothes."

"I whimper. But then I see you're the best looking man I've ever seen. You're tall and blond. You're wearing suspenders."

"Hooked to what? I'm naked! \: > O"

She laughed at the shocked expression on Mulder's glyph. "OK,

Mulder, no suspenders. I'll snap something else."

Their provocative and amusing cyber-foreplay drew her further and further into Mulder's IRC fantasy of a stranger seducing a married woman.

"HOT, you turn around so you can watch for your husband out the window," he typed.

"I don't want him. I want you. Kiss me more."

"No. You lean on the windowsill looking for him. I stroke the back of your bare thighs."

She felt his strokes. Her heart beat faster now.

"Do it, Mulder."

"I stroke your butt."

"I can't take it anymore. Lay me on the floor, Mulder."

Mulder didn't answer. She scanned the conversations for him. No, he couldn't leave now!

"I penetrate you from behind, HOT," he finally wrote.

"Oh my."

"You shudder."

"Oh yes!" Terra typed.

"You moan as I give you orgasm after orgasm."

"Mulder! Don't stop!"

"I thrust in and out, again and again."

She couldn't really feel the orgasms. Only increasing excitement.

"Oh no, I see my husband outside. He's come home. He's walking up the stairs. He's coming. He's going to kill you!" she typed.

"No. He's forgotten his briefcase in the car. He went back to get it. I give you one last orgasm."

"I'm weak with satisfaction, Mulder. But I hear him coming."

"I kneel in front of you and hand you a red rose. Thank you, HOT. I climb out the window and leave."

"You're the best, Mulder," she typed.

Immediately a host of people on the channel offered to be her husband and show her what real cybersex was. She groaned. She couldn't take any more. Mulder really was the best.

13 / Living on the edge

When Terra returned to work the next day, she probed darkside, Ranger's machine, using the back door she had created earlier. She noticed two significant changes. Ranger had finally bothered to uncompress Scout 5.0, and a new page on the Swede's SSIck hate site was devoted to insulting that unreleased software. Terra admired the obvious technical accuracy of the review, but was surprised that Ranger didn't brag about stealing the software. The warez-dealer seemed to treat Scout 5.0 as if it were particularly shoddy beta, not stolen alpha.

Things just weren't adding up. Ranger, a lousy cracker, seemed to be able to get into computers Terra herself couldn't. That could mean that Ranger was working with someone on the inside. Or it could mean that Ranger had recruited RogueKnight into helping him again. But why steal an early alpha version of Scout in order to write a nasty review? It was just as illogical as stealing code and putting it in shareware.

Which had happened, too.

An economic motive for the digital thefts seemed less and less plausible. But Terra refused to give up on the idea, because the destitute, now dead David made such a perfect inside man.

If only Ranger would tell her how he'd gotten the software, there might be one less loose end. She decided to just *ask* him. The worst that could happen was that he'd ignore her e-mail message, or that he'd lie to her.

Any attempt to pose as a fellow SSI-hater would lose credibility if she used her SSI.com e-mail address. So she hijacked another of her favorite computers, this one in Canada, and sent Ranger the e-mail from there. He'd reply to the same machine, so she monitored the Canadian computer daily.

★

When the Monday programmers' meeting rolled around again, Marc showed up. He questioned her, and only her. Ray appeared to be bewildered by their sparring, and her coworkers seemed shocked. Later, Ted told her that he and Lyle had come up with a reason for the CEO's actions. They thought that since Nancy Beck, the force behind development of personal agents, was dead, there wasn't any corporate support for the project. As a consequence, Marc was trying to scare Terra off by forcing her to defend her work at the programmer's meetings. She just shrugged at the bizarre scenario her friends had devised.

A few days after that, Marc ambushed her while she was alone in one of the basement machine rooms.

"Do the A & C guys still think you're dead meat?" he asked her.

"Sort of," she said. "They've decided that you're trying to make my life miserable enough so that I'll quit."

"Why do I want you to quit?" he asked.

"No corporate support for personal agents," she said.

His brow furrowed, and his dark eyes danced over her face, making her feel like she was the only woman in the universe, and he was the only man. She took a few steps away from him.

"That seems sadistic. Why wouldn't I just fire you?" he asked.

She laughed. "Why are you asking *me*? This is *you* we're talking about!"

"Speculating about," he corrected. "So how does this political explanation sit with you?"

"Well, it's a whole lot better than being fired because I'm a mediocre linguist," she said.

It wasn't until after he had left the machine room that she realized he never once asked her about the cracker.

128

By the time Peter came to pick up Terra early Saturday morning to go to Vail, her head hurt and she was out of breath because of anxiety. Why had Marc been so concerned about her feelings in the machine room? Did he intend to change their relationship? Whatever Marc's designs, she knew that being with Peter would not protect her at all.

"In a bad mood, Terragirl?" Peter asked after he'd slid in the car beside her.

"I'm just not a morning person, Peter."

He gave her a slow, seductive smile, and she smiled back, relaxing a little. She was on her way to Vail with one amazingly fun and sexy man. What was there to fret about? Besides, maybe Marc would bring one of his beautiful, passive girlfriends with him, and then her worries about him would be moot.

She imagined Marc looking at Velvet like *she* was the only woman in the universe. Terra yawned, trying to get rid of the tension that had returned.

"We'll get some coffee on the plane, Terragirl," Peter said. "You'll be ready for the slopes."

"Are you going to get to ski?"

"You bet," he said. "At least on Sunday. Maybe a short run or two today."

"Just exactly how good are you?"

"You'll find out soon enough," he said, giving her a sly wink.

She laughed. "I'm talking about skiing. What are *you* talking about?"

"Skiing," he said, and he slid his hand down her thigh and up off her knees like a ski jump.

She felt a little tremble. Marc was an idiot not to regard Peter as a rival.

The flight to Vail started out as a chaotic jumble of skis and strangers, but finally the group of about twenty settled down in the private plane. Marc sat a few rows in front and to the right of her.

He didn't seem to have a girlfriend with him. She couldn't decide if she was happy about it or not. Marc spent most of his time talking to Steve Myatt, the lawyer. After awhile Terra lay her head on Peter's shoulder and drowsed.

By the time they arrived in Vail, she felt refreshed. The entire group seemed exhilarated by the cold air and the startling blue sky. A van waited at the airport to take them to the lodge, a large cedar structure sitting directly on the slopes a mere fifty yards from a chairlift. The inside of the lodge was stunning. She stood in the middle of the expansive great room with its cathedral ceiling, and stared. A trapezoid window filled one wall, framing an incredible view of Vail Mountain.

Marc started making a fire in the imposing two-story river-rock fireplace. Everybody else trooped up the stairs to dump their stuff. She followed Kathy Myatt, the lawyer's wife, upstairs. Terra burst out laughing when she got there. There were only two bedrooms, the boys' and the girls'. Rows of bunk beds lined the walls in the girls' bedroom.

"It looks like an orphanage!" Terra cried, tossing her bag on one of the beds.

There were only six women in the room, which left lots of empty beds. Kathy organized a shopping party to go into the village. Terra, and another woman who was involved in the negotiations on behalf of Doering Group, declined.

Terra found Peter lounging on a couch in front of the fire; they arranged to meet at Eagle's Nest restaurant at two. She headed to the front door, where Marc was speaking to the departing skiing and shopping spouses.

"See ya," she said to him. She felt a prickling of danger as his dark eyes probed her.

"Have a good time," he said. "Be back here by five if you want dinner."

"I will," she said, and jogged off happily to rent her equipment. She loved the solitary aspect of the sport. No matter how many people were on the slope, she always felt like she moved down the mountain alone, hearing only the sound of her skis against snow and her own breathing. As promised, Peter met her at the summit restaurant for lunch. They brought their sandwiches and beers outside to a wooden picnic table on the balcony.

Sitting in the cold sunshine, gazing at Peter, Terra suddenly had a strong premonition they would never be lovers. The finance chief seemed to need her only as someone presentable to bring to company functions. She recalled how Carolina had remarked that she'd never seen Peter with a woman before Terra. Whatever sex life he had, it was completely secret, and apart from her. She wondered if he was gay, and again the thought disturbed her. What did being wildly attracted to a gay man say about *her* sexuality?

"How's it going with Doering Group?" she asked Peter.

"It's going," he said. "I doubt we'll be finished until late this afternoon, though."

"That's too bad. Hey, you never warned me I'd be sleeping in a bunk bed. How come the decadent luxury of the ground floor doesn't continue on to the second floor? Did SSI run out of money?"

"Nope. Everything about that lodge is planned," he said, pushing his sunglasses up on top of his head and squinting at her. "Marc actually owns the lodge personally, not the company. Although, as far as I know, he only uses it for corporate purposes. From the beginning, he decided that communal rooms like that would make it nearly impossible for anyone to have private conferences. The lodge was designed to put Silicon Silk at an advantage during negotiations."

She unbuckled her ski boots and wiggled her toes. "Marc has this fantastic Vail hideaway and he just uses it for corporate purposes? Weird. He doesn't make a big distinction between what's good for the company and what's good for him, does he?"

"Nope. He and SSI are one and the same."

"Is that why the company is still privately held? Marc can't bear to give up control?"

"You really want to know why the company hasn't gone public?"

"Are you kidding?" she said, laughing. "Everyone in the software industry wants to know that. SSI is the dominant force in information agent software. And it's profitable! Silicon Silk is *expected* to go public. Yet it doesn't. Sure I want to know!"

He took a swallow of his beer, and dropped his sunglasses over his eyes. "Well, you're half-right, Terragirl. Marc is against taking the company public. But I don't think he opposes an IPO because he'll lose control. It's more that he fears he won't be able to protect his baby anymore if it's publicly owned. And so he refuses to let SSI grow up. In the end, though, what happens to the company won't be up to Marc alone, because the company has more than one partner."

"Well, protection and control sound like the same thing to me," she said, shrugging. "So is it really true that the company even refused venture funding?"

"It's true."

"That's kind of rare, isn't it? I thought most Valley start-ups couldn't even get going in the morning without the sensation of the vulture capitalists' talons in their backside."

"So I've heard."

"So, how did you do it without the Sand Hill crowd?" she asked.

"We lived small. Macaroni and cheese was our staple back then. We worked hard, too. All of us made a lot of sacrifices along the way—Marc probably the most. But mainly we got where we are now because we had a good product."

She had a difficult time imagining Peter eating macaroni and cheese. He seemed so well-suited to luxury.

"That makes it even stranger," she said. "After sacrificing so much, how can Marc refuse the reward? How can he turn his nose up at millions, maybe billions?"

"Marc's not motivated by money."

"How about you, Peter?"

He chuckled. "I'm one partner who does want to take this

company public, Terragirl, but money isn't the reason." He emptied his beer. "Personal wealth is a pleasant byproduct, to be sure. But we should sell stock to the public so we have the cash to finance greater expansion, to entice the best employees, and to strengthen the Scout and Silicon Silk brand recognition."

She smiled at him. He sounded like he was reading directly out of a prospectus.

After their outdoor lunch, Peter returned to the negotiations. She watched him ski off toward the moguls and black double-diamond thrills. Elegant. Refined. She sighed. She loved the way he moved.

She got back to the lodge after six, feeling achy, exhausted, and wonderful. Just as she got to the lodge, the snow, composed of fat and dry flakes, started.

Inside, everyone was congenially gathered around the fireplace. Marc, wearing sweatpants and sweatshirt, worked in the kitchen. Seeing him at the stove reminded her that she was hungry, but she assumed everybody had already eaten because it was after five. She took off her parka, and plopped down on one of the couches. Peter relaxed on an overstuffed chair nearby, looking happy; he winked at her. That probably meant that SSI and Doering Group had reached an agreement favorable to Silicon Silk. Terra gazed at the large, cracking fire, contented, were it not for her growling stomach.

Marc brought her a bowl of stew.

"Thanks!" she said. The stew smelled wonderful. She ate a small spoonful. It turned out to be a delicious, spicy Mexican concoction. She took a bigger spoonful. She looked up at Marc, who seemed to be waiting for her response. "Yum," she said. A pleased look settled on his face.

"Hey Marc, how come Terra gets to eat late when the rest of us had to eat exactly at five?" Steve, the lawyer, teased.

"Yeah, and *she* gets fireside service!" someone else complained.

"Cook's privilege," Marc said. He slid into a spot on the couch next to her.

She watched him warily as he stretched his legs and bare feet out in front of him.

"Eat up," he coaxed.

He seemed friendly and harmless enough, so she resumed eating. She listened to Peter trying to entice Steve and some of the others to come with him for an out-of-bounds back bowl skiing adventure the next morning. Once Kathy was out of earshot, Steve eagerly agreed to join Peter's risky expedition.

"Did you a have a good day?" Marc asked Terra.

She described her ski runs. He listened to her with every part of his body—like he really cared about what she had done up on the mountain. She found his ability to listen the way he did arresting. When she'd finished telling him about her day, Marc gave her knee a brotherly pat, and got up.

"The bartender is on duty," he announced to everyone.

He started to serve his guests drinks from a bar near the fireplace. She watched him make an elaborate tropical drink for Kathy, and wondered if playing host wasn't integral to him. Maybe it wasn't an act at all, but something he enjoyed. She considered getting up and asking Marc to make her a drink, too. But it was too much work. Instead of drinking, Peter and some of the others went to the kitchen to hot wax their skis, anticipating lots of fresh powder. She took off her sweater, pulled her legs up on the couch, and serenely watched the fire dance and crackle.

Marc brought Terra a glass. It wasn't a froufrou drink. "What is it?" she asked him.

"Bourbon on the rocks," he answered, turning his attention now to reviving the fire.

She was surprised he'd even noticed, much less remembered, that she drank bourbon. She suddenly felt sorry for Doering Group again. Comfortable, isolated, and pampered by Marc, the little software operation would surely let down their guard. Just like her. Her internal warning sirens now mute, she sipped her bourbon, and drowsily watched him work the fire.

Terra woke up in the middle of the night, still on the couch, covered by Marc's heavy shearling coat. She sat up, dislodging the coat onto the floor. The fire blazed nearby.

"God, I'm hot," she complained.

She took off her turtleneck, and threw it onto the floor.

"Go back to sleep, Sweetheart; it's one-thirty in the morning."

Still half asleep, she turned to look at who had spoken to her. Marc. He was in the kitchen, sitting on a stool at the granite island, hunched over a laptop.

She stretched her stiff body, and walked over to him.

"What are you doing?" she asked.

"Working," he replied gruffly, without making eye contact with her.

Propping her elbows up on the island, she watched him poke at his keyboard, wondering why he was so curt. He wore nothing but a pair of sweat pants. The fact that Marc looked like *that* under his long-sleeved shirts would give her thoughts about him a new, and more concrete, erotic dynamism. She forced herself to look away from his bare chest and shoulders, and study his face. His curly brown hair was slightly damp. He must have just had a shower and wanted to get a bit of work done.

She glanced over at his computer screen, and realized he was connected to Crux, his computer at SSI, an impossibility for a house without a phone line.

"You cheater!" she said, laughing. "You have a secret telephone line."

He still didn't look up at her. "It's T1."

"Like that's *not* cheating?"

"It offers us an advantage," he said unapologetically.

"I'll bet. So, did you rob Doering Group blind today?"

He finally looked up from the screen and at her. "That's Peter's and Steve's job. Not mine. I'm supposed to be sociable."

"So said the spider to the fly. Right before the fly was trapped and devoured."

He grunted irritably. "It's you that's going to be devoured if you keep on leaning over my workspace wearing that."

She looked down at her chest. She had stripped down to her L. L. Bean pointelle longies. "These? You mean my thermal undershirt?"

"Thermal?" he scoffed. "I can see right through it."

She laughed, amused by the tension in his voice. "So, what's your point, Marc?" she asked, moving closer to him.

"My point is I'd appreciate it if you'd go back to sleep, Terra, either on the couch, or in the girls' room. It will save us both a lot of bother."

"Bother? What kind of bother is that?"

His glittering eyes skipped across her face, her body. "Good night, Terra," he said.

She found him irresistible, half-naked with a dead-serious expression on his face. *So.* He wanted to take it slow. She could hardly blame him—not after her extreme reaction to that kiss in Ray's office. He wished to feed her stew, cover her with his coat. He intended to *court* her. His circumspection and care touched her.

It also struck hard at a sexual nerve.

She walked around the island, trailing her hand playfully along his bare back, sliding over the ridges, the furrows, the mounds.

"What's your T1 connection doing in the kitchen?" she asked.

"I had it put in the kitchen. No one will accidentally find it in here. People generally stay away from kitchens because they think they might end up having to do the dishes. Now go to sleep, Terra. I really do have to get this done."

He hadn't touched the keyboard since he'd complained about her undershirt. She stopped to stand behind him, sliding her hands around his bare waist from behind.

"Go on doing what you're doing," she purred, delighted with the prospect of a challenge she knew she'd win.

She sensed new tightness. *Good.* Leaning against him, she rested her cheek on his back. She kissed him softly. *Make him snap, girl.* She kissed him again. His tension increased, and so did hers.

"Go *away*," he said irritably.

Pulling away from him, she moved around to his side. She ducked her head and her upper body under his arm. Grabbing onto his shoulders, she swung her leg over to climb up into his lap. They were chest to chest now.

"You tell me to go away to my face," she said.

At least one part of him didn't want her to go away. *Work him, Terra.* She put her arms around his neck, and repeated, "Tell me to go away, Marc."

Suddenly he held her waist tight and kissed her. The kiss was not exploratory like the first time; now his mouth and tongue calmly told her he was in control. When he stopped kissing her, she was clutching his upper arms, her heart beating wildly. Somehow, with only a kiss, he'd grounded himself in her.

She realized she was as scared as she was aroused. Her sexual power over him was only an illusion; it was *he* who had the power over *her.*

"Now what?" he growled, staring rawly at her with his deep-set black eyes.

"You know *what*," she replied. "The question is where."

He lifted her up off his lap, and set her down. Grabbing his sweatshirt lying on the island, he put it on. He strode to the couch, pulled his coat off the floor, and lay it over her shoulders. His boots sat by the door. He shoved them on, and they rushed outside.

The frigid air hit her. "It's cold!" she squealed.

He stopped, and carefully shifted his coat around her shoulders. "Do you want to go back inside?"

She looked up at the dark sky. The snow came down in fat flakes, but it didn't seem quite so cold now.

"I want you to make love to me," she said.

He gave her a soft, warming kiss and then guided her into the forest. After a short walk, he stopped. Gently, he backed her into one of the evergreens. And so, cradled in the flexible branches of a pine tree, he made love to her.

★

Terra woke up late the next morning, stiff and sore—and very happy. After showering and dressing, she came downstairs, glad to see some of her lodgemates were still there. They drank coffee by the fire, and planned their ski day. She knew Marc would be long gone, ice-climbing on an inhospitable mountainside somewhere. Rooting through the kitchen, she found a box of shredded wheat. She sat at the island with the secret T1 connection, eating dry cereal and watching as Peter's out-of-bounds expedition gained another follower.

"Hey Peter! I want to go too," Terra said.

"Are you sure?" Peter asked. "It's harder than any double diamond run."

Steve laughed. "Terra can handle herself, Peter."

Terra grinned at Steve; Steve was turning out to be a really nice man, even if he was a lawyer.

"Thanks for the vote of confidence, Steve," she said. "And as for you, Peter: I *can* handle myself."

Of course Terra had never been down a hill that difficult before, but she felt fantastic, and hey, life was for living.

★

Six people, including Terra, Steve and Peter, stood near the lip of the bowl, admiring the mountain ranges in the distance and the great white expanse below. The sight took Terra's breath away. It gave new meaning to the expression "living on the edge."

"Wow," Terra said.

"Fabulous, Peter," Steve said.

"Ah, spring skiing," Peter replied, smiling. "Nothing better."

The sky was brilliant blue. Even though they were above

timberline, the temperature was mild, probably even above freezing. She scanned the sun-warmed bowl and tried to plan her route. The slope at the top seemed a lot steeper than at the bottom. She noticed the more gently sloped part of the mountain was below tree line, yet a wide swath of white cut through the green.

Suddenly, the idea of actually skiing down the bowl scared her. The first part of the bowl was too steep and dangerous. And besides, there was probably a *reason* the bowl was out-of-bounds.

"They don't have avalanches or anything here, do they?" Terra asked.

"That's a risk you always take," Steve said.

"If you want to ski virgin powder, anyway," said one of the guys from Doering Group, grinning from ear to ear with excitement.

"So, are you ready, Terra?" Peter asked.

"Piece of cake," she said. Her attempt at macho swagger was ruined by her breathless, quavering delivery. All her instincts now told her she shouldn't go. But she couldn't back down, not after she'd practically forced herself on the group.

"All right then," Steve said, leading them to the lip. "We'll have to slide over one at a time."

"I'll go first," she gulped. The longer she stared at the bowl, the steeper it seemed. If she didn't go now, she never would.

"Wait a second," Peter said to her. He pointed down and to the left. "See over there, at the edge of the slope? It's not as steep there. Start over in that direction, and I'll catch up with you."

She nodded, and slid over the lip. She regretted it instantly. The hillside was even steeper and scarier than it had looked from above. Her passage broke a big chunk of snow lose. The fragment cartwheeled down the slope. She hoped she didn't end up getting down the mountain that way, too.

She worked her way over to the path Peter had told her to take, discovering the snow was not very powdery; it seemed mushy. Too bad. The day was too warm, and they had started too late for powder. The harder snow underneath her skis sounded hollow and settled under her weight as she moved over it. *Whumpf.*

The trail Peter wanted her to take didn't seem any easier. She pushed down another few feet and turned. Another turn. And another. The snow was getting wetter. She stopped and looked up the hill to gauge her progress. She hadn't gotten very far. The other skiers still waited at the lip. Steve, easily identified by his bright yellow parka, seemed to be giving her a thumbs-up.

Looking down the long expanse of the bowl, she wished she was already skiing on the path through the trees. She started her descent again, and heard Steve's whoop of pleasure as he slid over the lip.

Another few feet. Another. *Wumpf.* She stopped to catch her breath, and noticed her weight had started a big crack. The crack ran downslope about 200 feet. The hollow *wumpf* sound as she skied and the big crack gave her the creeps—like she was skiing on thin ice. A streak of yellow now skied down the center of the bowl, overtaking her. Others followed. She wondered if Peter was with them: maybe he'd decided to ski with the guys rather than over on the side with Terra the wimp.

She fought her way down a little more, hoping she wouldn't see any more cracks. Repeating the turn-ski-turn pattern, she forced herself to think only of the incremental progress she was making, not about how far she had yet to go, or about how ridiculous it had been for her to be here in the first place. Or the *wumpf* sound.

Suddenly, from above, she heard something even worse than a *wumpf.* An earsplitting crack—like a gun going off—vibrated in her bones, even in her teeth. She looked up. Her heart stopped cold. A slab of snow as big as a continent had ripped itself off the mountainside, and was coming down—toward her.

14 / Avalanche

Terra tried to ski away from the oncoming mountainside of white. Her progress was slow and agonizing. Her skis seemed to stick in the wet snow. A slab as big as a house slid by on her right with a deafening roar.

"Oh God," she yelled, terrified. The avalanche had caught up with her.

She started to shake. *Keep going, girl. Don't stop.* Suddenly, the snow beneath her collapsed and began to move. Her gloves and poles were ripped away, and her legs jerked forward, throwing her on her back. Through the cold mush of airborne snow, she saw one of her skis go sailing past her. Another ski flew by. She was on top of a chunk of the snowslide, heading down the mountain. She was surprised by how slow the slide seemed to move; the snow oozed rather than rocketed. Certainly she could jump off to safety, she thought. But like quicksand, the churning, freezing mass seemed to pull her in deeper. First her calves, now her thighs were buried. Crying with pain and terror, she tried to break free again and again. But she couldn't escape.

The snowy turbulence carried her downslope. She felt like she was in a cement mixer. She was in snow up to her waist, now her shoulders. She struggled to keep her head free, but the flying snow plugged her mouth, her ears, and finally, her nostrils. Panicked, she shook her head wildly, snorting and spitting like a animal. The snow dribbled out of her nose; she could breathe again. A stand of evergreen trees came towards her. She felt the sting of sharp pine needles in her face, and then she felt nothing at all.

★

Terra woke. She felt as if she were in a giant body cast. Then she slid into unconsciousness again. She must have awakened four or five times like that, not knowing where she was, only realizing she couldn't move, and was so cold it hurt.

Her awareness expanded; she heard muffled voices. Her body was numb, her face hurt. She couldn't move from the neck down; it was as if she was stuck in cement.

"Help," she whispered, opening her eyes to a brownish-green smear.

A female voice answered: "You're going to be okay. We're digging you out."

She remembered the avalanche. The snow slide must have slammed her into a tree and buried all but her head.

Rescue workers finally got her out of her snow-cement prison, and bundled her into a toboggan. As they pulled her down the mountain, she passed close to another group of rescue workers digging in the snow. She thought she caught a glimpse of a prone, bright yellow form, and a gray-blue face, the back of the head still encased in snow. He didn't move. A tear burned her cheek and dribbled off onto the blanket. Steve.

Please let him be alive.

Terra spent two days in the hospital. Diagnosis: concussion. The MRI scan had shown there wasn't any obvious brain damage, but the doctor said she wanted to be safe rather than sorry. You never know about head injuries, she said.

On the first day, Terra felt headachy and sleepy. She also thawed out. "Frostnip" was the medical term for her chilled appendages, and it wasn't as benign as it sounded. Her fingers and toes stung like hell as they went from hard and white to red and swollen, but she thought she deserved the pain. If she was going to survive an avalanche, she shouldn't get off easy. And maybe if she hurt enough, she wouldn't ever do anything so reckless again. Chastising herself for her stupidity, she concentrated on the pain. She never belonged on such a difficult slope. She had even *demanded* to go on that expedition!

On the second morning she felt more alert. She got a pretty bouquet of yellow tulips from her friends in A & C Group. Carolina called. But Carolina would change the subject whenever Terra asked about the rest of the out-of-bounds party. Marc didn't call her. Terra had a sinking feeling that Steve *had* died in the avalanche, and Marc's company was in chaos again.

On the second evening, Marc came to see her. She felt a rush of warmth and pleasure at seeing him. He looked like he hadn't slept in days. Dark circles puddled under his eyes. He'd apparently flown in from California just to get her out of the hospital. By making that effort, she realized their relationship had advanced yet another step.

The doctor seemed to be reluctant to let Terra go, even though Marc was at his forceful best. Only after a prolonged discussion in the hallway, where Marc promised they would spend that night in the lodge, and not fly back to California until the next day, did the doctor relent. With that accomplished, Marc hugged Terra gently, and told her he was glad she was all right.

As grateful as she was that he had come for her, his kindness disconcerted her. She'd expected a controller like him to yell at her. After all, he'd once ordered her to stop working on computational linguistics so she wouldn't burn herself out. Why didn't he tell her now that she couldn't risk her life like that?

All the way back to the lodge, he kept glancing over at her as if he was afraid she was going to faint. She suspected he would get mad at her once he thought she could take it. He carried her inside the lodge, and laid her down on the couch next to the fire. Covering her tenderly with several wool blankets, he sat next to her. He asked her how she felt. She shrugged in response.

"Nobody would tell me anything," she said. "Steve, and the rest of the guys, are they okay?"

He seemed to examine her face a long time before he answered. "Steve's dead."

"Oh, no." Another Silicon Silk partner dead. Tears stung at her eyes. "I'm sorry."

Nancy, David, and now Steve.

She recalled Peter standing at the lip of the bowl above her. His descent might have actually caused the avalanche. Was he okay?

"Is, is Peter…" She couldn't seem to get the words out.

"Peter's alive and well, Sweetheart. He didn't go down with you. But he saw it happen, and got help." Marc rearranged her blankets, and then looked straight at her. "Terra, you're the only one who made it."

"They all died?"

"Yes."

She recoiled. Four good people dead? And she was alive? She felt worthless and scared. Suddenly she *wanted* Marc to yell at her.

But instead, he put his hand on her blanket-covered feet. "Do your feet hurt, Sweetheart?"

"I'm fine," she said. She felt itchy, uneasy inside.

"Let me get you some tea," he said, and went into the kitchen.

She'd never had a close call before. But instead of being grateful she was alive, she felt superstitious, apprehensive, unworthy.

He brought her a mug. "How's your head? Headache? Sleepy?"

"Please stop asking me that over and over again," she said. "I told you, I'm okay."

He leaned over her so his face was mere inches from hers. He looked from one side of her face to the other, like he was trying to confirm that her eyes matched. Then slowly and sternly he spoke, as if she were a spoiled two year-old child.

"You had a run-in with some greenery and you blacked out. Your doctor ordered me to ask you specific questions, and look for certain things. She wouldn't have released you unless I promised I would. I fully intend to keep my promises."

Terra thought that now he'd tell her how stupid she was. But he didn't. He rearranged her blankets again. She pushed the blankets onto the floor.

"I gotta go to the bathroom," she said, getting to her feet. It hurt a little to stand.

He followed her as she took careful steps to the ornate little powder room off the kitchen. Once she sat on the toilet, he discreetly looked off in a different direction. He leaned against the powder room doorframe, waiting, his concern so earnest and intense. She realized she loved him.

When she finished, she studied her reflection in the mirror. She moaned. Scratches marred her right cheek, her nose, her chin. Her hair was a wild mass of tangles. A lump stood out on her forehead.

"God," she said, snorting unhappily. "You'd think I lost a fight with a cat or something."

She saw Marc's reflection in the mirror, moving behind her. He gently caressed her arms. She turned to him.

"Will you yell at me for being reckless, already?" she demanded. "I want to get your lecture over with."

He gazed at her with tired eyes, and led her back to the couch. She sat down, and he draped the blanket on her lap.

"Well?" she prodded.

"It's bad enough that you're beating yourself up over what happened," he said, still standing above her. He smoothed her knotted hair lightly. "I'm not going to add to your misery."

"But I think if you got really mad at me, I'd feel better."

He sat next to her, and put his arm around her shoulders.

"What could it hurt to try, Marc?" she asked, desperation now shading her voice. "Here, I'll help you. First you tell me how stupid I was to go on that mountain in the first place. And then you tell me that if *anybody* was supposed to live…"

"Nothing I say is going to magically make you feel any better. You've got survivor's guilt, Terra. It's going to take time, and a lot of thought, before you come to grips with what happened."

"I don't know why you're refusing to yell at me all of a sudden," she whined. "Being annoyed with me is second nature to you. What I did was dangerous. Just say it. Dan-ger-ous."

"I'm the last person who should lecture you about danger, Sweetheart. Climbing is dangerous. I just try to mitigate the danger by being physically prepared, and not doing anything foolish."

"See!" she cried. "You're getting the hang of it! Foolish. Tell me how foolish I was."

"If anyone is to blame, it's Peter," he said. "He should have known better than to take you out-of-bounds. There were plenty of avalanche warning signs. And he should have backed off the minute he saw them."

The doorbell rang, but Marc made no move to get up.

"How can you say that?" she asked. "I didn't see any signs warning us about avalanches."

Distracted by the sound of the doorbell again, he resettled her blanket once more. He then got up to go to the door. He opened it and invited his visitor in. A uniformed man stepped into the greatroom and looked around.

"You really don't have a phone here?" he asked Marc.

"No, sheriff."

"I'll be damned," the law said. "A computer guy without a phone."

"You have news?"

"Search and rescue has recovered the remaining body."

The two men started to discuss the logistics of getting the remains back to California.

The news shook Terra to her very toes. Marc hadn't told her that one of her skiing companions was still on the mountain, buried in snow. Someone was being pulled out, lifeless from an ice tomb, while she drank tea and self-indulgently whined about her knotty hair.

Only dumb luck had kept her alive. The realization of how close she'd come to dying in the avalanche, and how much she wanted to live, frightened her more than she thought possible. Finally the sheriff left, and Marc returned to her. She rose and sobbed into his chest.

The world was such a dangerous place.

★

Terra and Marc returned to Mountain View the next day. He wanted her to stay with him in the city. She declined. Taking her back to the condo, he ordered her to stay in bed while he went to Steve's funeral. He promised to be back as soon as he could. She tried sleeping, but she awoke, drenched in a cold sweat. Fear of death seized her. She had to go back home and heal herself.

She got up, showered, and worked on her injured face. After dabbing on some foundation to hide the tree scratches, she slicked her white-blonde hair off her face and tied it back into a ponytail. She put on a pair of giant gold hoop earrings. She desperately wanted to appear cocky and secure, because she couldn't shake the feeling that death might stalk her, even in New Orleans. Superstition dogged her, too. She hoped that if she didn't look scared, death might leave her alone, and pick on somebody weaker. Skin-tight jeans and a cropped, cotton sweater completed her look. Eyeing herself in the mirror, she arranged a smug look on her face. Carefree. A little slutty. Perfect.

The person in the mirror was fearless. Death would stay away.

The mirror reflected her blinking answering machine. She'd been back for hours, but she hadn't listened to the messages. She pressed the button to replay them and listened while she rechecked her travel bag. The first message was from Peter.

"Hey, Terragirl," he said. "This is Peter. Give me a call when you feel up to it. I'm sorry I couldn't get to you sooner. Carolina's been keeping me informed. Call me."

She grabbed some tissues to put in her purse, and listened to the second message, a get-well call from Carolina.

The last message was barely intelligible. "You there?" Marina

147

slurred. Was she drunk? Exhausted? Good thing Terra was returning to New Orleans. She could find out what was wrong.

Terra left a message with Marc's voice mail. "Marc, I'm going back to New Orleans. I've got to recharge."

She was nearly out the door when Marc arrived.

He looked potent in black; the dark suit emphasized his tanned skin and black eyes. Those eyes scrutinized her provocative attire, as if he were trying to gauge its significance. His gaze dropped to the overnight bag on the floor.

"Where are you going?" he asked.

"I left you a message. I'm going back home. Just for a day or two."

"You're leaving now?"

She nodded.

He picked up her bag. "Then I'll take you to the airport."

"Too bad you can't come with me," she murmured, scanning her apartment for something she needed but might have forgotten. She turned to face him again. An inexplicably fierce look had taken hold of his features.

"Ask me," he said.

"To come to New Orleans? I'm sure you don't have the time."

"Ask me."

It sounded like an order from someone who always got what he wanted. From women. From competitors. From allies. She could hardly breathe.

"Look Marc," she said, "I was just talking to myself. Don't make a big deal about it."

She held her arms stiffly against her body as he reached out with both hands to draw her closer. The memory of arriving at Silicon Silk eagerly anticipating her work on natural language, and discovering that Marc expected her to solve an industrial espionage problem instead, assaulted her anew. Terra and Marc were unequally matched: Ruthless C. Marc Elliott III had hurt her before, and he would hurt her again if it suited him.

Pulling her tighter against him, he caught her earring hoop in his teeth and gently tugged. Her fear dissipated, and she lost her train of thought entirely. His hands moved to mold her shoulders, and he stopped nibbling her earring. He gazed down at her with somber eyes.

"Ask me," he whispered.

She would love to find out what would happen between them away from the stresses of the Valley. She wanted him to see, and smell, and taste the land and culture that made her what she was. With a shuddery sigh, she dared to ask him.

"Will you come home with me, Marc?"

15 / Home

Home again. Terra slipped into the comfort of her French Quarter apartment so easily, she nearly forgot the fear that had driven her to come back. The dark, colorful rooms of the apartment also served as her consulting offices. Which meant most of the spaces were crammed full of computers and computer parts. She sank into her favorite overstuffed, paisley chair in the parlor, while Marc explored. She heard him making a little sound of amazement as he poked around her old motherboards and monitors.

He brought a shell of an old TRS 80 into the parlor. She'd cannibalized the TRS for parts for some hardware hacking project years ago.

"I haven't seen one of *these* in… well, a long time," he said. "I had no idea you were such a packrat."

"I'm not a packrat. I just can't get rid of anything."

He chuckled. "I have to admit I'm just as sentimental about my first Mac."

She scrutinized his dark, heavy-browed beauty, and doubted he had a sentimental bone in his body. He settled into a chair in the parlor. Showing that devoted, concentrated attention she found so appealing, he asked her detailed questions about her life as a consultant. What days and hours did she usually work? Which computers did she find most useful? Was that the chair she usually sat in when she worked? She basked in his interest, savoring the way he could make her feel so important.

He asked if she would mind if he made a few phone calls.

"Go right ahead," she said.

He spent a couple of hours in her office, while she dozed in the parlor. She felt superstition and fear lose their hold. Death wasn't stalking her anymore. By the time Marc had finished with his calls, night had fallen. He looked haggard and tense.

"Everything all right?" she asked.

"As well as can be expected." He sat on the satin loveseat. "I just spoke to Ray. He's trying to get the Mountain View police interested in investigating Nancy's and David's deaths. He thinks there's something fishy going on. Too many company founders have been killed. I don't agree with what Ray's doing, but everyone's got to deal with Steve's passing in their own way, I suppose."

"Maybe you should go back to Mountain View tonight, Marc," she offered.

"Peter won't have the short list ready for awhile. I can stay at least until tomorrow afternoon. We'll need a Chief Counsel before we can effectively attack the major problems anyway."

"Like buying out Steve's heirs?"

He rubbed his eyes. "That's not a problem. Hancock will be taking care of the buy-out. We have life insurance coverage on all shareholders."

Carolina had never mentioned the life insurance.

"So why didn't life insurance kick in to buy out Nancy's and David's interests in Silicon Silk after they died?"

"Hancock decided that SSI was, in part, liable for Nancy's death. The company infirmary didn't have the epinephrine that could have saved her life. And as for David, suicide isn't covered."

She noticed the way his eye twitched when he mentioned David. The loss of the VP of Platforms still bothered Marc a lot. He didn't seem to be nearly as upset by Steve's death.

"Is it going to be tough to find a new Chief Counsel?" she asked.

He nodded. "As a partner, Steve is irreplaceable. Besides being a good lawyer, he was totally immersed in the company culture. He understood what we are and what we're trying to become. But the company will probably survive, even though right now it doesn't feel like it." Marc rubbed his temples, and continued in a melancholy, thoughtful tone. "It would have been worse for the company if Peter had been the one crushed in that avalanche."

She got up and went to sit next to him on the loveseat, trying to offer him a little consolation. "Peter's a good CFO?"

"Peter is the best right hand man I could have," he said. "He and his logical mind can size up situations and personalities faster than anyone else on earth."

She agreed. Peter's perceptive nature was one of the things she appreciated most about him.

"Because of that he can exploit opportunities long before anyone else," he continued. "If an action benefits the company, he'll jump on it."

"Sounds like you're describing yourself."

"No, Sweetheart, I'm not a bit like Peter. I'm no quick thinker. I take a long time to mull the facts over before I come to a conclusion. Then I don't bend easily."

"Yeah, I know," she said. "On that first day, when you told me why you really hired me, and you snarled 'I'm not a negotiator,' it intimidated the hell out of me."

He seemed to silently chew over what she'd just said. "I regret telling you that." Reaching into the inside pocket of his jacket, he pulled out a folded set of papers. But he held the papers close to his chest, as if he didn't want to part with them.

"What do you have there?" she asked.

"I got this taken care of yesterday," he said, giving her the papers. "They're legal papers saying you've satisfied the conditions of the contract.

Her mind reeled with delight and relief. After all these months of anguish and pain, was she finally free?

"I don't have to hunt down your digital thief anymore?" she asked.

"No."

Giddy with triumph, her head swimming with the implications of finally being cut loose, she fanned herself with the folded contract.

"Is it because you finally accept that it was David who stole the code?"

"No."

"Then you're finally admitting that you were wrong to trick me into coming to Mountain View and doing your cracker hunt."

"I wasn't wrong to hire you, Sweetheart. I was wrong to hold you to your contract after we made love."

She felt a twinge of disappointment and confusion. "That's why you're letting me off the hook? Because I threatened to file sexual harassment charges after you kissed me in Ray's office?"

"It's gone one or two steps beyond kissing at this point, Terra. But now that you're free to come and go as you please, my conscience is clear."

"Well, your conscience *shouldn't* be clear!" she cried. She got up and began to pace the small room. "You tricked me. You pretended to hire me to do natural language interface design, and then forced me go cracker-hunting. You made me suffer like you wouldn't believe."

In one strong, fluid motion, he got off the loveseat, and stood in front of her. She understood how he would be able to change his position on a rock face with lightning speed.

"I never tricked you. I never cheated you. I offered you a contract. You had the right to read it carefully, and the right to refuse it. I gave you time to look at the contract, time to consider it, time to ask questions, time to say no. You tricked yourself, Sweetheart."

Everything he said about giving her time to read the contract was true. He hadn't pressured her at all. She had to accept responsibility for her own naiveté. But acknowledging her own foolishness made her feel vulnerable and small.

"Fine," she said. "Maybe you didn't trick me. Maybe you just exploited me. Some of us don't think that there's an ethical difference between tricking and exploitation." She creased the contract nervously with her fingers. "And don't call me Sweetheart when you're yelling at me. I don't like it."

His brow furrowed, and he held her face in his rough hands. "I didn't realize I was yelling," he said.

Of course he hadn't yelled, but his words had as much impact on her as if he had.

"How could you have tricked me like that, Marc?" she asked.

"Because I was desperate," he said. "I was convinced you were the only one that could rescue Silicon Silk from the thief."

But had she rescued Silicon Silk? Not if Ranger was still raiding the company. She felt herself frown as she forced away an unwelcome sense of responsibility.

Smoothing the cowlick on her forehead with the pads of his fingers, he said, "The thief is no longer your problem, Terra."

"What about Personal Scout?" she asked.

"The project is yours if you want it."

"That's an offer I'm going to consider seriously," she said. "So, are you hungry?"

"Sure."

"Well, if you want Louisiana cooking we'll have to go out," she told him. "People eat late around here, so if we go right now it will be a lot less crowded."

Within the hour, they were at Geoffroi's, sharing a platter heaped with spicy boiled crawfish, chunks of potatoes, and corn on the cob. She taught Marc how to eat the crawfish. His relaxed, cheerful attitude made her happy.

She was also amused every time the waiter gave Marc and her an odd look, as if a man in an Armani suit didn't belong with a cropped-top, bejeaned bimbo like her.

During the middle of dinner, she wiped her hands on her napkin and said, "I'll be right back. I want to go say hi to Geoff, he's the chef and owner."

She took a quick peek into the kitchen. Geoff was within, all in white—chef's hat and all—flouring a filet.

"Geoff!" she yelled into the din.

A man with sharp, narrow features turned to look at her. He

grinned, clearly delighted. Geoff was easy-going and fun, a treasured old friend.

"Terra!" He walked over to her, looked her up and down. "You back from California, or just visiting?"

She shrugged. "Um, I haven't decided."

He gave her a pat on the hip. "Welcome back just the same."

A waiter pushed his way into the kitchen and hollered a change in an order. Another cook screamed something in return.

Geoff gave her another pat and returned to his filet.

"You must have found Geoff," Marc commented when she returned to the table.

"Why do you say that?" she asked.

He just eyed her middle.

She looked down at her hips. There, in white, on her jeans, was a handprint. No, two handprints.

Acutely embarrassed, she brushed off the flour. "Oh, yeah. Geoff must have had flour on his hands." She sat down, and waved her hand dismissively. "It was harmless. That's just what he does. Pat people. He's an old friend, you know."

She had been concentrating so hard on acting innocent that it took her awhile to notice Marc was smiling at her. He was apparently amused by her excuses. Jealousy just didn't seem to be part of his makeup.

She couldn't say the same thing about herself.

"Are you really that modern?" she asked him, flicking her eyes in the direction of the kitchen and Geoff.

"You mean modern about you and other men? No, Dear, most certainly not. But I won't leap to conclusions just because of a handprint." He slipped off his jacket, draped it over the back of his chair, and loosened his tie. Leaning back, he watched the restaurant clientele.

She finished up the last of the crawfish, and had another swallow of her bourbon. "I guess I should be grateful for you not getting upset. Because it really was innocent. Except you never seemed to be very threatened by Peter, either. Why?"

"You know damn well I don't like your involvement with him," he said.

She propped her elbows on the table, rested her chin in her palms, and asked lazily, "Are you jealous?"

"No. I dislike that relationship because it gave you an out."

"What do you mean, an 'out'?"

"As long as you believed you had a relationship with him, you used it to keep me at arm's length. But involvement with him is nothing but smoke and mirrors. It has no substance, no permanence. You have no future with him."

She snorted and sat back in her chair. "You're so arrogant."

"That might be true. But it's also true that Peter can never give you what you need."

"Are you going to tell me that he's gay?" she asked. "Or that he actually *does* that creepy bondage stuff?"

He raised his brows. "What creepy bondage stuff?"

"You know. That S & M newsgroup he told us about at the launch dinner? Carolina's gross out contest?" And then she recalled Marc had been otherwise engaged with Velvet. "Oh, never mind."

"I don't have a clue if Peter's gay or involved in S & M," he said, "and I've known the man for fourteen years. What I do know is that beneath his suave charm lies pure, passionless intellect. And beneath that…" He shrugged. "Whatever sexual motivations or desires Peter has, they are buried deep," he said. "Too deep for even *you* to plumb. And I know you need *passion*, Terra."

"Oh, but I need challenges, too," she cooed. Slipping off her shoes, she slid her bare feet up his shins, and up over his knees. She scooted her feet along his inner thigh, until he rewarded her with a perfect look of surprise.

★

Terra woke early the next morning. Used to sleeping alone, she hoped she hadn't tried to kick Marc out of bed during the night.

She watched him as he slept, noting the occasional twitch of a muscle, the movement of a finger, the parting of his lips. His dark lashes lay against his wind-roughened cheek, brown hair curled around his ears and neck. So beautiful and harmless in repose. She wondered what he'd been like when he'd first founded SSI. Had he been innocent and sweet? Would he have exploited her back in those days? Leaning over, she kissed him gently on the eyelid. "I love you."

He stirred and, acting on instinct, caressed her cheek. "Sweetheart," he said, his eyes still closed. Then he drifted off to sleep again.

He was obviously accustomed to nights with the softer sex. A vision of Marc in the mild, yielding arms of Velvet slunk into her mind. She considered bringing him fully awake to subvert the thought of him making love to anyone else, but she decided against it.

She dressed, made chai tea, and brought it outside to her little balcony. Propping her feet up on the ironwork, she tried to fix the earring that had been twisted off-center during the ardor of the night before.

It was time to consider Marc's offer. Now that she was no longer hamstrung by the horrible cracker project, should she go back to California and work on natural language?

Her internal sirens screamed: Don't go back! He made you suffer professionally before. He will again. Now that you have your freedom, take advantage of it!

But this time I'll finally get to do what I've dreamed of: natural language work at red-hot SSI. I have to say yes. And besides, I love him.

The sirens now shrieked a reply: No! You can't trust him! Once he finds out you love him, he'll exploit it. He'll use it to figure out a way to keep you there forever.

I know what I'm doing.

Her earring was almost as good as new now. Putting it on, she went back in. He was awake, lying on her bed, gazing around her cobalt-walled bedroom. She launched herself onto the bed.

"You're already dressed," he said. He sounded disappointed.

"Marc, tell me something. Do you ever miss those early start-up days at Silicon Silk?"

"I suppose. Every once in awhile I miss the adrenaline surges, the all-nighters, the electrifying thrill of achievement," he said. "But that burning devotion to SSI cost me far more than I ever dreamed." A melancholy expression drifted over his face. "A lot more. So I don't see that period of my life in quite the same light as I used to. But back then, nothing seemed more important than reaching that first million in sales, and then after that, taking the company public."

She wondered just exactly what creating SSI had cost him. "So why don't you want to take the company public anymore?"

"They always say: 'Don't go too public, too soon.'"

"You still think it's too soon?" she asked.

"Never would be too soon." He fairly growled the words. "All sorts of new problems crop up when a company goes public; and every single one of them detract from technical progress. Suddenly SSI would be responsible to stockholders who don't know anything about software. Oh, but the stockholders *do* know about earnings growth."

Now she regretted having asked him, because the subject of going public obviously upset him.

"I'd end up spending every waking minute talking to analysts and CNBC," he continued, "about earnings growth, working to prevent our stock price from diving."

"The stock market is pretty erratic isn't it?"

"Especially the tech sector," he replied. "So, after a few years of that kind of hell, I'd ultimately get booted out of the company in a boardroom coup, because of a bad quarter." He ran agitated fingers through his hair. "I'd be replaced by a new CEO who had made his name selling ketchup. Ketchup! No, a company owned by a small group is far more intimate and satisfying." A pensive look now crossed his face, and he seemed to look at something far away. "Now

SSI is a company owned by a *very* small group."

Hoping to chase away his blues, she scooted closer to him. Her hands caressed his rigid chest and shoulders, yet he still gazed off in the distance, perhaps recounting the last terrible months.

"When do you need to get back?" she asked.

He now looked at her. "What?"

"When do you have to leave?" she asked, tracing a lazy path down the center of his chest with her forefinger.

"Two or so," he said. "In the meantime…"

Sliding a finger under the strap of her shift, he pulled it down to expose her shoulder. He kissed her there, sending a shock of heat through her body. In one smooth movement, he rolled over and straddled her.

To hell with Sunny and Velvet, she thought, her heart drumming. *Right now, Marc's here with me.*

With his rough hands resting on her shoulders, he bent over and kissed her in that grounding way he had. "Are you going to come back with me?"

"I want to," she said. "But you have to understand that if I do come back to work at SSI, we won't be having a public relationship. As far as anyone else is concerned, we aren't lovers. We don't go out. You ignore me. I ignore you."

"Why?"

"Because I care about my reputation as a computer scientist."

"That's ridiculous," he said, kissing her nose. "You didn't hide your relationship with Peter."

"That's different," she said as he softly kissed her cheeks.

Nuzzling her neck, he now began to stroke her thigh. "How is that different?" he asked as he slowly inched up her dress.

"As *if*!" she cried. "You're doing *that*, and you want me to *explain*? Get off me if you expect to have a coherent conversation!" She slapped his chest to push him away.

He rolled off her, clutching his chest, laughing. She jumped off the bed and stomped around her brilliant blue bedroom, scowling.

Before she went to Mountain View she needed to resolve this issue with him, and here he was setting her afire again. She moved a pillow here, kicked a rug there, closed the drapes. Finally after a few trips around the room, she sat down on the overstuffed armchair next to the bed.

"How, you ask?" she said, crossing her legs irritably. "Well for one thing, Peter doesn't come to programmers' meetings and make me look like I'm an idiot, and you do."

"So we're back to that, are we?" he asked.

"Yes, we're back to that! Look at it from my point of view for once, will you? You confront me about my linguistics work, and everybody thinks I'm about to get canned. Then suddenly, not only am I still employed, but we're kissing in the corner? It's going to look like I kept my job because I'm fucking the CEO."

"But you're okay with secretly fucking the CEO, just as long as he doesn't stoop so low as to take you out to dinner in a public place?"

"Yup," she said, annoyed with his ridiculing tone, "that about covers it. You should know what my computational linguistics reputation means to me, Marc. You've exploited it often enough."

"Yes. Your reputation. You want to explain it to me once more? How your reputation as a computer scientist was enhanced by going out with Peter, but would be irreparably harmed if you had anything at all to do with me?"

She threw up her hands. "There's a huge difference between Peter and you. *He's* not my boss."

He gazed at her with a devastating, "You'll end up doing what I want" expression, and lay back into the pillows, the very picture of confident virility. "Your arrangement doesn't suit me," he said. "But I'm willing to give it a try."

"Yeah, well," she said, disconcerted by his body language, which said something else entirely, "you'd better."

How would they ever work things out between them? He was too controlling, and she was too independent. She got up and walked over to her ornate rosewood dresser, and laid down her hoop earring.

"I really need to see if Marina's okay before I can go back to Mountain View, Marc. I was planning on checking up on her this morning."

"I'll come with you," he said.

★

As Terra and Marc headed over to the art shop where Marina worked, Terra told him about her sister's pregnancy, how Marina insisted on being independent, and her own profound concerns about the baby's father. She described Jared as someone who'd spent some time in prison, but did not mention he was a salami-slicing cracker.

The art store proprietor told them Marina was taking the day off. As they approached Marina's apartment building with its fancy iron balconies, Terra told Marc she thought it was one of the prettier houses in the Quarter.

According to the names scrawled above the mailboxes, Marina lived on the second floor. Terra knocked at Marina's door. It took awhile, but finally someone answered. Jared, dressed in his usual plaid flannel and his hair awry, opened the door. He leaned against the doorjamb, looked past Terra, and up at Marc, who was standing solidly behind her.

"Is Marina here?" Terra asked.

Jared spared Terra a dismissive squint, and then scrutinized Marc and his expensive suit.

"Jared, this is Marc Elliott. He's a friend of mine," she said, annoyed by Jared's peculiar rudeness.

She turned around to send Marc a smile that was supposed to say, "What can I do? Marina loves this guy."

Her smile died prematurely. Marc's face held an expression of raw hatred toward the younger man. She turned back to Jared. His stare had turned to glower. The dislike was obviously mutual.

She didn't have the time or the desire to analyze the two men's strange antagonism toward each other. She was here to check up on Marina.

"Well, is Marina here or not?" Terra asked impatiently.

"Not," Jared said.

Something didn't smell right to Terra. "Then I'll leave her a note." She pushed her way past Jared.

Marc followed.

16 / Dumpster diving

Marina's apartment looked terrible, and smelled even worse. Terra slogged through clothing strewn over the floor. Fast food cups and bags crowded the couch and coffee table. Dirty dishes overran the tables and counters. She was impressed that the girl even had that many dishes to get dirty. If she hadn't already known what a pig her sister was, she would have been worried that all the trash was a sign of problems with Marina's pregnancy.

Her sister was in the kitchen, standing against the sink washing dishes—obviously a rare occurrence. Jared had lied about her being home, maybe because he thought Marina might be embarrassed by the condition of the apartment.

A new PC, turned on and probably busily transferring fractions of cents from millions of bank accounts to RogueKnight's account, sat on a folding table in the living room. Curiously, the folding table was clean of debris, though the floor around it was littered with upturned cups and dirty paper plates. A sticky-looking purple stain splattered the computer tower and the keyboard. Marina's messiness was likely not an asset in the proper running of a salami operation.

"Hey, Marina," she said to Marina's back. The girl didn't respond or even turn around.

Terra walked over to her. "I was in town, and wanted to see how you were. See if you needed…"

A nasty greenish bruise marred one side of Marina's face, a pink splotch on her jawline promised a bruise later. Her lower lip was split and swollen. Her eyes were red.

"Please don't cause trouble, okay?" the girl begged Terra in a

163

whisper. "Okay? If you'll just leave, I'll be able to calm him back down. Okay?"

Trouble was the last thing Terra wanted. She knew from one short-lived brush with brutality that Marina was right. Confronting Jared would only make things worse. But there was no way she'd leave her sister with him. Her only option was to get Marina away from Jared without him realizing it.

"I won't," Terra promised softly. She looked down at the sink. Marina dipped her hands in the brown, detergentless water. Her sister's left wrist was swollen.

She took a deep breath. She had to figure out how to get the girl out. Grabbing a rag, she turned away from the sink and started to fiercely scrub down the stove. *But how?* She glanced over at Marc, who was standing near the door. His eyes flicked from Jared pecking at the keyboard, to the filthy floor, to Marina's back, to Terra's frantic cleaning, apparently trying to understand the bizarre scene.

She hit on a simple solution. "So," she said. "How about after we get the kitchen cleaned up, Marc and I take you two out for an early lunch? Our treat."

"You can keep your filthy data-hoarding profits," Jared said, cursing and now wiping at the dirty keyboard with a fast-food napkin.

"Marina?" Terra asked. "How about you?"

"No thanks," the girl murmured, bowing her head.

Scratch Plan A. If Marina wasn't going to leave, then Jared would have to. For Plan B, she'd need Marc's help. She bit her lip. Marc was a wild card. She couldn't just order him around and expect him to obey. Picking up a pile of food-encrusted paper plates from the floor near the folding table, she carried them over by Marc.

"I have to get Jared to go out somewhere with me," Terra whispered. She slipped him her keys. "Stay here and get Marina over to my apartment."

Marc gave her an incredulous, annoyed look, and moved across the room. He casually scooped up three or four dirty cups from the kitchen table, and set them on the counter next to the sink.

"Hello, Marina," Marc said. "Aren't you feeling well?"

"I'm fine," the girl mumbled. A tear glistened on her bruised cheek.

Marc turned around slowly, and regarded Jared with narrowed, contemptuous eyes. Terra's stomach dropped. *No, Marc, don't confront him!* For one horrible, endless minute, Marc just stared at Marina's tormentor.

And then Marc said, "You hit women, boy?"

Terra's heart stopped. She couldn't bear any more violence.

The salami slicer propped his legs up onto the folding table. "Who the fuck are you to call me 'boy'?"

And then all hell broke loose.

Marc leapt over to Jared, pulling him up by his armpits. The chair Jared had been sitting on crashed to the floor. The PC tower wobbled, and toppled onto the table with a loud pop.

"My Seagate Dazzledrive!" Jared screamed, trying to kick Marc.

Marc grabbed Jared's leg with both hands.

Marina shrieked. "Please don't hurt him!"

Marc twisted hard, and Jared lay face down on the dirty floor.

"Marina's pregnant," Marc said to Jared, "or don't you know that?" His voice was like ice: sharp enough to cut.

"Fuck her," said Jared.

"You piece of shit," Marc said.

Jared thrashed around, making sounds of pain. And then, abruptly, he stopped. Either he was dead, or whatever Marc was doing to him hurt worse when he struggled.

"What are you waiting for, Terra?" Marc demanded. "Take your sister and *go*."

She ran to Marina, grabbed her hand, and got her out of the apartment. As she pulled her shell-shocked sister down the stairs, she heard a stream of pained obscenities coming from inside.

★

After Dr. Dread told the three of them that Marina's baby was fine, and had applied a cast on Marina's fractured wrist, they all returned to Mountain View. The devastated and weeping girl kept asking Terra how Jared could care about that computer more than her. She had no answer for her. Marina also appealed to Marc several times, frantically begging him to reassure her that Jared wasn't hurt too badly. By the end of the flight Terra had a headache that started in the back of her scalp and stretched down to the middle of her back.

Marina was quiet and sullen by the time they got to the condo. She got her sister settled into the extra bedroom, and soon the girl slept, her cast cradled up against her thickening waist.

The violence left her churning. Finally, with her sister asleep, she joined Marc on the couch and confronted him.

"Why did you have to beat him up?" she asked him. "I was going to get him out of there."

"What's done is done," he said shortly.

"But you don't even understand what you did!" she cried. "Don't you see? You've turned Jared into a victim. Marina feels sorry for him. Sorry for *him*! That's the last thing she needs, Marc."

"Hmm," he grunted. He pursed his lips, and folded his arms across his chest.

"So you aren't even going to talk about it?"

"No," he said.

"Marc," she said, laying a hand on his arm. She was scared after having seen Marc twisting the younger man—even if Jared deserved worse. She wanted Marc to reassure her that he wasn't an uncivilized brute, that what he'd done to Jared was a rare event. "I need to know what you're thinking."

He stared at her coldly, like she was some stranger. She pulled her hand away.

"Marc," she said, "talk to me."

"That piece of shit had to be taught a lesson," he said.

The gulf between them seemed to yawn wider. "*Had* to? Like

you're obeying some natural law? Like water *has* to run downhill, heat *has* to travel to cold, and Marc *has* to beat the crap out of Jared?"

"The second he opened that door I knew that he'd mistreated Marina. Do you know how?" he asked. His black eyes glittered with awful intensity. "Because of the way he looked at you. Wrathful. Scornful. When Jared looked at you, he saw Marina."

"So my sister and I look a lot alike. Big deal. There was a way to solve this problem without violence." .

"You're not understanding me, Terra. The resemblance between you and Marina is uncanny. So much that when Jared looks at you, he sees your sister. By the same token, when I look at Marina, I see you. When I saw Marina—her face mashed, crying, hurt—I saw you. *You* were in tears, *your* cheek was bruised." He barely touched Terra's face, as if he were brushing away imaginary tears. "And I'm not going to let anyone get away with hurting you. Because I love you."

Gazing at him in all his heavy-browed, serious splendor, she had to admit that he hadn't asked to get involved in her sister's problems. He'd helped in the only way he knew how—even if it was through brutality.

An unexpected guilt snapped at her. He had let her off the hook because he loved her, not because he believed his company was safe from the cracker. If she pursued the development of Personal Scout full bore, she could be leaving him and his company in the lurch. She couldn't abandon Marc, no matter how much she hated hunting down the electronic thief.

"Marc, you need to know something about Jared," she said. "He goes by the name of RogueKnight. He's a salami slicer, among other things. That's someone who…"

"I know what salami slicing is," he interrupted, his voice tight. "Is he the one who's been stealing code?"

"No, I don't think so. But he knows the guy I think might be."

His eyes narrowed as he chewed that one over. "The kid in Sweden."

"Yeah. He goes by the name of Ranger. Anyway, what I've done…"

"RogueKnight, Ranger," he spat out contemptuously, "Those *names*. Those little assholes think they're noble, don't they?"

His vehemence caught her off guard. She had forgotten how much the CEO of SSI hated crackers and cracker sensibilities. She had forgotten how much he hated *her*.

"SSI was just another symbol of data-hoarding to RogueKnight," she said in a shaking voice. "But now it's going to be personal. You messed with his body, and worse, you messed with his computer. As if you *needed* another pissed off cracker in your life. And as for Ranger, I don't know for sure…"

He interrupted her again. "You give me whatever information you have on Ranger. And I will find out what his involvement is. This is going to end. Now."

"No," she said. "*I* will get the bottom of this."

He stared at her with his obsidian eyes, expecting her to back down. "This is not your job anymore."

"Yeah," she said. "It is."

Because I love you, too.

★

After he left later that night, she felt worn out and sad, smarting with the new and painful distance between herself and Marc. Defying him took every bit of strength she had, and she didn't have all that much to begin with. It was all so awful: her lover, roiling with violence and cracker-hatred; Marina, pregnant, concerned for the man who'd beaten her.

She peeked in on the girl. Sleeping. Dr. Dread had given her sister some painkillers, and they seemed to be working. After scrawling a quick note to Marina in case she woke up, she rushed out of the condo. Maybe Ranger had answered her e-mail by now. She hurried over to SSI.

With the exception of Lyle's nocturnal mice, she was alone in A

& C. She broke into the Canadian computer, the home of her purloined e-mail address. No mail for her. Damn. Ranger might never reply.

She looked at the time: eleven forty-two. Certainly Marina wouldn't be awake yet. Maybe she should finally investigate David's electronic correspondence. Hoping to find proof that the VP of Platforms had been the inside man, she penetrated his computer. But the experience was unpleasant: no leisurely exploration, no fun. This was slam-bam-thank-you-ma'am type cracking. David's e-mail had all been deleted; after all, he'd been dead for weeks. But the e-mail server or the backups might still have some of those messages. Working as fast as she could, she used the high-tech analog of dumpster diving, and managed to collect about 450 e-mail messages David had sent and received. She copied the messages onto a Zip disk, and rushed back to the condo.

Marina was still asleep, thank goodness.

Terra made herself some chai tea, and read about a hundred e-mail messages David had written. She nearly fell asleep. Poor David didn't have a way with words. The next hundred she only skimmed, scanning for words that might hint at extortion demands, or an offer to sell secrets. No cigar. Of course that didn't rule him out.

Next, she read the messages the Platforms Chief had received. They weren't dull, but they were largely unrevealing. She enjoyed reading the messages Marc had written to David—his letters were kind and encouraging. They had obviously been close friends. She found a scathing message Peter had sent to David. Peter accused David of having no backbone, and of being Marc's lackey. She snickered. Who *wasn't* Marc's lackey? In any case, the message didn't seem to have anything to do with stolen secrets.

She thought about the wiry, nervous man she'd met at the launch dinner. She could imagine David killing himself by carbon monoxide poisoning, even if Marc couldn't. Nancy too, had died of poisoning of a sort. Nancy had somehow accidentally eaten Kiwi, and because of it her throat had closed up, cutting off her air. And

Steve was dead because of an accident, too. But he hadn't died of the cold. He had been suffocated by the snow.

Carbon monoxide, cutting off air, suffocation. Nancy, David and Steve had *all* died of suffocation, she realized. But it was a pattern she didn't know what to do with.

★

The next morning, Marina encouraged Terra to return to work. Marina said she planned to rest up just a little more, and then she'd go out and get a job. More than a little anxious, Terra left Marina to her own devices and went to work.

Conversations stopped and everybody stared when Terra walked through A & C to her cube. She figured they all must have heard that she'd gone up to the Vail lodge with Peter, and narrowly missed getting killed. As she passed Jack's cubicle, he stopped his angry stomping around to glare at her with open jealousy. Just last week Jack thought she was dead meat, about to be fired by Marc because she was so incompetent, and now, suddenly, she was a hot-shit adventuress who was screwing the CFO.

His envy made her mad. She was no adventuress, and she'd never made love to Peter. And she certainly didn't want anyone to know she was involved with Marc. If her relationship with Marc became common knowledge, it would look like she was sleeping her way up the corporate ladder. Tense and unhappy, she plopped on her high-tech comfort chair, and listened to Jack snapping at someone on the phone.

One by one, her friends drifted into her cube asking to hear her story about nearly getting killed in an avalanche. It became harder and harder to dredge up the proper enthusiasm for the tale.

Peter popped in to see how she was, too. He winked and then glided back to his bean counting. She watched him leave, appreciating—only in the abstract—how attractive he was. It was a massive loss for womankind that man didn't come with passion.

Carolina also visited. "Hey, how are you? I tried to call you at home, but then I heard you'd gone back to Louisiana for awhile."

"Yeah, I did. I needed a break."

Carolina wore the gold drop earrings Terra had given her for her birthday. They looked fantastic on her.

"I can imagine," Carolina said. A smile spread over her face. "I am *so* happy you're all right, Terra. You have time to go for some coffee at the cafe?"

"Sure," Terra said.

Once they sat down with their mugs, Carolina looked directly into Terra's eyes and said, "So Ray told me that Marc went back to Colorado to get you out of the hospital."

"Yeah. He did. He came through in the clinch again." Terra glanced away and out the tall windows; she felt guilty. She longed to confide in her friend about Marc, but was afraid to.

"So, have you heard about that paternity suit Jack's involved in?" Carolina asked.

"No!" Terra cried, glad for the change in subject.

"Yup. This young woman is suing him for child support. She's supposedly the daughter of some high-powered, Valley mergers and acquisitions lawyer!"

"Uh oh," Terra said.

"Well it *is* possible that it isn't his baby."

"I guess." Being a defendant in a lawsuit sure went a long way to explain Jack's bad mood. She took a sip of her coffee. "It probably costs a lot to defend that kind of lawsuit, huh?"

"No doubt."

What about investigating Jack as the inside man? Last night's raid on the e-mail server hadn't fingered David Houle at all. And unlike poor, dead David, Jack been a suspect from the very beginning. The Surge-sucker had the knowledge to pull it off, and from what she'd seen during the programmer's meetings, he was inherently disloyal. And now, according to Carolina, Jack had good financial motivation for secrets theft.

True to her promise, Marina got herself a night shift job at the nearby Seven-Eleven. Terra was impressed with her sister's sense of responsibility, but at the same time she was worried. The girl refused to talk about Jared, or what he'd done, so Terra had no idea what her sister was thinking. She hoped against hope that Marina's anger at Jared's "fuck her" betrayal would win out over her compassion for him.

Terra rearranged her schedule so that she'd work the same hours as Marina. Not only could she protect her sister better that way, but she would also be able to investigate Jack in peace.

But working at night was lonely; she never saw Marc, even in passing, and she was no longer part of the gossip cycle. Just to keep her finger on the pulse of life at Silicon Silk, she began to spend a little time each night browsing the contents of the e-mail server. Much of Peter's correspondence was encrypted. *Still keeping secrets,* she thought. Marc's messages were not, and so she learned that the Chief Counsel's accidental death had hurled the company into disorder. Efforts to replace Steve were stalled due to a fierce power struggle between Marc and Peter. Still intent on an IPO, Peter insisted on hiring a Chief Counsel who had taken a company public before, and installing him on the board of directors. Marc refused. The only other shareholder, Ray, supported Marc. The Chief of Technology, like David before him, was rewarded with nasty e-mail messages from Peter. She thought that Marc might have been able to head off some of the antagonism if he had stayed in Mountain View after Steve died. But he had been absent, caring for her in Colorado and then in New Orleans. His concern for her had endangered his company and now he had to make up for it.

She wished she could see him.

Her cracker hunt wasn't going well. After rifling through Jack's computer files and his paper files, she had firm evidence that he was a pretentious jerk who'd fucked the wrong girl.

Jack was no more an inside man than David seemed to be.

One Thursday evening Marc called.

"How about a late picnic dinner on the coastside over by Half Moon Bay tonight, Sweetheart?" he asked.

"I'd love it," she said, thirsty for contact with him.

"Wonderful. I'll take you to see the house, too."

He promised to call her back within the hour to firm up their plans. He called within a few minutes, but it was to cancel.

"I'm sorry, we can't get together tonight, Terra." He sounded tense, even angry about something. "I have to be at a dinner meeting. We'll do it tomorrow. All right, Sweetheart?

She was disappointed, but hardly surprised. "I understand, Marc. It's okay."

"Before I forget, Keith finished searching the logs for communications with the Swede's computer. There were several connections between darkside and an SSI computer within the last three months."

"Yeah? Which one?" she asked. Now maybe she'd get somewhere.

"The SSI Web server. The logs show only http connections. Not even an attempt to try anything funny. Looks to be completely innocent."

"That's it?" she said, exasperated. "The guy looked at the Silicon Silk website?"

"That's all Keith could discover." She heard muffled voices as Marc carried on a conversation with someone in his office. He spoke into the mouthpiece again, harried. "I've got to go. Sorry, Sweetheart."

She went home early, discouraged with the progress she'd made in her self-imposed cracker hunt.

The next evening when she returned to work, she began hammering away at her natural language interface work. But tonight her great cerebral love seemed to give her no pleasure. What she needed was some leisurely high-tech fun to take her mind off her failures. *Yes.* She needed a cracking challenge worthy of her skills, with a sweet intellectual reward at the end. She settled into her high tech chair, and began the delicious deliberation. Which computer network did she wish to plunder? She'd heard Microsoft Research had been making some extraordinary advances in natural language interfaces. Certainly a worthwhile target.

Microsoft Research it was.

She began her attack. The intruder protection was not sufficient to keep her out for long. Inside Microsoft Research's network, roaming at will, digitally peering into this corner and that, she felt a satisfaction she hadn't felt in days.

"Oh, yes," she murmured.

And then a familiar voice from behind ordered her to log off the computer.

17 / Peachy-Pink

Terra turned around to stare into Marc's black-hole eyes, and felt a rush of guilty fear. Strolling through Microsoft Research's network was true industrial espionage.

"Oh, hi," she said, hurrying to log off Microsoft Research. Surely he hadn't realized she had been visiting a competitor's network.

"Finish up what you're doing, Terra," he said tersely. "I'm taking you home for the weekend."

Resentment now sent guilt into retreat. She didn't like being ordered around like that. Just because Marc was in a bad mood because he was having political problems, didn't give him the right to be rude. She gave him a dirty look, and faced her computer screen again, and diddled with a file. He could damn well wait until she was ready to go.

★

Marc's loft was in a converted factory in the heart of San Francisco's SOMA district. The large rooms and high ceilings made her uneasy, the hard-edged architecture intimidated her. The sparse leather and chrome furniture didn't help. Slick and cold, the loft felt like a museum without the art. The only spot of warmth might have been the wooden floor, except the deep red-brown surface was so uniform, and so highly polished, it almost looked metallic.

She lowered herself onto a black leather chair in the vast living room. The chair felt way more comfortable than it looked. "Nice," she said.

His bad mood long gone, his eyes flicked over her affectionately. Leaning closer, he gave her a warm, relaxed kiss, making her whole body feel like liquid rubber.

He clucked, "You haven't been eating right. I'm going to fix you a snack. In the meantime, make yourself at home, Sweetheart." He left her alone.

Hoping to find a bar, she got up and wandered over to a modern, polished wood affair along one brick wall. It was a bar. She fixed herself a bourbon, and carried it into the kitchen. There, among the gleaming, industrial steel appliances, he chopped up vegetables.

"You know, snacks are why they invented microwave popcorn," she teased.

He harumphed. "I don't even *own* a microwave."

She laughed. "Microwave too high tech for you?"

He threw the brightly colored mass into a contraption that looked like a fancy blender. "Can't cook with a micro," he said. "And I *know* the way to your heart is through your stomach."

"Not my stomach," she purred. "Think lower, Marc."

He gave her an amused look, and said something, but she didn't hear what because he turned his blending machine on.

Hundreds of cookbooks filled one kitchen wall. She went to investigate. Pulling out an exotic-looking Chinese recipe book, she wondered if his collection was for show. Marc, the poseur gourmet. Leafing through the book, she found a page bent over to mark it, and ingredient substitutions in Marc's measured script. She put the book back. The machine had stopped grinding. She idly opened a kitchen drawer. Rolling inside were some well-loved, dented things she couldn't put a name to. She shut the drawer, feeling a little like Goldilocks visiting the three bears.

"What are you making?" she asked.

"Something with lots of vitamins in it."

She returned to the living room, so sterile and lifeless. All of Marc's personal things must have been hidden inside the sleek, polished furniture. She saw no knickknacks, no treasured mementos, no art, no worn paperbacks. It almost looked like he'd borrowed the loft from a friend—who'd cleared it out first.

And then she saw a simple, silver-framed photograph on top of a low table. Curious, she walked over and picked it up. Two auburn-haired, freckled little boys laughed up at her. The sight of those little faces disconcerted her. What if they were Marc's children?

"Soup's on," he said from across the room.

She put the photograph back. "Who are the kids in that picture?"

"My ex-wife's boys, Spencer and Tyler."

"Oh," she said, trying to appear unconcerned. "I didn't know you had been married."

"Yes."

He didn't seem willing to offer any details about his marriage, so why would he cherish a picture of his ex-wife's children?

"Are you close to the children?"

"The boys? No. They were born long after Frances and I divorced. I've never even seen them."

Frances. So that was her name. Terra wondered what she was like. No she didn't. She didn't want to know anything about her. Not one tiny little thing. Except why he had a picture of her children.

"Do they live abroad or something?" she asked.

"They live in Los Angeles."

She wondered if he wanted children so badly he had emotionally adopted his ex-wife's kids.

He beckoned her to follow him into the dining room, were he served her a bowl of his vitamin-rich, cold soup. The soup was flavorful and spicy.

"Why don't you see those little boys? Frances won't let you?" she asked, still trying to understand why he had the photograph.

"Frances doesn't have a problem with me seeing the boys. It's Anthony, the boys' father, who does."

"So why do you have their picture if you don't feel any attachment to them?"

"That's overly harsh, to say I don't feel attachment," he said. "More soup?" She nodded and he served her seconds. "I care very

177

much about Spencer and Tyler. Even if I don't see them. But I suppose the photograph is mainly for Frances' benefit, so she feels more at home here when she visits."

"When she visits? You mean your ex-wife stays here with you?"

"Yes. We still have strong ties, even if we're not married."

The idea of Marc and Frances spending the night together, talking about her kids, made Terra feel uneasy and insecure. Just what kind of divorce did Marc and Frances have, anyway?

★

Terra woke late Saturday morning. Throwing back the sheet, she sprang out of bed. A little soup, a little sex, and a lot of sleep was just exactly what she had needed. She slipped on a long, tight skirt in flowered rayon, and a silvery silk tank.

Marc walked into the bedroom. "Hey," he said.

Her eyes moved over his damp, curly hair, and down the rest of his body. He wore nothing but a pale blue towel. That man was so sexy without clothes on. She walked over to him, and ran her fingers over his shoulders, admiring their edge. Putting her arms now around his terry-clothed waist, she pulled him closer. She enjoyed the strong, solid feel of him.

"Marry me," he said.

Looking up into his face and meeting those splendid, obsidian eyes, she realized he was dead serious. Disorientation flooded her. She'd never been the kind of girl to daydream about her wedding dress, about her husband and honeymoon, or about married life— because she never wanted to get married.

She'd never been proposed to, either. Even so, she knew he was doing it wrong. He wasn't supposed to tower over her, half-naked, and order her to marry him. A marriage proposal involved meekness, tentativeness. For that one deciding moment, a man had to prove he was worthy of the woman's trust.

He traced a finger along the ridge of her collarbone. "I want to take care of you," he said.

She imagined waking up every morning feeling satisfied and relaxed, looking forward to seeing her man. Why did Marc think those pleasures had to involve marriage?

"Well, then let's live together."

"No," he said, rubbing the center of her back.

She sighed roughly, closing her eyes, and tried to enjoy the worship in his caress. "Why not?"

"Because I asked you to be my wife. The proper answer to a marriage proposal is yes or no. A counterproposal isn't acceptable."

"Ughh," she groaned, her eyes still shut tight. "Counterproposal. What is this? A business merger?"

"Say yes," he growled in his uncompromising way.

She opened her eyes. His singular intensity constricted and frightened her. Yet at the same time, his rough fingers working her shoulders sent goose bumps of delight up and down her arms. She couldn't trust herself against his touch. Helpless against his powerful love, she was doomed to say yes to him.

But submission was against her nature. She had to give him a fight first. Her hands found the knot in the towel around his waist, and jerked it free. She stepped back from him to admire his beautiful, now completely naked body. This man had complicated her life horribly, and he was going to pay for it.

She snapped the towel, aiming for his chest. It hit. He looked surprised and then lunged for her, a wicked smirk on his face. Screaming, she got one more shot in, hitting him on the upper arm. She tried to hop on top of the bed to escape his grasp. But it was a struggle because her skirt was too long and tight. Somehow she still managed to elude him. From on top of the bed, she hooted and hopped up and down.

"You can't get me!" she cried, exhilarated.

She snapped at him. He dodged the towel and swiped at her. Shrieking, she got yet another shot in, hitting him on the shoulder. "You can't get me!" she taunted him.

"All done," he said.

He moved quickly. Before she could get away, she felt his fingers around her ankles. Suddenly she was lying on her back on the bed. He climbed onto the bed and straddled her, pinning her wrists.

"I thought girls didn't know how to snap towels like that," he said.

"Hah," she wheezed. All her screaming and hopping and laughing—and landing so suddenly—had winded her.

"Are you all right?" he asked, letting go of her wrists.

"Of course, you sissy!" she said, laughing.

"Sissy, you say?" He leaned down and gave her a gentle kiss on the lips.

For the first time she realized she didn't just love him, she didn't just respect him. She *liked* him. But she was also afraid. She feared that if she married him she'd lose. Just exactly what she'd lose, she wasn't sure, but it was something important to her.

"You know," she said, "even if we got married, I would still consult from New Orleans. I don't like it here much. I'd be leaving you alone in California most of the time."

He stroked her cheek tenderly. "In that case, you're going to have a fight on your hands."

"I *knew* you wanted to run my life!" If she could get him to confess to his commanding ways, maybe marriage had a chance.

He raised his brows, and barely shook his head. "No micro management, Sweetheart."

He leaned down over her, so their noses were almost touching, the very definition of domineering.

"Living with me is not a condition of marriage," he continued in a low voice. "But I'll find out what it takes to make this an attractive part of the world for you, Terra. And I'll transform the Peninsula if I have to. You'll stay with me because you want to."

"It's not going to work. I'm telling you that right now," she said, unwilling to surrender to his velvet threats.

"Don't be so sure about that." He slid his hands over her silk tank. "In the meantime, I think I'll explore that spicy, irreverent core of yours. Mmmm. Yes. I think I've found it. Oh, yes, very spicy indeed." He fondled her erect nipples through the silk, enjoying her response. "Irreverent as all get out, too."

Spasms of desire shot through her.

The doorbell rang. She sat bolt upright, bumping into his head.

"Ow," he complained.

The collision hurt her, too. Pain was at least as good as a cold shower, she decided.

"Who could that be?" he grumbled. He rolled off the bed and pulled on a pair of loose sweatpants. She followed him out of the bedroom, rubbing her forehead.

He opened the door to a petite, dark-haired woman. The woman's flowery perfume nearly knocked Terra down. Everything about her screamed Woman with a capital W. Her Barbie-doll body was clad in a sharply-tailored fuchsia suit. She walked in like she owned the place. Barbie cocked an elegant eyebrow, and her sapphire eyes slid down Marc's half-naked body.

"Forget I was coming?" Barbie asked.

"You're early, Jaime," he said.

"What a thing to say to me! *This* is when I had time, Marc. You can't expect better on such short notice, and arrangements made via telephone tag, at that." Jaime turned to Terra and smiled at her with perfect, white teeth. She thrust out her long-nailed hand. "You must be Terra."

She shook Jaime's hand gingerly, not wanting to get hurt by the nails. With a helmet of shiny black hair and bright pink lips, Jaime seemed harder than Marc's other women. But Terra didn't want to speculate about his taste; she wanted him to send Jaime home.

"Jaime's the interior designer for the new house," he told Terra.

She noticed the big portfolio under Jaime's arm. Was Jaime the one who'd created *this* place, in all its cold glamour?

"You're designing the inside of that house Marc's building on the coast?" Terra asked.

"You better believe it. That house is already causing a stir, and it's not even finished," Jaime boasted. "The construction guys tell me everybody on the coastside wants to know who owns it."

He didn't look too thrilled that his personal business was a topic of speculation up and down the coast, but the designer kept right on bragging.

"*Architectural Digest* has already contacted me about doing a spread," Jaime said.

He grunted, and put his arm around Terra. They both followed the designer into the dining room, where she lay out pieces of carpet and material, paint chips, plans, and drawings.

Jaime sat down in front of her designing hoard. She smiled at Terra. "Marc thought it was about time you got involved. So. Tell me what you like."

Terra glanced sharply at him, annoyed. She gave up a lovemaking session for this? She hadn't said yes to marriage, so why should she want to discuss the design of his house? As usual, he was pushing things. It suddenly occurred to her that he was trying to show off, impress her with all the wonderful things his money could buy. That settled it. No way would she get involved with his trophy house.

"No thanks. I think I'll sit this one out," Terra said sweetly. She had intended to go to the kitchen to search out some breakfast, but she saw the way the designer gazed at Marc with her spectacular blue eyes as he sat down in the chair next to hers. Jaime wore a faint, appreciative smirk on her bright pink lips. Terra probably had the same expression, minus the lipstick, when she first saw him half-naked at the Vail lodge. He was a magnificent specimen of a man, and no woman could fail to see that.

Terra decided to get interested in interior design. She walked over and stood behind him, laying a possessive hand on his shoulder. *Off limits.*

"I've worked up a design for the nursery," Jaime said, looking up at Terra. "It's the room directly off the master bedroom."

Terra quailed. *The nursery?*

"I think we might want to start with another room," he said, sensing her discomfort.

But the designer went on and on about cute curtains and even cuter wallpaper, lovingly detailing the drawing lying before her on the table.

The nursery?

"The room's pink," he interrupted. "And what if the baby's a boy?"

"It's more of a peach. Besides the color is supposed to appeal to your wife, not the baby. It doesn't matter if *you* don't like it. Your wife's the one who'll actually spend the most time in the nursery. And every woman I've ever known loves that color." Jaime looked up at Terra, tapping the paint chip with her long nails. "Am I right?"

Terra gripped his bare shoulder like a life raft, speechless, unwilling to admit to Jaime that she hated peachy-pink, the color that every other woman in the universe loved. How had this creature managed to intimidate her?

"Terra doesn't go for pink," he answered for her. "And neither will any son we might have."

Terra doesn't go for pink? Terra doesn't go for *babies*! Her stomach hurt from hunger and tension. So there it was: he expected a son to carry on the family name.

Why had he started building a house before he'd found a wife? Had he intended to find a woman to fit the house, like prince Charming searching for the girl to fit the glass slipper? In that case, Terra was the wrong Cinderella. All those sweet, pink-loving women in Marc's life and he wanted *her*? She recalled how Velvet had sold him the land. No doubt she dreamed of sharing the property with him. Or how about Ms. Barbie-Jaime herself?

"But Marc, once the baby is old enough to know he's a boy, he's out of the nursery anyway," Jaime was saying, "he gets kicked upstairs to the kid's rooms."

"Kid's rooms?" Terra choked out.

"Just rooms, Sweetheart," he said. "Well, Jaime, we're all agreed

183

that pink is out of the question for the little room off the master bedroom. Let's move on to something else."

Terra noticed he didn't call it a nursery anymore. She almost felt sorry for him. If he wanted a house with rooms for millions of children, that was his right. If he dreamed of living in a cold and airless place like the loft they now conversed in, that was up to him.

She didn't care what Marc's house was like. *Her* home would always be in the French Quarter, its rooms colored like jewels, crowded with comfortable antiques, old computers and everything else she loved.

Everything else she loved—but Marc.

18 / The compromised FTP Site

Terra wanted to spend some time with Marina before she went to work, so Marc drove Terra back down to Mountain View on Sunday night. They said their goodbyes in the nearly empty SSI parking lot where Terra had left her car.

"Well?" he asked, lowering his head so their eyes were on the same level. "Are you going to think about it?"

"Yes," she replied.

His hands gently molding her shoulders, he nudged her up against the side of the Rover. She felt the pressure of his hip region against hers, her pulse pounding where their bodies met.

"You know if I married you," she said, "I'd keep my own name. No Mrs. C. Marc Elliott the second for me. Can you deal with that?"

An amused expression crossed his face. "I'm C. Marc Elliott the *third*, Terra. C. Marc Elliott the second was my father."

"Stop being flippant with me," she said.

He smoothed back the cowlick on her forehead tenderly. "Yes, I can accept that, Ms. Breaux," he said.

"And I hope you know I wouldn't be making babies for you either," she said.

"I can accept that, too," he said.

He kissed her. *Say yes,* his lips urged. *I'll take care of you,* his tongue promised.

★

Marina was lying on the couch in the living room, staring into space. She seemed contemplative, dreamy. Terra wondered if her sister was thinking about her baby.

"Hi, Honeybunch," Terra said. "Everything all right?"

"Yup," the girl replied, pulling her legs up to make room. "So did you have a nice time with Marc?"

She sat down next to her sister. "Yeah. I did. I guess I needed a little time off."

"So what did you computer geeks do?"

"We coded together, of course," Terra said, laughing. She decided not to tell Marina about Marc's proposal unless her answer was yes. "Actually, he fed me soup. And he had this hoity-toity designer come by. He's building this house on the coast by Half Moon Bay, and she's doing the inside. According to her, this monstrosity is famous up and down Highway One."

"Why do you say it's a monstrosity?" Marina moved to sit cross-legged on the couch.

She flashed to the pink nursery, and the kid's bedrooms on the second floor. All the ambivalence she felt toward his proposal, and their future, was transferred to utter hatred for the house.

"Oh," she said, "the house practically hangs off these cliffs. It's got a helicopter landing pad on the roof. The back of it is almost all glass, and it has these balconies that seem to jut out over the ocean."

"Sounds neat."

She shrugged. "Not to me. Living in that house would be like living in one of those glass elevators. Creepy." She got up and headed into the kitchen. "Have you had dinner?"

"Yup."

Terra saw a pile of dirty dishes in the sink that told her Marina was being truthful.

"I got a letter yesterday," Marina said.

"Yeah? From who?" she asked, tying off a bag of kitchen trash.

"From Jared. I already wrote him back."

Terra dropped the bag and stalked into the living room, disgusted and dismayed. She thought for sure her sister had rejected him for good. "I can't believe it! After what he did to you? Why would you want to write him?"

"I wanted to *see* him, Terra." Her voice was hard, sure of herself. "Why?"

"Here." Marina handed her a Hallmark card embossed with pink roses. "Read it."

She opened the card. In large, sloppy letters, Jared said he was sorry. He loved her more than life itself. He would never, ever hurt her again; he wanted her back. He just knew that they could work out their differences just as long as Terra and her "rich data-hoarding boyfriend" didn't interfere.

Terra hoped Marina hadn't been completely conned.

"Are you going back to him?" Terra asked.

The girl looked up at her with a yearning, sorrowful expression. "I didn't tell him I would. But I love him."

"How can you love a person who beats you?"

"Is that all you think there is to it? That he hits me? Give me some credit, will you? He cares a whole lot about me and our child. He can be the softest and sweetest guy in the world..."

"Did his sweetness make your bruises disappear? Stop your pain?"

"Look, it wasn't that simple. I wasn't an angel either. Okay?" Marina smoothed her shirt over her little stomach.

"What do you mean, you were no angel?" Terra demanded. "Are you telling me that it's *your* fault that he hit you?"

Marina got up, her hand still over her stomach.

"Jared's nothing but a low-life loser who'll end up killing you!" Terra cried.

"I gotta go," Marina said. She picked up her purse and walked out of the condo.

Terra realized with numbing horror that her sister had tied herself, her unborn child, her happiness and Jared together into one neat and deadly package.

And there wasn't a damn thing she could do about it.

★

As was her habit, Terra checked her e-mail on the hijacked Canadian computer when she got to SSI. She had begun to work normal hours, now that her sister had enough seniority to work a regular day shift. One day she finally got an answer from Ranger.

The e-mail message started with, "Dear Newbie,"

She snorted in response. "Like *you're* real Internet."

The e-mail continued: "I got the latest release of Scout by anonymous FTP from the SSI FTP site, where else?"

She read that line over again, stunned. Ranger claimed he hadn't broken into SSI at all. He was saying that SSI *gave* the software to him by FTP. Impossible! An FTP site was a kind of electronic clearinghouse used to deliver digital files, like software, over the Internet.

This was bad news. If Scout 5.0 was available by anonymous FTP, that meant *anybody* with access to the Internet could download this defective software. Thousands and thousands of people might already have done so.

The Swedish SSI-hater had to be lying.

It didn't take her long to discover that Ranger hadn't lied; the source of the unreleased software *was* the Silicon Silk FTP site. Scout 5.0 was so crude, so defective, that nobody outside the company was supposed to have access to it. To give this pre-release software away through the corporate FTP site was self-destructive. How had it happened? Accidental screw up? Intentional? Within the hour, she found definitive proof. She bolted out of her cubicle.

She had to let Marc know—if he didn't already suspect that the FTP site had been compromised.

She ran to Building A. She jogged through the halls, slowing to a walk right before Marc's outer office to catch her breath. Once inside, the receptionist smiled at her expectantly. Terra realized she should have called for an appointment.

"Uh, hi," Terra said. "I'm Terra Breaux from A & C. Is there any way I could get in to see Marc?"

"Mr. Elliott's out of the office right now. He's scheduled to be out for the rest of the afternoon. Would tomorrow afternoon work for you?"

Terra bit her lower lip. *No, tomorrow won't work. The more people that download that pre-release software, the more it will hurt Marc's company.*

"I guess I could e-mail him, or leave him a message on his voice-mail," Terra said, distracted and worried.

Maybe I should shut down the FTP site myself. Or get Keith to do it.

The receptionist must have sensed Terra's distress. "Could you tell me what this is in regards to?"

She had to make the receptionist think it was important without revealing too much about the real problem. "It's a computer security issue."

"Is there someone else other than Mr. Elliott who could help you?"

"No."

Marc probably won't like it if I bring Keith into this. So I'll have to do it myself. But he'll probably be pissed about that, too.

"If tomorrow afternoon is the best you can do," Terra added, "then I guess I'll take it. I really need talk to him."

The receptionist nodded sympathetically, and Terra turned away. Just then Marc entered his outer office.

He seemed tired out. Whatever he'd just been doing, he obviously hadn't enjoyed it. Still, an air of optimistic hope glittered in his eyes as his gaze moved over her face. It hurt her to see his sweet expectancy. He thought she was there to say yes to marriage. Instead, she was about to figuratively punch him in the stomach.

"I need to talk to you," she said. "Do you have time now?"

"Of course," he said. "In my office?"

She nodded.

Once inside his office, he shut the door, and placed his hands on her shoulders. "You feel so good, Terra."

She was rapidly losing her courage. Telling him was much harder than she thought it'd be. He bent closer, about to kiss her. She'd like nothing better than to lose herself in his kisses, but it wouldn't solve the problem.

"Marc," she said, pulling away. "Something's happened."

He stared at her, concerned, waiting for her to explain herself.

"The company network has been compromised again," she said, her mouth dry.

The warmth receded from his eyes. "What did they take this time?"

"They didn't just take something. I'll show you."

They walked over to his desk. Marc sat down in front of his machine, a solemn expression on his face.

"Go to the external Silicon Silk FTP site," she told him.

Marc followed her instructions. "Looks normal enough," he said, eyeing the collection of links that, when clicked on, would start the FTP process of transferring SSI software over the Internet.

"Run your cursor over each link," she said. "Do you see the URL that's odd?"

He didn't move the mouse. "Just tell me what they did, Terra. I don't need a show and tell."

Ignoring his comment, she placed her hand on top of his hand on the mouse. She pushed the mouse and his hand purposefully so that the cursor drifted over each link. Then she stopped moving the mouse.

"See that? This address is different," she said. "This file resides on a computer named AC10. That's an A & C server. It's rarely used, near as I can figure. All the rest of the files are where they're supposed to be—on a server called ftp." She clicked the link to start transferring the digital file from AC10 to Marc's machine.

"Since when is the public allowed to FTP something off an A & C server?" he asked, a deep crease forming between his brows. "What is it that we're transferring anyway?"

"It's supposed to be version 4.0 of Scout. But it's not. It's Version

5.0. Pre-release. Early alpha."

"We don't need pre-release software out in the public domain, certainly," he said. "But maybe it was a simple mistake. How do you know that somebody didn't just accidentally mess up?"

"It's not an accident. And I'll prove it to you."

The electronic transfer was complete. She now decompressed the file, putting the white spaces back in.

"Open the README file, Marc."

He did, and read the contents aloud: "Beta-testers, please send comments, bug reports, etc. regarding this software to marce@crux.ssi.com..." He rubbed his chin. "Well, I'll be damned."

The e-mail address was Marc's.

Like an unlisted phone number, Marc's e-mail address was supposed to be a secret to everyone outside of SSI, and known to very few within the company.

"I'll be damned," he said again. "So everybody and his brother can now FTP pre-release, subpar software directly from A & C. Then, being massively dissatisfied, they are invited to send *me* the bug reports. Not good. Shut AC10 down, will you, Terra?"

He got off his chair and she took his place in front of the computer.

"Huh," she exclaimed. "AC10 is an IBM RS/6000. I didn't know A & C had an RS/6000."

She tried to log on to AC10 using her regular A & C account and password, and failed. Odd. She was supposed to have an account on all A & C servers. Next, she tried to log on as root, using a password she'd recently obtained by judicious shoulder surfing.

"This is weird," she said, perplexed. "I can't get in. I seem to be locked out by an internal firewall that's not even supposed to be there."

19 / An unnatural pattern

Marc read the screen from over Terra's shoulder. "Remote access denied. If this is in error inform your local firewall administrator." He grabbed her hand to pull her to her feet. "It's an error all right. Come on, let's shut down AC10 locally."

On their way to A & C, she realized she didn't know where server AC10 was. But Ted, the alpha geek of Applications and Commerce Group would. He knew where just about everything was. Once they got to Building B, she collared Ted in his cubicle.

"Hey, Ted," she said.

She noticed Ted wore a suit and shoes. Never having seen Ted in anything but shorts, a T-shirt and Birkenstocks, she concluded he must be interviewing for a new job. He was probably going to visit another company during lunch. She wanted to find out which company and why, but couldn't ask him now, not with Marc right behind her.

"We're looking for AC10; it's an RS/6000 workgroup server. Do you know where it is?" she asked Ted.

Ted eyed her, and then Marc, and then her again. A tiny smile touched his mouth, and he got up.

"Sure do," he said. He led them to a tiny room. Shelves full of obsolete manuals, tapes, and disks lined the walls. The server sat in the middle. "It's our backup to the backup server," Ted explained. "We obviously don't use it much."

Once Ted left, she hunched over the keyboard, preparing to break into AC10 in order to shut it down.

Marc reached over and twisted the key. The terminal went dead. "This is the way us *regular* guys turn off an IBM."

She chuckled.

"This server not accepting connections," he commented dryly. "Try connecting later." He physically removed the external SCSI disk.

He carried it out of the little room, and she followed him.

She had expected him to be upset about the latest break-in, but he seemed merely thoughtful. Maybe he didn't fully understand the ramifications of this intrusion. One conclusion was inescapable: David hadn't messed with the FTP site. The high-strung VP of Platforms had been long dead when the FTP site was compromised.

They returned to Marc's office. He put the SCSI disk on his desk, and stared at it.

"SSI doesn't need early alpha software out in the public domain. This attack is potentially far more damaging to the company than the first two intrusions. How many copies of pre-release Scout were downloaded, Terra?"

"Forget about that. This isn't about Silicon Silk. This is about you. Don't you see? This invasion was directed at you—not the company. *Your* e-mail address was listed for a reason. They wanted you to know SSI was penetrated."

He turned to gaze at her.

"If you really think about it," she continued, "all of the break-ins were focused on you. And it's getting worse. I can't shake the feeling that something bad is going to happen to you."

He came over and planted his hands gently on her hips. "Sweetheart, off-the-wall e-mail isn't any kind of threat to my safety. But the compromised FTP site is a danger to the company. I should finally let Peter and Ray know about the break-ins."

"And you have to call in the FBI Computer Crime Squad now, Marc."

"No," he said, staring at her with his dark, deep-set eyes. "And you know why. It invites our vulnerabilities to become public knowledge."

They'd had the same argument before, and she suspected he

would never budge. She moved closer to him, hoping the contact would allay her anxiety. It didn't.

"Sweetheart, stop worrying," he said. "There's nothing to be afraid of."

"That's not the only thing that I'm scared about," she said. "Jared wrote Marina this card. He seems to blame you for screwing up their great relationship."

"And you think he's out to get me?" he asked, sounding completely unconcerned.

How could she be nearly overcome with nebulous visions of doom, and Marc could just shrug everything off? Maybe it was a man thing. "I think the whole world is out to get you," she said.

"That little shit only hurts defenseless women. He's no threat to me, Terra."

"He has the skills to hurt you electronically, Marc. And it's more than just Jared, anyway." She struggled to solidify her vague feelings of dread. To make him understand. "I've been thinking about all those company executives that have died. Do you realize that Nancy, David and Steve all died of suffocation?"

"Okaaay," he replied, waiting for her to elaborate.

"There's an unnatural pattern there, don't you think?"

His brow furrowed. "I'm not following you."

"Well, three people die. All of them are company founders. Doesn't it bother you that they all died from lack of oxygen?" She looked up into his dark eyes, hoping she'd get through to him. "Don't you see it? What if Nancy, David, and Steve were *murdered*? And Marc, what if you're next on the list?"

"I think I need a drink," he said.

He went over to the miniature kitchenette in his office, where he'd once prepared her espresso. Now he made her a bourbon on the rocks, and poured himself a Scotch. She wondered if he needed fortification because she'd convinced him or because he thought her accusations were crazy. Bringing the drinks over, they sat down together on the couch. He leaned back into the cushions, one hand holding his drink, the other hand drawing her back, too.

"Terra," he said, "remember back in New Orleans when I told you that Ray tried to get the Mountain View police interested in investigating the deaths after Steve died? Well, the police did come and speak with some of us. And it had no impact. As far as the police were concerned, the deaths were completely unrelated. And I have to agree. There isn't a pattern, Sweetheart." He briefly shook his head. "Unless it's a pattern of tragedy. And that doesn't add up to murder."

"You told me yourself you don't believe David Houle killed himself. So what else is there besides murder?"

"Accident," he replied.

"By carbon monoxide?"

"David accidentally forgot to open the garage door when he started the car engine." Again his eyelid twitched. Marc still hadn't accepted David's death.

"Okay," she said, "let's say that David's death was an accident. Well then, you have to admit there is a pattern. Nancy and Steve's deaths were 'accidents,' too."

"A lot of other people died along with Steve. You can't believe that somebody created an avalanche, ending those other lives, just to kill Steve?"

"I don't know," she said, now uncertain. "Can you set off an avalanche on purpose?"

He took a sip of his Scotch. "I suppose you could to some degree, given the right conditions."

She clutched his knee. "Marc! I heard a gunshot right before the snow came screaming down at us! Could a gunshot start an avalanche?"

"That gunshot sound you heard *was* the avalanche," he said. "A loud noise wouldn't set off an avalanche, anyway."

"Okay, so how do you start an avalanche on purpose?"

"Just ski on it. That snow was unstable. Maybe you'd luck out and kill only those below you, rather than yourself."

"How can you can tell that the snow's unstable?" she asked.

"Long cracks; strange hollow noises when you traverse it; felled trees indicating another avalanche has been by—things like that."

"I saw those things," she said with a shiver. She took a long drink of her bourbon. "I especially remember those long cracks in the snow. They gave me the creeps."

He put his drink down on the low table, and gazed out his windows at the darkening skies. A rainstorm was coming.

"Everything about that slope was bad," he said. "The openness, the angle of incline, the exposure. Peter was extremely irresponsible for taking you there."

Was Peter irresponsible? Or was he a killer? Had he lured the group to the back bowls, knowing they would be crushed by a snowslide, one that they themselves would cause?

No. Peter had no reason to destroy the company he'd worked so hard to create.

"Well, maybe Peter doesn't know as much about avalanches as you do," she said.

His eyes then narrowed, and he seemed almost hostile. "Then he had no business taking you to the back bowls."

Marc seemed even angrier about Peter's role now than he had right after the avalanche. She wondered if his animosity toward Peter had something to do with the political battles between the two.

"I haven't had time to think this avalanche thing through," she admitted, uncomfortable with the way he blamed Peter. "But take what happened to Nancy. Everybody knew that she was allergic to kiwi. And they also knew that she drank bottled water. It would be so easy to slip some kiwi juice into her water. How can you explain why that drug that could have saved her life was missing from her purse, *and* there wasn't any of it in the infirmary? Somebody set out to kill her by doctoring her water, and then painstakingly removing all of her fail-safes."

"Terra, Sweetheart, listen to yourself. You're saying there's a suffocation serial killer on the lose, with a taste for murdering only SSI's founders." He patted her hand.

She drew her hand away, stung by his patronizing tone.

"Let's look at this logically," he continued. "Why would the killer go though the bother of creating avalanches or spiking water or poisoning with carbon monoxide? If he wants to kill by suffocation, why doesn't he just choke his victims?"

"Now *that's* easy to explain," she replied. "Because then it would *look* like murder."

★

Not long after, A & C was in an uproar because of a massive overhaul of the computer security protocols. Gossiping about the reason for the sudden security consciousness took far more time than actually implementing the procedures. Lyle—he of the fake stock market ticker—was convinced it meant a company IPO was imminent. Jack claimed the tight security was designed to torture the peons like him. The old-timers like Sherry simply shrugged. They'd seen it before: laxness followed by great paranoia. It was all part of the natural security cycle.

Terra didn't participate in the speculations, because she knew the real reason. Ray and Peter, and the rest of the higher-ups, belatedly informed about the security breaches, had agreed with Marc. They decided to solve the problem in-house by overhauling security rather than call in the FBI. She knew it was a mistake. The new precautions wouldn't stop a knowledgeable insider.

By the time Friday rolled around, she sat at her desk, unmoving, depressed by the futility of the company's actions. Marc and the company shareholders should have called in the FBI.

Since they didn't, it was still up to her to figure out who the inside thief-saboteur was. Jack had been ruled out. Damn. He was a made-to-order suspect. Disloyal and needing money—what else could you ask for in a suspect? What about revenge as a motive? She recalled Ted in his interview suit and shoes. She'd heard of people so mad at a company, that they'd sabotage something vital before they left. Not that Ted would ever do something like that. She hoped.

It was time to find out if Ted really was looking for another job. And if he was mad. She went to go look for him. Ted sat at his terminal, looking dazed. His bear frame was clad in his usual T-shirt, shorts, and Birkenstocks.

"Hey," she said.

Ted turned to her, "Can't think my way out of a paper bag today."

"Me either. I noticed you were wearing a suit the other day. Are you job-hunting?"

"Was job-hunting. I gave Ray my notice today. I'm out of here in two weeks."

"To where?"

Ted scratched his thick, curly beard. "Over to the enemy."

"No! Not Microsoft!"

"The enemy up the Peninsula," he clarified.

"Oh, Oracle. So is it a big step up?"

"No," he replied. "It's not a job I'm going to particularly enjoy. The pay isn't that great compared to here, either."

"Then why go?"

"Because," he said, "Oracle is a public company. Stock options mean something." He pulled out a folder from a drawer, opened it, and handed her a letter. "This is my original employment offer with SSI. I got 37,500 SSI shares, vested in two and one half years. I would have been vested in six months. But what are non-voting shares in a non-public company worth? Absolutely nothing. And they never will be, because this company is never going public. I'm moving to Oracle because I have to start thinking about *me*." He snatched the letter back from her.

"You're leaving a job you absolutely adore because of *stock*?" she asked, incredulous.

"Well, not all of us get those special Silicon Silk incentives."

"What are you talking about? I'm a consultant. I don't get stock."

"I'm talking about your arrangement with Marc."

Her heart stopped. "What do you mean, arrangement?"

Ted stabbed his forefinger in the air at her. "You tell me. All I know is I see you slide into his car one night."

"Big deal," she said. "Maybe I had a flat tire."

"And maybe you didn't. You're a hypocrite, Terra Breaux. You have something going on—first with the CFO, and then with the CEO of the company—and yet you think you're fit to judge *me* for looking out for myself?"

Ted's accusations cut her to the core. She'd never gotten any special favors from Peter or Marc, nor would she ever ask for them. Preserving her independence and her reputation were vitally important to her. That's why she'd desperately tried to keep her relationship with Marc a secret—so she wouldn't be the subject of filthy and inaccurate innuendo. And yet here it was.

But she never, ever expected to be confronted with those nasty rumors by a *friend*.

"Go to hell," Terra spat. She turned and hurried out of Ted's cube.

Hurt and angry, she headed back to her cubicle, intending to pick up her purse and go home. More than anything, she wanted to have a good cry. If she was going to have to put up with that kind of crap from her coworkers, she might as well just go ahead and marry Marc.

Carolina was waiting in her cubicle, tears glistening in her eyes.

"Hi Carolina! What's new?" asked Terra, hiding her own pain.

"I've weaned Emily," Carolina said in a small voice.

"Is that something bad?" Terra asked, settling into her fancy chair.

"No. It just hurts. Inside. I feel a big empty space there now."

"It sounds awful." Terra wasn't sure why weaning would leave a big empty space, but she reached over to hold Carolina's hand.

One tear spilled out of Carolina's right eye. "Ray and I had a big fight about it. I've been upset all day. He doesn't understand that I miss nursing my baby. That it hurts." She poked her fist into the center of her chest. "All he cares about is that now we can go on trips together, just me and him, and not have to worry about Emily starving. He actually went out and made arrangements for us to go down to San Diego this weekend!"

Terra instinctively understood a man's physical rhythms far better than the cycles of a mother. "You can't blame him for wanting to be alone with you, Carolina."

"I just finished weaning her! Can't he wait a little longer?"

"He's probably been waiting to be alone with you ever since Emily was born. How long ago was that?"

"Eight months, two weeks and three days."

"Almost nine months," Terra said.

Carolina wiped away the tear, and sniffed. "I guess that is a long time. Before we had Emily we used to go on these excursions up and down the coast all the time. We'd stop at some cute little bed and breakfast inn and shut ourselves up and..." She smiled, her brown skin darkening. "Well, anyway. I guess he must have missed doing that, huh?" She got to her feet. "Thanks, Terra. For helping me see it through Ray's eyes."

"Have a good time," Terra said, winking broadly.

★

When Terra got home, she put on a Johnny Adams CD, and treated herself to a bourbon. She didn't expect Marina home for a few hours yet, so with deep soul blues as her sympathetic companion, she relived Ted's betrayal for a good long time. Finally, she decided Ted had been a jerk about her private life because he was defensive about leaving SSI for stock. Perhaps someday they'd be friends again.

On Saturday, she began to weigh the pros and cons of marriage to Marc. Why not take the chance? Marc was a gorgeous man she loved, admired, liked. A man who'd make sure she got regular nutrition and regular sex.

Yes. She'd tell him yes.

Waking up before dawn on Sunday morning, she felt strong and energized. She took it as a sign that she'd made the right choice. Marrying Marc was a good idea. Slipping into a pair of slim jeans and a loose-fitting, white T-shirt, she drove into work just as the skies began to lighten. She could get in a good coding session before she called Marc with her answer.

Sauntering into the dark spaces of A & C, swinging her ID badge, she noticed the door to Ray's office was ajar, and his lights were on. She was surprised Ray would be at work on a Sunday morning when he was supposed to be enjoying a romantic weekend with Carolina.

"Ray?" she called. "Ray?"

No answer.

It occurred to her that maybe Ray was too embarrassed to reply. What if he and Carolina had another blowup over weaning Emily, and he got kicked out of the house, and he ended up having to sleep in his office?

She headed over to his office tentatively and knocked on the partially open door. "Hey, Ray, you in there?"

No answer. Obviously Ray wasn't here; his lights must have been left on accidentally. She slipped inside his office, intending to turn the lights off.

What she saw made her insides squirm. "Oh, no."

Ray lay face down on the carpet.

A marital squabble hadn't put him there. He wasn't asleep. Not with a double coil of black Ethernet cable wrapped around his neck.

20 / The crude attack

Terra's first impulse was to flee. Let somebody else find Ray. The CPR she had learned wouldn't do him any good now. But this was a friend who was lying on the floor in a large, meaty heap. She knelt down and put fingers to his wrist. Cold. No pulse. She stood up, backed out of his office. With trembling hands, she called SSI security from her cube.

It didn't take long for A & C to be swarming with uniforms. She even caught a glimpse of Marc before a female police officer drew her aside into Jack's cubicle to interview her.

The Mountain View Police officer asked her questions about when and how she found Ray. Terra answered slowly, carefully, and yet the officer asked her the same questions over again, as if she might have forgotten what had happened only minutes ago.

A male police officer soon replaced the female one and asked her different questions.

"What is your job here?" the police officer asked.

"I'm a programmer."

"Do you come into work on Sunday morning often?"

"No," she replied. "I usually work late at night instead of in the morning." She craned her neck, trying to find Marc again.

"Can you use a computer like the one on Mr. Iverson's desk?" the officer asked.

Terra finally saw Marc's dark head. She wondered if he would tell Carolina about Ray, or if the police did that. Grief suddenly threatened to overwhelm her. Ray and Carolina were supposed to be getting to know each other again in a bed and breakfast inn in San Diego. Now he was dead; Carolina had no husband, and baby

Emily had no father.

"Miss?" said the police officer.

"I'm sorry," she said, focusing on the officer. "I was paged out for a minute there. Could you ask me that again?"

"Can you use a computer like the one on Mr. Iverson's desk?"

"Probably," she said. She didn't remember what kind of computer Ray used, but she assumed she could. Distracted again by the thought of Carolina's and Emily's life being torn up, it took her awhile before she became aware that the officer had asked her another question.

"Huh?" she said.

"Did you use Mr. Iverson's computer?"

"No." She wondered when they were going to stop asking her questions, and when she could finally search out Marc.

"Do you recall if Mr. Iverson's computer was on this morning when you discovered him?"

"I don't even remember looking at his computer," she said. "I looked at *Ray*. I felt his wrist, looking for a pulse. And then I called security."

"Have you ever seen anyone other than Mr. Iverson use his computer?"

"No," she said, shaking her head irritably. "Why are you asking me all these questions about Ray's computer, anyway?"

The officer wouldn't answer her. After a few more questions, he left. Soon the rest of the law was gone, and she was alone in the vast warehouse that housed Applications and Commerce Group.

She dialed Carolina's home number.

An unfamiliar and weary voice answered. "Iverson residence."

"Hello, this is Terra Breaux. I'm a friend of Carolina's. What can I do?"

"Nothing. Carolina and Emily have gone to be with family now. But thank you for asking."

"Oh," Terra said. "Thanks." She hung up.

She wished she knew how Carolina was. Most of all, she wanted to know who had killed Ray. An unwelcome image of the Chief of Technology on the floor, with the cable twisted around his neck, assaulted her. Just days ago Marc had pointedly asked her why a serial suffocation killer wouldn't strangle his victims, instead of using more elaborate forms of oxygen deprivation.

Ray *was* strangled. Of course! Why hadn't she seen the connection before now? The Chief of Technology was the fourth SSI founder to die of suffocation, dying like Nancy, like David, and like Steve. And Ray was clearly murdered. Didn't that give credence to her suspicion that the other company founders were murdered, too? Even Ray himself thought the deaths of Nancy and David weren't coincidental.

She picked up her purse, and headed over to Ray's office, intending to find out what his computer had to do with his murder, before she went home. Yellow police tape still barricaded the door. She slipped in between, and then examined the screen of Ray's old Sun workstation. Someone had attempted to break into the computer. That someone hadn't succeeded because they couldn't guess his password. That someone had tried again and again.

Now she understood why the officers had asked her so many questions about Ray's computer. The police must have decided that whoever had tried to break into Ray's Sun had murdered him, too. But this failed electronic attack was crude beyond belief, making her bristle with suspicion. Randomly guessing passwords? The cracker that had been plaguing SSI was an order of magnitude more sophisticated than that.

But the police wouldn't know enough to make the distinction. If they found out about the other cracker attacks, they'd attribute this break-in attempt to the same person. And then they'd assume the Chief of Technology had surprised the computer criminal as he was trying to do his dirty work, and got killed for it. The police would say that Ray was in the wrong place at the wrong time.

Maybe she shouldn't go home after all. Perhaps if she stayed she could uncover clues to the identity of the murderer.

She felt eyes on her. Her head jerked to look. Someone was standing outside Ray's office, staring at her. She cut off her surprised little scream when she realized it was Marc.

"Do you think it's a good idea for you to be in there?" he asked.

"Marc," she breathed. "Am I glad to see you." She hurried out of Ray's office, nearly tearing the police tape. He grabbed her upper arm and guided her away from Ray's office. She had a hard time keeping up with him as he hustled her out through Building B.

"Why are you doing this?" she asked him, bewildered by the way he moved her across the campus.

"You have to go home," he said, "it's not safe here."

She pulled loose at the edge of the parking lot. "Marc! Stop dragging me!" Facing him squarely, she said, "What's going on?"

"Did you see Ray's computer screen?" he asked.

"Yes."

"The police asked me what it meant," he said. "I told them about the other attacks. They concluded that Ray was murdered when he caught the cracker by surprise. That clearly puts you in danger."

"But it couldn't have happened that way," she said. "Sitting in front of the computer, trying to guess a password by typing in trials, one at a time? Strictly amateur. It's not the work of our cracker. He knows the ins and outs of SSI systems. He'd test passwords remotely with a software program. I mean, a program like Crack can test 50,000 passwords a second! And while his cracking software did all the work, he'd take a nap. Don't you see? This stinks of a setup."

Marc knit his thick brows. "Terra, I want you to go home."

"You're not listening to me, Marc!" she cried, frustrated. "Ray wasn't murdered by our electronic thief and saboteur. This is a false lead."

He put his hands on her shoulders. "I am listening to you. You're telling me that the cracker doesn't meet your high standards. But that doesn't change the fact that Ray was murdered. By a good cracker, bad cracker, I don't care. I want you out of the way until we find the person who murdered Ray."

"Out of the way?" she repeated, suddenly suspicious. Why didn't he want her to remain at SSI?

Out of the corner of her eye, she saw a Mercedes drive into the nearly empty parking lot. The new Chief Counsel, Steve's replacement, got out of the car and made a beeline for Marc.

"I meant to say out of *harm's* way," Marc said.

"Then maybe you should have said that. But I'm not about to leave," she told him, standing her ground. "Not now. Not with electronic clues just waiting for me."

Marc spared the approaching lawyer a look; his body seemed to throw off sparks of annoyance. He raised his hand, like some imperious judge, to stop the lawyer's advance. Marc turned back to Terra.

"You're going to have to let the police handle it, Sweetheart. Please go home."

She suddenly felt compassion for him. His company was crumbling around him, and everyone expected him to fix it by force of will alone. Yet he still worried about *her*.

"All right," she said.

She turned away from Marc, and walked toward her car. Peter's black Porsche pulled up alongside her as she unlocked her door.

Peter got out. "How you holding up, Terragirl?"

"It's just so awful, Peter! I'm so worried about Carolina. And Marc, too. I just saw him. He seems wound up tight." She took a glance at Building A; Marc and the Chief Counsel were entering. After a deep, steadying breath, she asked, "What's going to happen to the company now that Ray's dead?"

"The same thing that has been happening," Peter said, "SSI will grow and prosper."

His callousness left her cold. "Geeze Peter, how can you say that? Ray was Chief Technical Officer. He was the creative genius behind the company."

"There's more to SSI than code and coders."

"You're talking to a coder," she snapped.

"As important as programmers are," he said, "Marc is the heart and soul of this company. And he isn't dead. That's why SSI will still thrive."

Tossing her purse into her car, she recalled how Marc had once said a similar thing about Peter. But all their talk about the respect they had for each other didn't gibe with their personal e-mails.

"Well," she said, unhappy with the way Peter seemed to be brushing off Ray's death, "Ray was a friend of mine. And I feel like I'm running out on him. That maybe if I stayed and obsessed about it, I could somehow figure out who killed him."

"I thought it was some computer hacker."

"Cracker," she corrected. "That's what the police say."

"You know, Terragirl, just because you discovered him doesn't mean you have to find his murderer all by your lonesome. That's what police are for."

"I suppose."

"Ray's funeral is Tuesday at two. I could pick you up around one-thirty and we could go together if you'd like."

She wondered if she should go to the funeral with Marc instead. After all, he was going to be her husband, even if he didn't know it yet. But Marc hadn't asked her to go with him, and Peter had. Peter was a friend, too, and despite his surface heartlessness, deep down inside he was probably disturbed by Ray's death and wanted some company.

"Yeah. Sure. Thanks."

He smiled at her in his serene, confident way. "Good enough," he said. He glided off to the turmoil waiting inside.

She got into her car, and sat there awhile, pondering the fact that she'd fallen into her usual role of accompanying Peter to an SSI function—this time to a funeral. Dammit, this was the fourth funeral for an SSI founder.

She couldn't leave it alone. And she didn't care what Marc or Peter thought about her getting involved.

Throwing open the car door, she leapt out, slamming the door shut. Running all the way back to Building B, she vowed not to leave SSI until she discovered who had killed Ray.

Once within her cube, she called her sister to let her know that she wasn't coming home until late. Marina seemed excited about something, but she wouldn't tell Terra what. Marina did say that Marc had called, and wanted her to call back. Terra didn't bother.

Instead she paced, rapping a pencil on all the hard surfaces, her thoughts tumbling over one another. A handful of her coworkers drifted in and out of A & C. They saw the police tape and asked her what happened. She shrugged, told them a crime must have been committed, but she wasn't sure what it was. No way would she discuss finding Ray with them, reliving those awful moments.

She resumed pacing, her thoughts now more organized, and focused. One conclusion kept surfacing: the attempted break-in of Ray's computer was a planted and false lead. Not just because the intruder wasn't sophisticated. No. What bothered her was that guessing passwords one at a time in front of the computer was too obvious. It was the high-tech equivalent of making robbery look like the motive for murder by taking the wallet from the victim, and then, on top of that, leaving a note saying, "FYI: I took the wallet."

So, cracking was *not* the reason Ray was murdered.

She got up, headed over to the coffee area, and started to make herself a pot. She knew if she ever wanted to figure out who killed Ray, she'd have to figure out the motive. Sighing loudly, she was glad it wasn't dark yet. Pretty soon she'd start to feel scared contemplating murder motives in the vast space of A & C, where Ray had just been killed. When the coffee was ready, she poured herself a cup, and returned to her desk. She sipped and reviewed.

So if the last attempted break-in was intended to provide a fake motive for Ray's murder, she wondered, what did that say about the other electronic invasions? Those intrusions could have also been planted to set up Ray's murder.

She propped her elbows on her desk, and rested her face in her hands. Things still weren't adding up. Like, why were the first penetrations so slick, and the last one so crude and unsuccessful? Didn't that mean that the attacks couldn't have been carried out by the same person?

An answer came to her. One individual could have been the attacker all three times, if the first three break-ins were a message to Marc, and the last attempted break-in was a message for the police.

Her head came up with a snap. She was overpowered by a sensation of horror. Long ago she'd concluded the cracking had been carried out by an SSI insider. That could mean the killer was also an insider.

Maybe Marc was right, and she was in danger hanging around here. Like, what if the murderer was Jack? She took a quick look over the half-wall, just to make sure her cube-neighbor wasn't lurking there with his can of Surge.

Scared as she was, she refused to leave. She stayed all Sunday night in her exotic executive chair, thinking and napping, with an occasional visit to the Building B vending machine room. Bells and Whistles made a racket with their wheel, and she was grateful for the living company. Lyle's mice made her feel less lonely.

At about six Monday morning, as she dozed in her cubicle, her phone rang, nearly sending her through the roof.

"Geeze," she breathed. "Scare me to death, will you." She picked up the phone, prepared for a wrong number. "Yeah?"

"So you *are* at work," Marc said. "Go home, Terra. Leave on your own accord or…"

His attempt at strong-arming her fell on deaf ears. "Or what? You'll drag me to my car again? Leave me alone, Marc. I know I can contribute something here."

She hung up, and turned the ringer off.

Hardly anyone showed up for work; they had probably heard about Ray's murder. Except Jack. Listening to him chattering away on his keyboard in the cube next to hers, she convinced herself yet again that Jack wasn't involved in industrial espionage or Ray's murder. He wasn't a spy or a killer.

She got up and stretched, recalling how Peter thought Ray's death hadn't hurt the company much. What crap. Programmers were far more important to a software company than bean counters—or, for that matter, charismatic, controlling CEOs.

After fetching herself some coffee—now nasty and old—she returned to her cube. Sitting down in front of the computer screen, she decided to do a little ego-surfing on behalf of Ray. She asked Google to fetch the number of web pages that contained the name Ray Iverson. Sometimes she had searched for her own name on the web like that when she had felt under-appreciated and needed an ego-boost.

Ray was listed 4,951 times.

She now did the same search for Peter Donohue. The search engine found Peter's name a mere 702 times.

"4,951 compared to 702. So there," she said aloud, feeling only a *little* petty.

She couldn't resist looking at the summaries of the sites that contained the name Peter Donohue. Scanning through the first entries in the list, she wondered if Peter's name might be on some S & M sex websites.

Not so far.

When she came upon a link to thevalley.com, she decided to explore that website. The buzz was that major players in Silicon Valley often threatened to sue what amounted to a weekly multimedia gossip column, but never did. Apparently, they themselves scanned thevalley.com for dirt and information about their competitors a bit too often to shut thevalley down.

She settled down to a good investigation, guiltily aware that her activities weren't getting her any closer to discovering who killed Ray. Once the home page of thevalley.com appeared on her screen, she clicked on the link to "Silicon Haul." In an entertaining way, ripe with links to related sites and photographs, the Haul page described which Silicon Valley personage was acquiring a private plane for his son, and what famous computer company founder was planting an orchard next to his house in Palo Alto, and which CEO was planning to diversify by purchasing a professional ice-hockey team.

Finished reading the uber-materialistic Haul, she clicked the link to the "Silicon Finance" page. Here is where she expected to find Peter's name. In a slightly more formal format, this week's page mentioned that Intel's earnings had exceeded the street's "whisper number," laid the rumor of the acquisition of Intuit by IBM to rest, and provided a choice tidbit about SSI:

"Silicon Silk Inc., the closely-held Internet software company, has hired William E. Douglass to head the Platforms group. Douglass held a similar post at Adobe Systems for six years. In a surprising development, SSI has apparently refused to allow the loss of several key officers to impact plans to go public. Sources close to Peter Donohue, finance chief, say that the long-awaited initial public offering of Silicon Silk stock will take place before the end of the year. The lead underwriter is slated to be Morgan Stanley Dean Witter."

Since when is the company going public?

Had Marc really relented? Of course she could call and ask him. If she was an idiot, that is. She didn't dare to contact him, not as angry as he was with her. So how would she find out about the initial public offering? Ask Peter?

And then understanding took her by the throat. The IPO and the deaths of so many important people at Silicon Silk were tied together. Someone was killing off top SSI executives to thwart an SSI stock offering.

Of course.

She felt sick to her stomach, repulsed by her conclusion. A competitor systematically killing people just to prevent infusion of money to Silicon Silk? Impossible. Nobody was that cold and ruthless.

211

Were they?

And if company leaders were being murdered one by one… she reached for the phone and pounded Marc's number.

Marc was the one that was in danger, not her.

She heard a rustling behind her. Hoping it wasn't somebody wanting to ask her about the police tape again, she swiveled her chair around to shoo them away. It wasn't a coworker.

Instead two grim-faced SSI security men stood in her cube.

"Terra Breaux?" one of them asked.

"That's me," she said, her ear to the phone. Why wasn't Marc answering? Why didn't his voice mail respond?

"If you'll gather up your personal effects," the security guard said, "we'll escort you to your car."

21 / Fired mode

Terra stared at the security guard who'd spoken to her. She tried to get her bearings by studying his freckled face. What was going on?

"Now if you'll just gather up your things..." the other guard prodded.

She turned to stare at him now. His stubby hair and a permanent-looking scowl labeled him as former military.

Was this was a new safety precaution because Ray had been murdered? If so, she wouldn't trust either one of these men to escort her safely to her car.

"I didn't ask to be escorted," she said.

"You're trespassing, Ms. Breaux. Please come with us now," answered the scowling guard.

"What do you mean, trespassing?"

She put down the phone, and reached for the badge around her neck.

"You got your facts mixed up, boys. I work here. See?" She shoved the badge into the marginally friendlier freckled man's face. He blinked at it with his pale eyes, looking unimpressed.

"Not anymore, you don't," he said. "You've been let go."

She dropped her badge. What in the hell was going on? Had the killer convinced the guards to kick her out of SSI because she was getting too close to fingering him? Were these guys even real company security guards?

"On whose authority?" she demanded. She studied the freckled guard's face, carefully looking for signs of deception.

"The CEO's," he replied.

Either the kid had iron balls or he was telling the truth.

"The bastard *fired* me?" she asked, stunned. "Why would he do that?"

"Maybe it's because of your foul mouth," the scowling guard suggested.

"Oh shut up." She swiveled her chair to face her computer, intending to log off. A heavy hand on her shoulder stopped her.

"Please come with us," the mean one said.

Leaving the computer as it was, she grabbed her purse and got to her feet. She passed Jack's cube flanked by the two guards. Jack looked up at her, his face radiating hatred and sneering satisfaction, as if he always knew she'd end up getting dragged out by security. The high brought down low.

Her face burned as she walked through A & C. Didn't Marc realize how humiliated she'd be? How could he allow her to be hauled off as if she'd been caught stealing office supplies?

Behind her she heard the squeak of wheels on carpet, followed by a soft thousand-dollar swoosh. Jack was taking her fancy chair.

The guard's words, "You've been let go," rang in her ears. Fired. Marc had fired her. She'd never, ever been fired before. She walked faster, not wanting the guards to see her cry.

They took her to her car, whereupon they peeled the entry sticker off her bumper. They took her ID badge. She bit her lip to stop the tears: handing over her badge was one of the worst moments of her life. She'd worked so hard to gain the industry's respect. And to what end? Here she was being kicked out of SSI like some petty crook.

She drove off the campus with as much dignity as she could muster. No way would she cry. She was stronger than that. So what if the man she was going to marry had fired her.

Veering off onto a residential street, she stopped the car. Sobbing into the steering wheel, she asked herself how he could have degraded her like that? All her misery spilled out; she grieved for her ruined love, her sorry life, her tattered career. How could she have ever thought she'd have one moment of happiness with a bastard like C. Marc Elliott III?

After who knows how long, she sat up, staring blindly out the car window. Why hadn't she listened to her intuition? A million sirens had gone off warning her not to get involved with Marc. And why had he been so eager to get her away from A & C? Oh, God, what if he was the killer?

A soft rain began to fall, making sympathetic dripping sounds on the windshield. No, Marc wouldn't have murdered Ray; he'd sooner chop off his own hands than harm his company. Just like Peter. She searched her car for some tissues to clean her face, but couldn't find any. God, what a mess she'd gotten herself into, she thought as she wiped her eyes with a Starbuck's napkin. But she'd figure out a way to overcome this latest disaster. Just like she always did.

She headed back to the condo.

"Marina?" she called out when she arrived, "you home?"

Her sister either wasn't home or wasn't answering.

She strode to the phone sitting on the kitchen peninsula. She'd wallowed in self-pity long enough. It was time to let Marc know how she felt. But first, she retrieved her messages, irrationally hoping he had come to his senses and had already left her an apology.

The first message was from the doctor's office, reminding Marina about a change she'd made in the appointment for Wednesday. Terra wrote down the information on a note pad. The next message was from Marc, apparently before he realized she hadn't left the campus as he had ordered her to. The fact that she wasn't home yet obviously made him anxious.

"Call me when you get home," he said.

"Yeah, right," she said.

The next message was also from him, his tone more urgent. "Where are you, Sweetheart?" he asked, almost pleading.

"I was at SSI trying to find out who killed Ray," she replied, unmoved by his anguish.

She heard a few clicks on the machine telling her she'd gotten more calls, but they hadn't left a message. The last message was also from Marc. He'd finally discovered she'd stayed at SSI, and had by then probably made arrangements to fire her.

"Dammit, Terra," he said. "I haven't got time for hide and seek. Once you do get home, stay there, and I'll be by to come pick you up as soon as I can."

"*More* orders?" she sneered at the machine. *We'll see about that.* She pounded out his work number. This time she got through.

"Elliott here."

"How could you?"

"You're still angry."

His easy arrogance infuriated her. *Still* angry? "You *fired* me! Of *course* I'm still mad!"

"You refused to understand you were in danger, Terra. If you won't protect yourself, I will."

"*You* will? Your hired guns tossed me out!"

"Now you're being unfair," he replied. She could just imagine him running his hand through his dark hair, just about now. "I walked you to the parking lot. I assumed you'd leave. Once I understood that you hadn't..." He paused and cleared his throat. "I don't have the time to stand guard over you. Everyone, from distributors to company middle managers are scared witless that the company won't be able to deliver the next version of Scout on time. I have to convince them everything will be all right, even when I don't believe it."

She recalled Jack's sneer as she was escorted by the security guards, sending a fresh, red-hot shaft of anger and humiliation though her.

"I never asked you to stand guard over me," she said.

"Too many people have died. And I'm not going to let you be one of them."

"What bothers me the most is that you pulled the strings," she said. "How could you let those goons toss me out, without even the decency to confront me face to face?"

"I warned you in advance, Terra."

"You think *that* makes it right?"

"My love makes it right."

"Love? It's called control."

"I'll be over to the condo in a few minutes. We'll settle this disagreement then."

"Give it up. I'm not your employee anymore. And this isn't Silicon Silk. Don't bother showing up here or you'll be trespassing on *my* property," she said, warming to the subject. "You come and I'll call the cops and have *you* tossed out of here."

He chuckled.

"It's not funny," she said, wondering why he wasn't stung by her words. "You *will* be trespassing. I *can* have you tossed…" Suddenly she figured out why he was so confident. The company owned the condo. If she ever pressed the issue, she'd probably be the one getting kicked out.

"Don't come, Marc," she growled. "I don't want to see you." She hung up.

Propelled by anger, she pulled a stack of neatly folded moving boxes out of the living room closet. She dropped them to the floor. They landed with a nice thud. Time to get back to New Orleans and her real life. She put on a Zydeco CD, and turned the volume up high, hoping the roaring accordion and droning fiddles would stop her from recalling Jack's contemptuous look as she was "escorted" off the campus.

"Ughaah!" she cried. "How could Marc *do* that to me!"

She rummaged in the kitchen drawers for packing tape and scissors. But what about Marina? How could she bring her sister back to New Orleans when Jared was there? One by one, Terra reassembled the boxes with tape. No way should Marina go back to New Orleans. She needed another solution. Clenching her hands in frustration, she took a quick, sharp look at all the boxes scattered about the room. Where could Marina stay and be safe and cared for? Other family? Suddenly she felt like an orphan again. She didn't *have* any other family. No kindly, distant relatives would take pity on poor, pregnant Marina.

Poor, pregnant Marina was Terra's problem.

She gathered up some of the boxes too mutilated to reuse, and carried them out to the apartment trash bin. When she returned to the condo, she loaded up the dishwasher, then taped a few more boxes. She spent some time in her bedroom e-mailing a few select people to tell them she was available for consulting assignments again.

Her stay at SSI had been a failure. She felt the pained impact deep in her heart. Why couldn't Marc have left her alone, never hired her in the first place? The irresistible force had met the immovable object, and now he had hurt her too grievously for her to ever forgive him.

She ripped the note about Marina's doctor's appointment off the paper pad, and headed to Marina's room. Why couldn't he ever say sorry? Why couldn't he ever admit he was wrong? She knocked on Marina's door, just in case. No answer.

She pushed the door open.

"No," she whispered.

For the first time since Marina had moved in, the bed was made. The floor was clean of worn hose and shoes. No pregnancy books, or pistachio shells, or Kleenex tissues littered the nightstand.

Marina was gone.

A note lay on the bed. She grabbed it and read:

"Terra, I've gone to be with my man. I'll call soon. Thanks for everything. Marina."

"Oh, God," Terra moaned.

Still clutching both notes, Terra raced out of Marina's room. Snatching her purse, she ran out to her car. She had to get to the San Jose airport to stop her sister from making the worst mistake of her life.

Once inside the terminal, Terra moved from one departure gate to the next, hoping that *this* was the flight to New Orleans that Marina would be on.

At about eleven, when the last flight to New Orleans left San Jose and she hadn't seen her sister at all, Terra wondered if maybe the girl had flown back via San Francisco. Great. Then again, maybe Marina hadn't left at all yet. Perhaps her sister would be taking a flight first thing in the morning. She decided to stay at the airport to find out.

Besides, she thought, there was no better place than a gloomy, silent airport to feel sorry for herself. She got some chips at a vending machine to stave off a headache. Pain surged through her chest when she remembered that vitamin-rich soup Marc had made for her. She tossed the chips uneaten in the trash. Why couldn't he have been the *good* guy?

Of course, she'd invited her own doom by seducing him. This had to be the last time she would ever let her libido do her thinking for her. And, she couldn't ever, ever again fall in love with someone who had power over her.

Tuesday morning she woke up, feeling tight and depressed, thinking again about the deaths of Nancy, David, Steve and Ray. The murders were so bloodless and controlled. It troubled her that she'd probably never be able to convince anyone that Ray wasn't killed by a "hacker."

Soon the airport came back to life, and she repeated the circuit of last night, searching for her sister. No luck. Terra called Sally in New Orleans alerting her to Marina's return.

She vowed to do whatever it took to protect Marina. The gloves were off. She couldn't be afraid of the girl's anger anymore. If she had to kidnap her sister and deprogram her, then she'd do it. How could Marina not realize that Jared would end up killing her? She sighed. It didn't matter. If her sister was too stupid to protect herself, she had to do it for her.

A feeling of displacement and déjà vu nagged at her as she drove back home to get ready for Ray's funeral. She recalled Marc's explanation of why he had her booted out of SSI. "My love makes it right."

She got home with barely enough time to shower. Standing in the spray, she wondered: if she had the right to protect Marina, didn't Marc have the same right to protect her? She toweled herself off and dried her hair. Even if she understood why he had fired her, she wasn't ready to forgive him. At the minimum he should have fired her with *tact*. She would have to teach Marc a lesson he wouldn't soon forget. He could never treat her like crap again.

She combed her hair and pulled it back severely, tying the ponytail with a silk, paisley scarf. A disgusted perusal of her closet revealed nearly nothing black. In fact, she hated the color, because with her pale complexion and nearly white hair, black made her look like a ghost.

An image of her mother's funeral darted out of long hiding. She and Marina had worn black, but her father—the man who would eventually kill himself because the loss was too great—wore navy. The family had grieved before a large framed photograph of her mother instead of at a casket or an urn. The airlines had never recovered her mother's body, or even any identifiable part of it, from the crash site.

She finally put on a short, pleated, black rayon skirt and a deep gray cashmere sweater set. It was June, and she'd bake, but this outfit was the most conservative dark thing she owned. She put on pearl earrings. Satisfied that she looked as horrible as she felt, she waited for Peter to come and pick her up.

Dutifully, Peter arrived. He complimented her in his usual smooth way, and asked her how she was doing.

"Not great," she said. What she meant was: *yesterday was one of the worst days of my life.*

He nodded sympathetically.

Once at the funeral, she realized how well liked Ray was. So many of his colleagues and friends were there. Carolina wept without making a sound, and Terra cried with her.

After the service, she went to give Carolina a hug.

"I'm so sorry," Terra said, "I'm so sorry."

Carolina didn't speak. More of Ray friends came to give the new widow their condolences, and Terra moved away.

She glimpsed Marc's dark figure across the room. He spoke to an older Hispanic woman, probably Carolina's mother. His face held immeasurable sadness. Terra had fallen in love with far more than Marc's perfect body and razor-sharp mind. She had been drawn to that intense, incongruous compassion, even if he hadn't always shown much kindness to her.

The wisest course would be for her to run from him and never look back. Teaching him a lesson was doomed to failure. Even so, she couldn't run from her moral obligation to tell him about her IPO theory, and warn him that his life was in danger.

"I'm going to see if I can have a word with Marc," she told Peter.

She headed over to him, and Peter accompanied her. As she got closer, Marc glanced over and saw her. He spoke another few words to the older woman, and then strode toward Terra.

He scoured her with his black eyes. "Where have you been?" he asked, his voice rough with emotion.

"It's Marina. She's…" Terra suddenly stopped, paralyzed by the sight of a beautiful creature who came to stand beside Marc. The woman put her hand on his upper arm.

Terra crumpled up inside. He had gotten himself another woman. Already. Any designs to teach him a lesson about respect for her were futile: he intended on *destroying* her. Numb, she gazed at his companion.

She was tiny, like Sunny and Velvet. Wavy, reddish hair hung down to her waist. His love looked up at him with concerned, sorrowful eyes. He patted her hand, an intimate gesture. They knew each other well.

Enormous pain bubbled up inside Terra, threatening to choke her.

"Terra," Marc said, "I'd like you to meet…"

Before he could finish the introduction, a small, strangled sound escaped Terra's lips.

22 / The replacement

Terra turned away quickly, horrified that now Marc would know how hurt she was. She mumbled some excuses, and ran out to the parking lot. Pain roiled within her. Did he actually think that she'd stand there and be introduced to her replacement? Especially someone like *her*? So tiny, so lovely, so *helpless*.

Of course he expected her to stand there and take it! He wanted to rub her nose in the fact that *this* was the kind of woman he preferred. Compliant. Dumb. Well if that's what he wanted, fine. Good thing she found out before...

She paced next to Peter's sportscar. *Before what?* Before she fell in love with him? She hadn't saved herself one bit of heartache. Not one little bit.

Things couldn't get much worse. No job. No sister. No love.

But she did still have some pride. She spied Peter coming toward her. Sending him a small smile, she hoped Peter had assumed she'd broken down because of Ray's death, not because of the red-haired woman.

"Sorry I left like that," she told him, "but it's starting to get to me."

"No apology needed," he said. "It's been tough on everybody."

He opened the car door for her, and she slid in. He got in, too. When he looked over at her, his usual urbanity was marred by an intensity that unnerved her.

"What's going on with you and Marc?" he asked.

"Nothing," she said. She looked away from Peter, and gazed out the side window when she felt her face flush. She couldn't lie worth a crap.

"Marc's concerned about you, Terra. He seems to think that you're in some kind of danger. He wants you to call him. He's going to be over at the new house most of the day, so you'll have to call his cellular. He says you know the number."

"With that woman?" She gazed down at her hands lying limply in her lap. Why would Marc want her to know he was going to the house with that red-haired woman? To sink in the final blade? Even in a lover's quarrel, he far outclassed her.

"That woman?" Peter repeated. "You don't know who she is?"

"No," she said, her voice losing its strength. "And I don't care to either."

She sensed Peter shifting in the car seat, perhaps to get a better view of her face.

"All that hostility you've always had towards Marc. A very effective smoke screen. I never believed those rumors about you and him. So how long have you two been lovers?"

She refused to answer. Her unhappiness at being introduced to her replacement must have been obvious to everyone at the funeral.

He started the car, and backed out of the parking space.

"I promised Marc I'd take care of you until you called him," he said. "Since you're inclined to make him suffer awhile longer, do you want to go out for a drink?"

Pain flashed through her again. *Until she called Marc?* She'd never give that bastard another chance to hurt her.

"Okay," she said, turning her head to stare at Peter's profile. "But you can forget about that promise you made to take care of me. I can take care of myself."

"You and Marc make a good match," he commented.

"I don't want to talk about him."

He flicked her a curious glance, as if he refused to believe that her relationship with Marc was over.

"I know a place not far from here that will knock your socks off," he said. "Views that won't quit, intimate and quiet. But if you don't mind, I'd like stop off at the company first to pick up a couple of things."

"Uh," she said, trying to stall him. "I don't have my badge with me."

"To be expected. But I think I can sneak you past the lobby sentries." He winked at her.

And she didn't think he could. By now she was probably on some list of undesirables and would be refused entry. The last thing she needed was for Peter to learn in such a graphic way she'd been fired.

"I'd really rather not, Peter."

But it was too late. They were already driving into the SSI complex.

"We won't be long. A few minutes at most." he drove past the gatehouse. The guard waved.

Her mouth began to dry up. She squirmed in her seat.

He parked the car directly in front of Building A, and looked over at her. "Marc's not here. Look around the parking lot. We're practically alone. You can come inside."

"Yeah," she said. Peter apparently thought she was nervous because she didn't want to encounter Marc. She could see the lobby guard through the black glass. "I'll just wait for you here anyway, all right?"

"Suit yourself. But the man-who-shall-go-nameless is probably already at his house by now."

Once Peter entered Building A, he spoke to the guard. Through the black glass she could see Peter gesturing, probably telling the guard that her life was in danger and to keep an eye on her. Dismayed, she realized the guard was the freckled punk who had smirked at her yesterday. Sliding down deeper into the seat, she hoped he hadn't gotten a good look at her. She started counting the seconds until Peter came back.

So Marc was probably already at his ocean hideaway, she thought. Making love to the tiny beauty, no doubt. A vision of him pumping the woman to the rhythm of crashing waves took hold of Terra.

She seemed to hear the woman gasping in pleasure. She imagined Marc stopping once to push back a strand of her red hair, damp with perspiration. And then he worked her again. Terra seemed to hear the seagulls scream, and then finally Marc's lover, too, cried out in ecstasy.

Terra's heart pounded. Where was Peter already? She needed diversion—and bad. She dared not peek out the window and look for him, or else that young freckled snot might recognize her and come investigate.

The driver's side door opened. "Hey," Peter said. He slid a sheaf of papers under his seat and got in.

Inching up in her seat to sit upright, she asked. "Get what you wanted?"

"Everything's all set."

His blue eyes inspected her face with ferocity that she'd never seen before. Did Peter finally recognize her as a sexual being? Something like fear rippled through her. In her fragile state of mind, she couldn't bear to be swept off her feet by a man again.

She should go home. Alone.

"Peter," she said. "I think maybe…"

But his strange, predatory expression was suddenly gone; all she saw now was his usual offhand, smooth sexiness. The change in him bewildered her. Leaning back into her seat, she forced herself to breathe evenly. She was wound up way too tight.

"Yeah?" he prodded. "You think maybe what?"

"I think maybe I'm bad company. Why don't you take me home?"

"I won't take you home yet. You'll just brood," he said. He drove out of the SSI complex, giving the guard at the gatehouse a curt wave.

After a short drive on 280 through the foothills, Peter headed over the Santa Cruz Mountains. He worked the Porsche hard up the narrow, winding road, as if his car required domination. The way he shifted got on her nerves more than usual. He seemed to enjoy hearing the engine scream and whine. She tried to concentrate on the wild beauty of brush-choked canyons, the roadside juniper, dillweed and eucalyptus, as they sped past.

"Are you still hunting for Ray's killer?" he asked.

"I've hit a snag," she admitted. That snag, of course, was being fired. She was still convinced there were trails to follow at the company. With a jolt she realized she should have risked going inside SSI with Peter; it was her last chance to learn anything about the murder. But her fear of being kicked out again had stopped her.

"Anyway," she continued, "I guess I should tell you what I've figured out so far. I wanted to tell Marc. He was supposed to figure out the best way to tell you. But Marc probably wouldn't have believed me anyway, and you..." She shrugged dismally. "I guess I should try telling you."

Peter sent her a baffled look. "Tell me what?"

"That I think you might be killed next. I'm convinced Ray wasn't the first company founder to be murdered. Nancy and David and Steve were killed on purpose, too. Out of the original six, only you and Marc are left."

Finally they reached the coast highway, and he stopped tormenting his poor car.

"Okay, suppose I just take you at your word, and accept that they were murdered. Who do you think did it and why?"

He sounded genuinely interested, which surprised her. "Well," she said, hurrying to re-examine her thoughts right before security had dragged her off. "I think some ruthless competitor is out to destroy the company."

But now that she'd said it out loud, her theory didn't add up. Certainly the deaths of four founders was devastating to the company. But the stolen computer secrets had been more of an annoyance than a real threat. Why would a cutthroat competitor kill people, yet only steal useless software?

"It's an interesting conjecture," he said.

"Yeah," she said, gazing at the ocean sparkling to the west. Breathing in deeply, she savored the scent of the sea and sealife.

Some Californian things she'd truly miss. "But you think it's crap."

"No. I still think this is a job for the police, not an amateur detective."

Don't worry, this amateur detective has been forced into early retirement.

Wasn't Marc's new house around here somewhere? Surely Peter wouldn't bring her to Marc's place.

Peter now turned right onto a dirt road, nearly hidden by a large grove of eucalyptus. The bar really *was* out of the way. Fear flared. What if Peter was the killer?

She dismissed the thought again. Peter wouldn't destroy the company. A ruined Silicon Silk could never go public and make him a millionaire.

Now that they were off the highway, he again abused his car, making the engine howl as they sped along through the trees. At one point he had veered to the right to make room for an A-Plus Painting truck coming the other direction.

He stopped the car when they emerged from the little forest. An ultramodern stucco structure perched off the seaside cliffs in the distance.

"This isn't someone's house, is it?" she asked, uneasy.

He nodded. "And the views from inside are incredible, Terragirl."

She gave him a dirty look for his troubles. Why did he suppose she would want to socialize with some Silicon Valley mogul?

He pretended not to notice her foul face, and started his car again with a shriek of gears. The dirt road wound through acres of tall, dry grasses to end in a circular drive. He parked beneath the broad portico.

"Come on," he said. He jumped out of the car, and opened the car door for her. "There's someone I want you to meet."

She took a long look at the house. A feeling of déjà vu crept in on her. The house seemed familiar, but she knew she'd never been here before. She walked up the imposing concrete stairs. Peter's hand rested in the small of her back, guiding her up. With each step she took, her trepidation increased. The sensation that she knew this place became stronger. She stopped at the top stair, reluctant to go any further. Peter increased the pressure on her back, urging her forward.

Once on the porch, he put his arm around her, and smiled serenely. He rang the doorbell, and they waited in front of a pair of inhumanly-sized steel doors. After a time, one of the unwieldy doors opened a crack. She fully expected to hear the door creak and moan like in a horror movie. It didn't. The door opened a bit more. Silence. Her eyes roved about as she waited for the hunchbacked servant to win the battle with the heavy door. Wires stuck out of the wall near the door, begging for a light fixture. A large chunk of granite with the owner's address engraved on it leaned carelessly against a ladder. She blinked and looked at the slab closer. She tried to read the name engraved on it. But the angle was wrong. She read the letters one by one: E... L... another L... and an I. The door made a soft sound and she looked up, her heart racing. Ellison? She hoped to God that the CEO of Oracle was going to open the door, and not...

Marc's beautiful lover stood at the partly-opened door. The shock stretched Terra's nerves to the limit. She bit her lower lip to stop herself from making another strangled sound of pain.

How could Peter do this to her? Had Marc ordered Peter to give him a second chance to rub Terra's nose in his latest conquest?

Apparently unaware of Terra's turmoil, the fragile-looking woman smiled at them.

"Sorry it took so long!" she said. "I can't seem to get the hang of these doors. Come on in."

Peter guided Terra inside. The smell of fresh paint nearly knocked her down.

"It does stink, doesn't it?" said the woman. "But you know those type A personalities. Marc thought up some painting project and he couldn't possibly wait for the regular crew to do it. Oh, no. It had to be done now." She laughed softly. "Me, I'd never trust anything I came up with in the middle of the night, much less move heaven and earth to get some poor slob to come out and do it."

The woman's affectionate, intimate criticism of Marc stung Terra. She stole a look at Peter, who still had his arm around her shoulders. He smiled back, guilelessly. Was he playing matchmaker, trying to patch things up between her and Marc? Didn't the presence of Marc's fragile sweetie pie throw a wrench into his plans? Terra couldn't help but notice the woman's incredible cheekbones, or fail to see the way an artful sprinkling of freckles warmed her flawless skin. But the woman's hair, reddish, brownish blonde, worn loose, and waving down to her waist, was clearly her glory.

She tried to shrug away from Peter, but he pulled her closer. She felt victimized, but she wasn't sure by whom. Marc or Peter? Both? The woman herself seemed to be an innocent party. Terra forced herself to relax in his hold, not wanting to cause another scene like she had at the funeral. She hoped the other shoe would drop soon, and she'd know for sure if Peter was benign or Marc's sadistic ally.

"In any case, you just missed Marc," the woman continued. She sighed softly. "Come on out to the balcony. It doesn't smell so bad out here."

The woman walked toward a balcony on the other side of the room. Terra moved to follow her, and Peter finally let go. Despite the summer sun shining through massive windows to the west, she felt cool. Huge stone pavers, laid out in intricate designs, dominated the cavernous, furniture-less room. Her eyes were drawn horribly to her right, to the very spot where the master bedroom was supposed to be. She saw only closed double doors. Swallowing nervously, she tried to get herself under control. Why had she remembered that small fact about the plans, and why did it matter so much now? She jerked her head away from the master bedroom and looked straight in front of her.

She stepped out onto the concrete balcony to join the woman. The curved, multi-level balcony stretched across most of the back of the house, seeming to cling precariously. Horizontal metal pipes formed the railings, following the curves of the balcony. Though not to Terra's taste, the railings were an art form in themselves, irregularly spaced, colored various hues of red. The house itself appeared to clutch the rocky cliffs. She now remembered Marc had shown her a drawing of the back of the house. That's why the house had seemed familiar, but she hadn't recognized it.

Walking over to the railings, she looked down. She took in a sharp breath. A lovely, crescent-shaped beach lay below. She turned to gaze at the woman. The beauty leaned against the railings, the impeccable lines of a black wool crepe suit enhancing her tiny, perfect figure.

"I know Marc would be upset if I didn't try to get you to stay until he got back," the woman said. "I'd call him in his car, to let him know you're here. He left his cell phone here, though. Please stay with me until he gets back, Terra."

Uncertainty and hurt swept through her. The woman knew her name. What else did Marc's new sweetheart know? Why did she want her to stay and wait for Marc? Was she less innocent than Terra had initially surmised?

The woman's eyes, a singular shade of turquoise, flicked about Terra's face as if she were looking for answers too.

"Oh dear," the woman said. "Please forgive me. I don't think I ever introduced myself to you. I'm Frances. I'm really happy to meet you."

Just like the front of the house, her name sounded familiar. "It's nice to meet you, too, Frances," Terra said, feeling ridiculous. *Nice to meet you?* She'd practically rather be dead!

"Frances is Marc's ex-wife, Terra," said Peter.

Terra tried and failed to lift her jaw up into its proper position. "Oh," she murmured. *Frances. Of course. The mother of the two little boys.*

The knowledge that this beauty was once married to Marc didn't make her feel any better. There was a lot of history between Frances and Marc; they must have been taking up where they left off.

"Well, I suppose we ought to go," Terra said, holding back tears. "Thank you for showing us around."

Frances reached over and put her hand on Terra's forearm. "Didn't Marc ever tell you he was once married?" She sounded genuinely distressed.

Terra shook her head no. Of course she knew he had an ex-wife, but the supposed shock of learning that bit of news from Frances might give her a graceful way of fleeing Marc's house with her pride intact.

"I've got to go," Terra said.

She didn't care anymore about finding out if Frances or Peter was evil. She just wanted to get the hell out of California. Turning away from Frances, she walked into the cool house. Frances followed.

"Please don't go, Terra," Frances said, an inexplicable anxiety tingeing her voice. "It's just Marc's nature to complicate things. You know that. He told me he really wants to show you the house himself. Please wait for him with me."

"What would be the point?" Terra glanced behind her. Peter had joined them in the house. "Are we done here?" she asked him coldly.

Before Peter could answer, Marc's beautiful ex-wife ran to block Terra's way. "Wait a second," she said. "You don't think there's anything going on between Marc and me, do you?"

Terra shrugged indifferently. *It doesn't matter. I concede defeat.*

"Well, Peter, you could help me out," Frances said. "Tell Terra that I'm not involved with Marc."

"Only one small problem with that," he replied. "You and I both know that's not true."

23 / Capture

Profound bewilderment marred Frances' beautiful face. With a woman's sure instinct, Terra knew that Frances' shock was genuine. That meant Peter was lying about Marc and Frances being lovers. But why? What could he gain?

Terra studied Peter. He wore an expectant expression, like he hoped something exciting was about to happen. Maybe he was one of those men who loved cat fights, getting thrills out of watching women claw at each other, pulling out each other's hair, the whole time imagining that the women were fighting over *him*.

But tussling with fragile Frances, screaming, "Leave my man alone, you bitch!" wasn't Terra's style.

"I've had it, Peter," Terra said tightly. "No more of your fun and games. I want to go home." She turned and stalked over to the massive doors.

Frances cried out a warning.

He grabbed Terra from behind, his nails digging into her neck. His fingers tightened, and she raised her shoulders and whimpered. Tears burned her eyes. Still in her assailant's grip, she twisted to face him.

"Is that what this is?" Terra hissed. "Some kind of invitation for rough sex? Well I'm game, Peter, just as long as I get to hurt you, too."

His blue eyes flickered over her face, tasting it.

She suddenly realized his knowledge of the S & M newsgroup hadn't been due to mere curiousity; he was part of that perverse society.

Whispering a silent *one... two... three...* to focus her anger and subvert her pain and fear, she kicked him in the shin as hard as she could. The impact made her foot throb fiercely. But he let go of her.

Terra hopped toward Frances. The woman's pale face held a look of utter terror, which made Terra even more afraid. What did Frances know that she didn't?

"Where's the cell phone?" Terra gasped.

Frances pointed to a spot in the center of the huge room. Her foot now throbbing less, Terra raced to reach the phone. But Peter, even though he was limping, was far closer. He picked up the phone and hurled it against the stone floor directly in front of Frances. It shattered into a hundred plastic and metal fragments.

Frances screamed and darted away, like a rabbit from a hawk, to some far corner of the house.

Trusting Frances' instincts, Terra scurried to the entry doors. But he blocked her way.

"It's time to get to work, Terragirl," he said.

She backed away from him, turned, and ran toward the double doors of the master bedroom. The plans she'd seen indicated that the nursery had a door to a private garden. The nursery might offer her a way out. She slipped into the master bedroom. The smell of paint was much stronger. If she could just get to the outside nursery door before him, she'd be home free. Out in the open she thought she'd be able to outrun a man with a limp.

She dashed through the master bedroom, full of makeshift tables and power tools, and hurried into the nursery. The stench of fresh paint came from this room. She spied glass French doors to the outside. Her goal was only a few yards away. She took a sharp glance behind her. Peter was in the room too, limping toward her.

She ran toward the French doors, but she had to dodge massive, drop-cloth covered pieces of furniture to get there. And as she did, the brilliant hue of the room itself seemed to shake her, slow her. The nursery wasn't peachy pink as she expected. The walls had just been freshly painted a fiery rust color—nearly the same shade

234

as the walls in her New Orleans office.

Marc had this room repainted for her?

Don't think about the color of the room! Just move!

Just a few more feet and she'd make her escape. She reached for the door knob. She made contact. She twisted it. Her heart stopped cold when she heard the sound of a gun firing. Turning away from the wall, and turning away from the bullet lodged there, she faced Peter.

He held a tiny, glistening silver weapon in his hand. If she hadn't heard it fire real bullets, she would have sworn the gun was a toy.

"I don't much like blood," he said. "But if I have to, I will wound you."

He didn't say kill. He said wound.

"Okay," she said, her mouth paper dry.

That was all she could think of to say with a gun pointed at her. She had no thoughts of fighting him, or escape, or tricks. She only had thoughts of wanting to live—another second, another minute, another day. Her heart pounded, more and more wildly. Her mind skittered—afraid, useless.

He stared at her dispassionately, as if he were trying to figure out what to do with her. Ripping off a nearby drop cloth, he exposed an ornate, walnut desk with an SGI O2 on top of it. He pushed her down to kneel beside the desk. She submitted quietly. The action gave her another second of life. If she were lucky she could overcome a man with a limp, but she couldn't overcome a man with a gun. And she wanted to live as long as she could.

Workmanlike, slowly, he tied her wrists to the table leg with black Ethernet cable. It was the same stuff that had choked the life out of Ray.

She shivered. Peter was the killer. She suddenly needed to pee.

Just as calmly as he had tied her up, he'd murdered four shareholders of SSI. He thought he could gain control of SSI by killing them. He obviously didn't realize he would also destroy the company in the process.

He straightened up, and looked down at her, just as smooth, as composed as ever. She wasn't a shareholder. Killing her would net him nothing. Maybe she wasn't going die.

"Why are you doing this to me?" she asked.

He knelt down beside her. "You mean this?" He tested the knots in her cable.

She winced, and his eyes brightened in response, like a machine coming to life, energized by her pain. Reaching out, he grabbed her neck and held her immobile. She gasped. He cocked his head and smiled.

"Or could it be this?" he asked. With his other hand he pressed the little gun into her chest, right in between her breasts. The hard metal of the weapon bit her.

"Ow!"

He pushed harder, and the pain traveled up her collarbone into her shoulders and arms. She cried out. Without letting off any pressure, he closed his eyes. A low growling sound came from his throat. He opened his eyes again. Gazing at her with a look of consternation, he seemed to be struggling for self-control. He pulled the gun away from her chest, and stood straight.

"Not now, Terragirl," he said. His voice held a tremor of internal fight. "Not now. I have to find Frances. This won't work without her."

Terra hoped that Frances was long gone, that she had saved herself. Silent until she heard his limping footsteps crossing hard stone, she sighed, attempting to relieve her terror. The sigh sounded more like a moan. Sliding her tied hands up the desk leg, she touched her raw neck with trembling fingers.

How had she managed to get tied up by a killer? And Peter *had* killed. He'd murdered Nancy and David and Steve and Ray to get control of SSI. Only one man—the last living founder—stood in his way. Marc. And for some reason, he needed Terra and Frances to kill him.

Well, at least I'm still alive, she thought, hoping to force off her misery. She studied the bulky, shroud-covered objects in the splendidly orange room, wondering if this thing or that thing was the last object she'd ever see. One lump she had pegged as a Sun workstation, still in the box. The other shape was probably an unpacked Mac on top of a desk. Was that an HP printer? It seemed to be the exact same hardware she had back at in New Orleans.

Marc had brought in the computer equipment for her. The nursery had been transformed into a consultant's office. Knowing that tore her up inside. What could she do with love now? Neither she nor Marc seemed to have a future.

Refusing to hurl herself any deeper into that pit of sorrow and despair, she decided that even if she couldn't overcome a man with a gun, there had to be something she *could* do. Like slow Peter down. Or not be part of his plans to kill Marc. Somehow she'd thwart Peter. She sighed again, this time not so pitifully.

She considered the fact that her pain had excited Peter. His cruelty didn't seem at all consistent with the way he'd killed Steve and Nancy. He'd murdered them without direct contact—bloodless and cold. Perhaps sadism was just a different facet of his warped psyche. She didn't know how she would use that understanding against him; her chances of surviving didn't seem to be any better because she knew he enjoyed hurting her.

She shuddered. He had nearly lost it when he'd rammed the gun into her chest. His arousal had caught him by surprise. And that little tidbit of hard-won knowledge didn't improve her chances either. She had to get herself loose.

Twisting and fighting with all of her strength had no impact on her imprisoned condition. The hard, slick cable burned her wrists, but the knots didn't loosen.

"Ugh!" she cried in frustration. She wasn't making any progress, and the smell of paint was making her nauseous. "Shit!"

Torn between cursing and whimpering, she gave one last tug. Futile. If she was going to die, couldn't she at least die in fresh air? She gazed around her. If only she could lift up the table and slide her bonds off the table leg. But how? The table was massive. Plus it had a workstation on it. Twisting her body, she got under the table. She pulled her hands up as high on the table leg as she was able, and grasped it for support. Hunched underneath the table, she slowly got to her feet. Using her back, she managed to rock the table back and forth. After a few agonizing minutes of rocking, and pushing and pulling the table leg with her bound hands, she got the hang of it. The workstation unsteadied and crashed to the floor. Out of breath and gasping, she waited to hear Peter's footfall on the stones outside the bedroom. Maybe he hadn't heard the computer tumble to the floor. Perhaps he was on the other side of the house. She stared at the dented, breadbox-sized computer on the floor next to her. What a nasty thing to do to an O2.

She returned to rocking the table again, lighter now without the workstation on top. Finally, with a grunt and a powerful heave, the table toppled over to its side. She slid her hands off the exposed leg.

With the cable still wound around her wrists, she got up and ran to the French doors. The private garden she'd seen in the plans wasn't in place yet, so she got a clear view of the circular drive in front of the house.

She blinked, unwilling to believe what she saw.

Jared, aka RogueKnight.

She blinked again. No. Jared's long, lean, flannel plaid-shirted figure was heading toward the house. Her heart constricted. God, that probably meant Marina was here, too. Jared must have learned about the house from her sister, how it was famous up and down the coast, how it had walls of glass and a helicopter pad on the roof.

Terra opened the nursery door and slipped outside. She wanted to slap Jared silly before she fled. How could he bring Marina into this danger?

But then she heard Peter's voice, and her blood froze. And so did her muscles. She couldn't seem to move.

"Did you see a little red-haired woman wearing black as you

drove in?" Peter asked Jared.

She swallowed convulsively, withdrawing back into the nursery as silently as she could. Shutting the door, she moaned, deeply afraid. Peter must have been standing out on the porch.

Peter's going to win. He's stronger than I am.

She hadn't expected to react so intensely to Peter's voice alone. But then again, she'd never come across pure evil before. Evil that wanted to hurt her.

I'm going to die.

She peered through the glass doors. Jared stood on the walk, looking up toward the porch hidden by the bulk of the front of the house.

"Who are you?" Jared asked.

"I own this house, son," Peter said.

"Bullshit. Where's Marc?"

"Who's asking?"

"My name's Jared. You remember that."

"And why would I?" Peter said, contempt souring every word.

"You tell Marc that Jared was here looking for him."

"Son, I can't imagine Marc has a clue who you are," Peter said. "So, did you see a woman out there?"

Peter's voice was tight, irritable. Jared was in peril, and he didn't know it.

Peter's going to kill us all!

"I'm not looking for your woman," Jared said. "I'm looking for Marc. He's been messing with my life, so now I'm going to mess with his."

"Your life," Peter repeated icily. "Uh, huh. I have things to do, sonny. Go on home."

"You tell that motherfucking data-hoarder that he never should have come to New Orleans and interfered." Jared's voice was raised. "And you tell him it's payback time. That it was *me* that destroyed his house."

"What do you mean, destroyed?" Peter asked.

Terra saw Peter now. He had limped down the steps onto the walkway to stand face to face with Jared. Her heart beat rapidly. Peter eyed something in the distance, and a look of annoyance settled on his face.

"Son," Peter said, "you shouldn't have done that."

Peter pulled the little gun out of his jacket pocket. He shot Jared in the chest, point blank. The sound of the gun seemed to ricochet off the cliffs. Terra reeled away from the glass door.

He'll do the same to me—if I let him.

Seeing Peter kill set her in motion.

Running out of the nursery, she raced through the master bedroom. Thankfully, the massive double doors of the entry were already shut. She hurled herself towards them. But she overshot and landed hard against the metal with a clang. Her left cheek burned from the impact. Dizzy, she fumbled for one deadbolt, and pushed it shut. She shut the other deadbolt. She stepped back from the doors.

She'd done it. Peter was locked out.

"I've won," she whispered. "I've beaten you."

The door rattled as he tried to get back in. He spoke to her; his vile words tried to hack through the door and rekindle her fear: *Let me in, Terra. I'll go easy on you if you open the door. But if you don't let me in, I'll hurt you more than you can even imagine.* He listed the ways.

And then suddenly he was silent.

She whirled around with a dismayed cry. There was another door to the house, and she'd left it unlocked.

24 / The well

The massive front doors would be impossible for Terra to open fast enough. She'd never get out before Peter reached her. She had to stop him from coming in the nursery door. She ran back to the master bedroom, and into the nursery. She was too late. The nursery door was unlocked. He limped through it, staring right at her, sending her a satisfied smile.

Again she was alone in the house with a killer.

There has to be another door out of this house.

She snatched a sharp computer stylus off the desk as a weapon, turned tail, and bolted away from him, into the huge central room. Maybe Frances had known the way out. Hurrying in the direction she'd seen Frances go, she ran into the kitchen, scanning for outside doors.

"Shit!" she cried, her eyes resting on the large kitchen window. Nothing but ocean outside. The kitchen was perched over the cliff. There'd be no outside exit from this room. How had Marc's exwife gotten out?

Terra heard Peter's slow, syncopated steps on the stones of the central room. He was even whistling. He wasn't a whistling sort of man. But there was no clearer way to let her know that she didn't stand a chance against him.

Dashing toward a hall off the kitchen, she hoped to find an exit. She found herself scrambling down narrow stairs, her heart hammering in her throat. She hated basements. They seemed unnatural, like dungeons. But she'd probably hate dying more.

The stairs seemed to go on forever. Finally they stopped, ending in a gloomy hall. She shuddered, and not just because the air was cool. Dungeon was a good word for her surroundings, all right. She took a quick look back at the stairs, wondering if he had followed. Her left shoulder hit the cement wall painfully. She rubbed it.

In the dim light, she could see a series of doors on her right. She had trapped herself. The only thing she could do now was hide or defend herself. She opened the first door. It led to a tiny room carved out of the cliff. The little chamber was intended to be a wine cellar, but it had no wine. It also offered no place to hide.

She couldn't open the middle door, wide and made of heavy metal. It seemed to be locked.

The last door led to a rock room with a furnace and other mechanical devices. She squeezed behind the furnace, and started practicing breathing without making a sound.

She thought about the metal door she couldn't open. What if the door had been locked from the inside? And what if Frances was hiding in that room, and Frances had locked it? The idea horrified her. Frances was supposed to be safe. Outside the house. Getting help.

Terra peered around the furnace at the door. It couldn't be locked. If Peter found her she'd have to fight back. She rotated the stylus nervously in her hand, imagining striking him with it. Did she even have the guts?

The locked metal door nagged at her. If Frances *was* in that room, she would be a lot safer in there with her. But why take the risk of finding out? He probably stood outside the furnace room right now, waiting to grab her. Her breathing became more ragged.

She finally made her choice: getting away from him was worth any price. Moving out from behind the furnace, she then peered out into the dim hallway. No lurking Peter. She ran to the locked door and tapped gently.

"Frances," she whispered, "are you in there?"

Nothing.

"If you're in there, please let me in."

She anxiously looked down the hall, straining to hear Peter's footsteps.

"Frances?"

She thought she heard a shuffling sound from behind the locked door. Someone *was* inside!

"Frances!" Terra cried, now knocking frantically. "Open the door!"

"Is that you, Terra?" asked a small voice from the other side of the door.

"Please, Frances, let me in," she begged.

The door opened a crack. Terra pushed the door open wide enough to slip in. Once Terra was inside, Frances slammed the heavy door shut and slid the deadbolt shut.

"I thought you were dead," Frances murmured, staring at Terra like she wasn't real. "I heard a gunshot."

Those words brought Terra closer to hysteria than she'd ever been in her life. She scurried as far away from the door—and from Peter—as she could. She found herself on the other side of the room, terrified, her back plastered to the wall, staring at the door. "I'm okay," she repeated over and over again, hoping to subdue her extreme panic. Why was she so scared now—now when she was safe?

After what seemed to be an eternity, her body ran out of the chemicals that made her heart hammer and her muscles ready to run. She sat on the floor, exhausted. Frances was standing near her, her expression strained.

"Thanks for letting me in," Terra whispered once she found the strength to speak.

"You're very welcome," Frances said, regarding Terra with her turquoise eyes.

After a glance at the door, Terra gazed around the room, trying to figure out where she was. The room was like a well: about two and a half stories deep, with walls made of rough masonry. There were no windows at all, but small skylights adorned the ceiling 25 feet up. Four gas torchlights, the flames providing scant illumination, jutted out of the oceanward wall. Terra now realized this dungeon was for climbing; it was the very same room that had Velvet so upset. Marc must have wanted to feel like he was climbing an ancient castle wall.

Terra got up and walked over to investigate an alcove. Inside the little chamber there was a primitive shower, a sink, and a toilet. They could last for days down here if they had to. Rejoicing, Terra slid the stylus up her sweater sleeve.

Sliding her fingers over the wall, Terra found a sharp section of brick, and used it to saw viciously at the Ethernet cable. Frances watched her, distressed at the sight of those black bonds.

Where was Marina? She hoped her sister wasn't waiting for Jared. What if she began to worry and went looking for him? She stopped and examined the progress she'd made. Slow but working. And what had Jared done to Marc's house that had earned him a bullet hole in the chest? Whatever it was, the cracker obviously thought Marc valued his fancy house above all else; Jared had hit Marc where he thought it would hurt most. But Jared was wrong. What Marc loved most was Silicon Silk. And then, after his company, he probably valued her... and Frances.

Terra glanced at Marc's delicately beautiful ex-wife, and the memory of his tenderness towards her at the funeral washed over her. Even if he wasn't screwing Frances, he clearly loved her. She wished he didn't. It would have been way simpler. At least Terra had no past. Well actually, she had a past—a big past—but of all the men she'd made love with, she'd never been *in* love with anyone but Marc.

One cable was nearly sliced clean through. She lifted the cable off the brick and pulled her hands apart. The cable snapped. Her wrists, though still wrapped with black knots, were free of each other. She made a sound of relief.

"Peter did that to you?" Frances asked somberly.

"Yeah. He wanted to keep me in one place while he went looking for you." Terra took a deep breath. "I was hoping you had made it out."

"That's the big problem with cliff houses," Frances said. "No back door."

Her hands free, Terra now used the facilities. With that chore done, she felt an order of magnitude better.

The torchlight seemed to dim. She wondered if the light intensity was cycled to make a nighttime castle climb more realistic.

"Peter's been killing off SSI's founders," Terra said, "one by one. First he slipped some kiwi juice into Nancy Beck's water. Then he made it look like David Houle killed himself. I don't know how, exactly. But it was probably murder. Even Marc couldn't believe he'd killed himself."

Frances nodded as if she agreed.

"And then Peter suckered Steve Myatt and a bunch of us into skiing on a slope just begging for an avalanche," Terra went on. "I just about got killed, too."

She recalled how Peter had tried to discourage her from going on that back bowl adventure, and then, when she had come along anyway, Peter told her to ski down a different path than the others. Had Peter tried to protect her? She got goose pimples all up and down her arms. Had she actually ignored a killer's warnings? How dumb could she be? And what about that sadism newsgroup he had described at the launch dinner? Wasn't that a clue that he was abnormal? Why had she dismissed it so easily?

After a shuddering sigh, Terra continued. "And then, Peter strangled Ray, making it look like a homicidal computer cracker had done it. So who's left of the founders? Only Marc and Peter. And Peter means to control the company. Marc's in danger, Frances."

"You and I are in danger," Frances replied.

Terra laughed sourly. "Yeah. I suppose we are."

She spotted a set of hand weights in one corner of the room. They might come in handy as weapons. Climbing ropes hung neatly on racks on the walls, too. She imagined knocking Peter out with a barbell and then tying him up with the ropes. And then hitting him with the barbell again. Suddenly she felt light-headed; her unaccustomed violent thoughts were making her ill. She sat on the concrete floor and waited for the dizziness to pass.

Frances sat down next to her. In the soft light, she appeared even more frail. "I think Peter wants the company, too. But he won't kill Marc. He can't."

"He *can* kill Marc," Terra said. She wondered if sentimentality made Frances unable to accept Peter's intentions. "Marc's the only one standing between him and a nice, juicy IPO." She picked at the knotted cable around her wrist, musing. "Anyway, Peter likes to deprive his victims of air. I figure he's going to drown Marc. That's why Peter is here, by the ocean, waiting for him to come back."

"You're wrong, Terra," Frances said. "He could never carry off an IPO without Marc. Marc isn't his intended victim at all. In fact, Peter arranged to draw Marc away from here."

"What do you mean?"

Terra thought she heard a faint whirring sound by the door. Both women glanced over at the door.

"Did you hear that?" Frances asked.

Terra nodded, and started to get up to investigate, but then the noise stopped. "So why do you think that Peter was trying to get Marc away from here?"

"Marc got a phone call soon after we got here. He thought it was from you. He told me he could barely understand what you said, you were so scared and whispering so quietly."

"But I didn't call Marc," Terra said. She remembered Peter going back to the office after the funeral. Had he made the call to Marc's cellular pretending to be her?

Terra heard the sound outside the door again. A thrill of fear coursed through her. What *was* that?

"Yeah. I figured you hadn't made that call," Frances said, "when you showed up here with Peter about forty-five minutes after you supposedly had called. By then it was too late; Marc was gone. The second he got that call, he tore out of here like a bat out of hell. Apparently he thought you were heading to San Simeon, and you were desperate for him to come and meet you there."

"Well, Marc will come back once he figures out I'm not in San Simeon," Terra said. "And I sure wish we could figure out how to warn him about Peter."

"San Simeon is a long way from here. And when he doesn't find you in San Simeon, he'll tear that little town apart."

Of course Frances was right. Marc wouldn't just shrug and give up. Terra got to her feet. The movement was harder than expected. Gravity seemed to want to drag her down. *Hiding from a killer with her lover's all-knowing ex-wife must be taking a physical toll*, she thought.

She walked over to the door and rattled it. Solid. A future seemed possible. But she wondered who would save them from insane, gun-wielding Peter. The hapless workmen that would arrive to work on the house at some point? Marc? Terra and Frances themselves?

"We should be safe in here until help arrives," Terra said. "Why do you suppose Marc even bothered to put a deadbolt on this door anyway?"

"I don't have any idea." Frances looked so small and vulnerable, sitting hunched against the wall, her head resting in her hands. "We aren't responsible to each other anymore." A note of bitterness and regret crept into her voice. "I should have done what Anthony wanted me to and returned them. If I had listened to him, maybe I wouldn't be here now. But I thought I deserved them as repayment for all the tears." She sighed wistfully.

Terra had no idea what Frances was talking about. "It'll be okay," she soothed.

Frances' raised her head and looked straight at her. "Ignore my rantings. I'm just scared, and I'm going through the 'if onlys.'"

"We're going to make it, you know." She pulled at the doorknob again.

Frances smiled weakly. "Yeah."

Terra had a strong sensation that a shadow had just passed over her. Frances must have felt it too, because they both looked up at about the same time. Terra scoured the skylights two and a half stories up. The sky was cloudless, nearing dusk. Could Peter do anything to hurt them from above?

Frances looked away from the skylights, and hugged herself. "If we make it, are you going to say yes to Marc's proposal?"

"I, uh, haven't decided," Terra said, surprised and uncomfortable that Marc had confided in Frances.

How would their relationship, already rocky, fare when he was so close to his ex-wife? Terra gazed down at the huddled beauty; wouldn't she always be a temptation for him?

"Was Marc faithful to you?" Terra suddenly blurted out.

Frances unfolded herself and stretched her legs out in front of her. "He was faithful. He didn't cheat. And I hope you believed me when I told you there's nothing going on between me and Marc. I have a family I adore."

"I believe you. It's Marc I have doubts about, I guess. I'm having a hard time shifting gears, you know, and trusting him. And Peter *knew* I was insecure. I was devastated when I saw you and Marc together. He kept putting salt on the wound, trying to make me believe you and Marc were lovers. He gets his jollies out of hurting me." Terra rattled the door again just to make sure, recalling Peter's excitement over her pain. "He's sadistic, Frances. Did you know that?"

Frances was silent for a long time. "No. I didn't know that. I do know that Peter's a brilliant opportunist, though. Coldly logical. He pressed you hard because he thought your feelings toward me offered him a way to gain control of the company." She curled her legs up to her body again, hugging her knees. "You're supposed to kill me in a jealous rage."

Terra blinked, disturbed. How could Frances jump to such an outrageous conclusion? Marc's ex-wife had seemed so perceptive. She'd been suspicious of Peter from the start, trying to keep Terra at the house until Marc got back, attempting to stop her from leaving with Peter. Of course Terra had misinterpreted Frances' motivation at the time.

"Kill you?" Terra said. "Because I think you're my rival? I'd just go home and lick my wounds."

Hoping to relieve the staleness in the air, Terra walked over to the toilet and flushed it, and then ran a little water into the sink.

"You're missing the point," Frances said. "You don't actually have to kill me. Peter is perfectly capable of doing that. But he needs someone to frame, and to create a motive. He already did that once with Ray and that hacker, didn't he?"

"But this is a lousy frame-up," Terra argued. "Because nobody knows Marc and I are involved. We kept our relationship a secret. Except Marc told you, I guess. And Peter knows. But I just told Peter this afternoon. I never told anyone else."

"A lot of other people were at the funeral, Terra. And some of them saw how hurt you were when you and I met. They're going to assume that you *do* have a relationship with Marc."

"Was I really that obvious?" Terra asked unhappily. "I was really kind of hoping people would think I was upset about Ray—which I actually was."

"You were obvious enough to suit Peter's purposes, anyway; he'll exploit your reaction to kill me."

"But I still don't understand. How will your death let Peter get control of SSI?"

The gas lights suddenly went off. The climbing room was dark, except for the weak, dusky light coming in through the skylights.

"Terra?" Frances called. She sounded panicked. "Are you still there?"

"I'm here. Peter turned off the gas; he's just trying to scare us."

"Well, it's working."

"Look up and concentrate on the light coming in from the skylights, Frances. I'll get over to where you are."

Darkness had never scared Terra. After all, she still had her other senses, like touch and hearing. She moved along the wall until she reached Frances. She sat down next to the trembling woman. Gazing up at the skylight too, Terra felt a little breathless and uneasy, and wondered if Frances' anxiety was rubbing off on her.

Terra yawned. How could she feel sleepy when she was so scared? After awhile, she realized Frances had stopped shaking.

"Why did you and Marc get divorced?" Terra asked.

"I suppose it's because I wanted a real family. Kids, husband. He wanted Silicon Silk. His devotion and concern went to the company. Not to me. After two and a half years of being neglected, I finally got mad about it. What's the point of being married to someone you never see? So finally one day he was at home long enough for me to tell him in person that I wanted a divorce. It turned out I demanded the end of our marriage on the same day of his greatest triumph, but there was no help for that." Frances sighed loudly. "SSI was incorporated that day, you see. The incorporation agreement had been formalized, and the company had a product ready to sell. Marc was so happy and optimistic and proud. His driving dream of entrepreneurship had come true. And he thought giving me a piece of the company would make me happy and proud, too. It didn't occur to him that a marriage needed to be nurtured more than once every few years."

"So what did he do when you said you wanted a divorce?"

Frances chuckled. "He reacted in his usual patronizing way. Patting me on the shoulder, 'It's all right,' that kind of thing. He obviously didn't believe our marriage was over. Even when I moved out, he was sure I'd eventually come back to him. Even being served the divorce papers didn't seem to bother him."

"He seems to regret the divorce now." Terra suppressed another yawn. She tried to blink away the sparking lights in front of her eyes. Her head was starting to hurt.

"Oh, the regret happened later, when I married Anthony. My remarriage nearly killed Marc. Marc couldn't very well expect we'd get back together when I was married to someone else, could he? At that point, when it was far too late, Marc finally understood why I'd left him. He tried to right the wrongs. He desperately wanted to make amends. Prove how much I meant to him. But like I said, it was too late. I was married to another man. So about the only thing Marc managed to accomplish was alienating Anthony."

"I still don't think he's over you, Frances."

Frances yawned. "Sorry. Didn't mean to yawn in your face like that. I'm just tired, I guess. For a long time Marc couldn't accept that we would never get back together, that's true. He was in such pain. His reaction used to worry me sick; I divorced him because I was miserable in the marriage, not because I wanted to punish him. I hoped he'd find love with someone else, like I had with Anthony. Finally Marc started to date. But it didn't seem to me that he was making any progress. His choice of girlfriends seemed driven by the failure of our marriage. He'd get involved with these incredibly high-maintenance women. I think he thought he could fix his mistakes with me by being a devoted, caring lover to a woman who was impossible to please. Only then could he prove himself."

Terra had to admit Frances had a point. Dependent, needy Velvet and delicate Sunny had even looked a little like Marc's ex-wife. But Terra herself wasn't anything like Marc's other girlfriends.

"I'm not high-maintenance," Terra said.

Frances yawned again, followed by a little chuckle. "I know. And Marc knows, too. He's finally let go of the divorce, Terra. He's over me, and loving you proves it. Listen, I'm really tired. I'm going to lie down for just a minute. Is that okay with you?"

"Yeah, sure, go ahead."

Her apprehension, and the feeling of being trapped in a well, grew stronger. Something seemed to be wrong with the air. The stale odor had turned pungent. She rubbed her temples. Her head now throbbed. Peering up at the skylights, so far above, she saw a dark form, a head maybe, looking back at her.

Peter; it had to be.

Oh, God. The air. He must have done something to the air. Had the torch light extinguished itself because there was no more oxygen for the flame to burn? Was he up there waiting for them to suffocate?

Terra heaved her unwilling body up and lumbered to the door: she needed air. She slid the deadbolt open, and pulled at the knob. The door didn't budge. Either she was too weak, or Peter had somehow closed them in.

Before Terra blacked out, she felt for the stylus inside her sleeve. It was still there.

She vowed she'd use it when she saw Peter again.

25 / Sensation play

Terra's head blasted pain, so she figured she was still alive. She gulped down air, greedy for more.

When she finally opened her eyes, she realized she lay on the stone floor of the large central room. Someone stood above her. Maybe Marc had returned in time to rescue her, and he had pulled her out of the climbing well.

"Marc," she heaved.

Her eyes tried to focus. But her vision seemed to drift about randomly. Finally her eyes fixed on two wide stripes.

"Marc?" Now anchored by the suspenders, her eyes moved up to his face. Handsome and refined. One of his eyes closed and opened again. A merry wink.

Peter. Not Marc.

Her head swam. "Peter?"

"Yes, Terragirl. It's me."

Peter had saved them? He must have had second thoughts about killing. He didn't like murdering anymore. She took more deep breaths, grateful that somehow he'd regained his sanity.

"Can you get up?" he asked.

"I don't think so."

She took more breaths. Rolling her head to the side, her gaze fell on the windows to the south. She blinked. The sky was dark, but the ground glowed. Why would the ground be bright, and the sky black? She smelled smoke. Fire. The grasses around the house were aflame. She looked to the north and saw the same thing. Burning grasses. Jared must have set the grasses on fire as revenge against Marc.

And this last prank against a data-hoarder had earned Jared death.

They had to get out of here. With a groan, she pushed herself up to sit. After the dizziness passed, she scanned the room for Frances. Why wasn't she here? She tried to stand, but she couldn't seem to get her feet in the right place, and kept falling. Her feet were hobbled. The paisley scarf from her hair was knotted tightly around both ankles, separating them about a foot apart. Peter's handiwork. Why had he snatched her from death only to tie her up again? And where was Frances? She looked up at him. He rolled up his sleeves slowly, a faint smile on his lips.

"Can't have you kicking me anymore, Terragirl."

He loosened his tie and then tightened it again so the knot fell a little lower. Staring at her, he smoothed the front of the material with his long fingers. The movement was caressing, seductive.

Icy terror settled over her heart as she recalled his tranquil description of newsgroup torture tips. Had he saved her so he could hurt her?

"Frances needs you, Peter," she gasped, her lungs seeming to constrict with fear. "Please go get her, too."

"She's already dead."

No. Peter's lying. Frances is small. She doesn't need as much air. She's still alive.

"You must hate Marc so much," she said.

"Do you know what I'm going to do to him?"

"It's what you've already done. You've murdered four SSI shareholders so you alone can own SSI, and then you'll take the company public."

He gave her a smug look as if he had a lot to congratulate himself for. "Not a bad guess."

Even if she couldn't kick him, she *would* be able to slap his murdering face, because he hadn't retied her hands. The ends of the black cable still dangled from her wrists. Except that right at the moment, she couldn't seem to get to her feet, let alone walk over and hit him.

"Well, you're never going to be able to kill Marc," she said. The faith that Marc would thwart Peter, somehow avoiding the fate of Ray and the rest of SSI's founders, gave her pained satisfaction.

"And I won't even try," he replied. "I need Marc to run the company for me. He'll still be the charismatic, brilliant leader we all know, except on a short leash."

So, Peter believed he would control the company without killing Marc? She didn't understand how.

He walked around her once. Would he hurt her now? Her fear was fresh, pungent. Her oxygen debt must be partly repaid if she felt alarm so strongly. And Frances, could she breathe at all? Or was Marc's ex-wife already dead, like he said? How did Frances figure into his plans at all?

Once he completed his circuit, he actually moved further away from her.

"Marc isn't going to be on anyone's leash," she said, hoping to burst his bubble. "After the IPO, he'll sell his SSI stock, and start a new company. You'll be eating his dust, Peter."

"Interesting idea, but wrong. Even if Marc wanted to abandon his baby after the IPO, he couldn't. As an insider, he wouldn't be able to sell his ownership for six months. By the time he could cash out, he'll have discovered the rewards of being the head of a public company."

"A paper millionaire," she said dismissively. "Big deal."

"Money is hardly the only reason to go public," he said. "Selling stock makes our success and our superiority concrete. SSI isn't an operation running out of Marc's spare bedroom in Sunnyvale anymore. It's time to expand, to dominate the competition, to control the entire industry. SSI is finally going to get the respect it deserves."

"Respect? You're destroying the company!"

"No. I'm saving it, Terragirl. The founders were strangling the company with their short-sightedness."

"Is that why you suffocated them—because they were strangling the company?"

"Poetic justice isn't it?" he replied.

He obviously thought he was powerful and clever. And the way she cowered on the floor probably made him feel even more potent. *Damn!* She tried again to stand up. This time, knowing her feet were hobbled, she managed to stand. But as she rose, he advanced toward her. His eyes were on fire.

She backed away. One tiny hobbled step, then another.

I can't run for my life when I can't even run.

His eyes seemed to devour her.

She took another step back, her heart pounding. He moved closer. She inched backward, and then again, until her back was against the wall. There was nowhere she could go.

"How are you going to explain Frances?" she asked, desperate to get him talking again. "No one's going to buy that I killed her in a fit of jealous fury."

He smiled faintly as he drew near. "I had intended a little drowning accident for you both. But being able to shut off the climbing room vents was a stroke of good fortune I just couldn't pass up. I have a dead boy out there, Terragirl, someone who obviously hates Marc. He's going to take your role as Frances' killer now. In the meantime…" He reached out, outlining her cheekbones with his forefinger.

Her fear made his touch feel like sandpaper. "Peter, don't," she said.

He took a step away from her, and she thought for one agonizing moment that he might leave her alone. But then he smoothly closed the distance between them. Resting his right hand around her left hip, he pushed her up against the wall.

"Oh God," she moaned, wincing at the contact. What happened to her desire to slap him? Where was her courage?

His eyes razed her up and down, and he grunted with pleasure. "I like you scared."

She swallowed convulsively. Peter wasn't excited by her pain—

but by her fear.

"Strong, angry, self-sufficient Terra," he continued. "I didn't think you had it in you."

"What are you going to do to me?"

His blue eyes flashed with an emotion she couldn't name. "What comes naturally," he said. He ran his hands over her shoulders, down her arms.

She tried to take a few deep breaths so she could clear her head enough to figure out what to do, but she could only gasp spasmodically.

He caressed her wrists, and found the severed ends of the cable. First an experimental tug on the cables, and then he pulled her arms up over her head by the cable, pinning her hands up against the wall behind her.

He shifted the ends of the cable to free his right hand. Leaning over her, he moved his fingers over her breasts. He did not actually touch her, though his eyes shimmered with sexual intensity. She felt his breath on her face.

"Peter, listen to me," she gasped. "The house is going to burn."

"This house is stucco and stone. We'll be perfectly safe here."

Safe? She couldn't seem to catch her breath as he moved his hand down, above her stomach, still not touching her.

"Let's get Frances and leave," she pleaded. "And then I promise that you and I, we'll go off and have a lot of fun afterwards."

He chuckled. "Fun? Afterwards? Oh, but Terragirl, as they say, a bird in the hand is worth two in the bush."

She felt him press his palm against her crotch. She shuddered.

His hand moved lower, pushing through the cloth of her pleated skirt to rest between her legs. Terra tried to wriggle away from his touch by standing on her toes. She squeezed her thighs together. But it was futile. He began to stroke her through the cloth, with those long, strong fingers she had once admired. Cajoling. Persuasive. Skillful.

"Sugar," he murmured, looking straight at her, still stroking.

Tears sprang to her eyes. If her wrists weren't held above her head, if her brain weren't swimming from fear, and if he had asked her, maybe she would have been encouraging him with little sighs of delight. But this was rape.

"You don't have to do it this way," she whimpered. "You don't have to force me. I wanted you, remember?"

He pulled his hand out from her legs and gazed at her with vibrant eyes. "But I don't go for plain vanilla, Terra."

With a slow, insistent tug on the cables binding her hands, he pulled her wrists higher and higher, stretching her arms up against the window. Her elbows sang with pain. She couldn't relieve the pressure because she was already standing on her toes. He pulled tighter. She thought her arms might snap in half. She screamed.

His free hand now caressed her breasts through the knit of her sweater. She couldn't feel his touch there, because he made her hurt so bad in other places. He paused and stared at her chest, a small smile curling his lips. He seemed to be admiring his handiwork, as if he were an artist, and she a canvas. And then he started sliding his hand over her again.

"Yes," he said, as he fondled and teased. He pulled on her bonds once more, shifting her up a fraction. "Better," he murmured.

Her whole body shook. The trembling made her shoulders hurt even worse. A long, low moan emerged from deep inside her.

He answered with a regretful sound. "I'm taking you too fast." After grazing his palm down the front of her body in one long, sliding movement, he released her wrists.

The unexpected respite made her cry out. Her arms tumbled down, numb, useless.

"You are so responsive," he whispered. His eyes flicked over her hungrily. "I want to gorge myself."

She heard him breathe in and out through his teeth, making a whistling sound. He was clearly in turmoil. Agitated. Hot. Impatient.

She couldn't understand how this could be the same man who

killed his partners so dispassionately. Or had he?

"Did you do this to Ray and David too?" she asked.

"Of course not." He looked her up and down, still breathing heavily. He pulled her numb right hand up, sliding it underneath his suspender. "What a lover you're turning out to be."

Lover. Her stomach cramped up into a tight ball.

He slid her unfeeling left hand under his other suspender. "Looking down and seeing you in the climbing room, watching the way you fought to open the door, I knew I had to experience the ultimate with *you*."

She tried to pull out of the grotesque parody of an embrace, but her arms had no strength.

"How right I was." He brushed her lips with his fingers. "This is it, Sugargirl," he whispered, his eyes bright, insane. "Let's make it last as long as we can."

Feeling returned to her arms. And it was stinging pain. She tried again to pull her hands out from under his suspenders and defend herself. But the motion was feeble and impotent. How long would it take until she could finally make a decent attempt at hitting him? The stench of scorched grassland now seemed to envelope the room.

He leaned over, propping his left elbow on the wall behind her. Draping his forearm casually over her neck, he bent to kiss her. She held her breath, stiffening, steeling herself for more pain. But his kiss was tender. His wiry arm hair grazed her throat. If she didn't excite him by giving him the terror he craved, maybe he wouldn't hurt her so soon.

His kiss became more insistent and seductive. At the same time, he rested his forearm on her throat. Panicked now, she pushed at his chest. He answered by leaning his forearm more forcefully against her. She couldn't breathe. His kiss became rougher, impassioned. She tried to pull to one side, but he held her neck fast against the wall with his forearm. The pressure on her throat was crushing. His kisses deepened. He ground his hips into hers, so she might feel his arousal. She tried to scream, but the sound was muffled by his mouth.

Frenzied with fear and self-survival, she bit down on his tongue as hard as she could. He pushed away from her, and her hands snapped out of his suspenders.

He stood a foot away from her, his eyes wild. Blood dribbled from the corner of his mouth.

Her ankles were tied. Now what?

"I didn't mean to do it," she said in a shaking voice. In a way it was the truth; she had bitten him more out of instinct than plan.

Reaching out, he gave her a calculated slap. He seemed to strike her for effect rather than to hurt her.

But he *would* hurt her again.

Her arms still burned and tingled. She flexed her elbow experimentally. Stronger than she was minutes ago, but she couldn't protect herself. And she sure couldn't run from him with her ankles bound.

"I'm sorry," she said, trying to buy more time. Her fingers twitched as feeling returned to them.

"Blood," he said, "turns lovemaking short and ugly." He pulled a handkerchief out of his pant's pocket and dabbed his lips.

She shook her arms, hoping to bring strength to them. Something sharp poked her forearm. The stylus! If only she could get the stylus out from under her sleeve. Hoping he wouldn't get suspicious, she put her arms behind her back, and worked to slip the stylus out of her sleeve. Almost. Almost.

He folded the handkerchief, and put it back in his pocket. He stared at her with shimmering eyes.

What if he guessed what she was doing? She finally got the stylus out of her sleeve. Now she clutched it in her trembling hand. The sharp end was pointed toward her wrist: she needed to turn the stylus around before it would work as a weapon.

He pulled the decorative gun out from the back of his pants and fondled it. "Would you prefer brute, Sugargirl?"

"No," she said through a dry mouth.

He put the gun on the windowsill, turned, and gave her a lazy, seductive smile. "We've had enough foreplay."

Despair forked through her. She knew she'd never survive his climax.

Faster than she had any idea he could move, he grabbed her around the waist. He hefted her onto his shoulder. Striding through the central room, he carried her out onto the brightly lit balcony. Her body bouncing, the stylus nearly dropped to the floor. He crossed the balcony, and sat her on the top railing. She heard the ocean below whisper her name.

"No!" she cried.

He was going to push her off. He'd come when he heard her body smash below. Grasping her firmly around her waist with his hands, he stared at the horizontal metal bars that formed the railing. Distracted and thoughtful, he lifted her up. She thought he'd drop her now. Vertigo and terror washed over her.

But instead, he lowered her so her feet again touched the floor of the balcony. With sudden, bruising force, he pushed her head and neck to the side and back under the top bar. She screamed. The top bar now pressed against her collarbone, the middle bars bit her back, imprisoning her. But it wasn't over. He pulled her legs apart roughly, the silk scarf tearing into the flesh of her ankles, until finally the scarf ripped. Lifting her lower leg off the ground, he pushed her foot and calf backward through the lower bars. He did the same thing to her other leg. She was kneeling now, pinned in the railing.

Peter had woven her body in and out of the bars.

He studied her, squinting. Again he seemed to be the artist of pain, regarding his sculpture.

A small cry escaped her lips as he approached her again. His eyes fairly glowing, he grabbed her ponytail through the rails, and pulled. Her neck arched back. He nudged her knees backward so they slipped in behind the bar. She'd surely slip through and fall to the beach below. Pushing and jerking, he stretched and squeezed her limbs.

When he finally stopped, every muscle in her body seemed to be on fire. And no wonder. Her back and neck were now arched back unnaturally. The bar that had pressed down on her collarbone now gnawed at her breasts. The bar she had kneeled on now bit her splayed thighs just above the knee. It was if she'd been caught midair in a backward flip.

Her arms hung down towards the beach. Miraculously, she could still feel the stylus clutched in one hand. If she could only get it turned around. But if she messed up, the stylus would fall, and she'd have no weapon.

"I wasn't sure I could do that to a human body," he said. Moving closer, his hands swept down over the exposed arc of her middle. "Perfect."

He folded her skirt up neatly onto her waist.

She tried to squirm away. But she could only manage to twitch.

"You don't want to move, Sugar," he said. "You're balanced on a pinhead. You fight me and you're likely to break your back. And that wouldn't suit either one of us."

He slid his fingers under the crotch of her panties, pulling the silk to one side. He sighed hoarsely, and moved his forefinger on top of her tender nub.

"I can feel your heartbeat here."

She wept as he nicked and pulled at her sensitive folds.

Marc had once claimed that Peter was pure, passionless intellect. Marc was wrong. There was more to Peter than cold logic. Though he had probably killed Ray and David without pleasure, something dark and depraved had always surged beneath Peter's smooth exterior. Now, with his plans to control the company completed, and feeling invincible, he wanted to celebrate, and relish someone's suffering.

Hers.

He stepped back as if to delight in his work of art. "Quivering.

Ready. Sugarsweet. You'll be mine soon."

She heard his whistling breath. She hated his easy charm as he hurt her. She despised the way he had killed his partners. But most of all, she detested how his eyes licked at her exposed crotch.

I'm not going to die this way, not raped by a murderer.

With renewed strength, she got the stylus turned around. Slipping her arm through the bars, she waited.

She heard his zipper, felt him grab her hips hard.

Now.

"Fuck *this*," she hissed. With hatred and fright giving her power, she struck him with the stylus.

26 / Rescue

The stylus hit. Peter's lips twitched and his eyes clouded over. He didn't seem to realize who had injured him. Howling in pain, he jerked away from her. He staggered backward, holding his crotch, his face contorted in agony. Stiff and scared, she watched him move around the balcony spasmodically. He seemed to be blinded by the pain. She began to moan softly. When would he stop screaming?

And then, suddenly, he did stop. He seemed to have disappeared altogether. Maybe he'd pitched himself off the balcony. She strained to hear the sound of him landing heavily on the beach. Only the wet whispering of the ocean reached her ears.

She felt him near and alive, even if she couldn't see him. Now he would pull the stylus out of his body, and rise up. He'd come toward her. He'd see her skirt was still flipped up, and her thighs still spread wide. He'd get closer, making that whistling sound. He would stroke and nip her again, showing her how lovemaking could be transformed into pain.

"No!" she sobbed.

Panicked and bawling, she struggled to get out of her high-art metal prison. She writhed and twisted. Still stuck, but bruised and battered, she stopped to catch her breath. She'd end up killing herself if she kept it up. She wasn't some helpless, trapped animal. There was a logical way to get herself lose.

If she had time. Her weeping and panting made it nearly impossible to hear if he was coming towards her. So she forced herself not to think of Peter's pulling and snapping. She reached out and grabbed onto the bar with both hands. Scraping and sliding, inch by inch, she finally pulled her legs free of the trap. Though her feet couldn't reach the ground, and her chest was still pinned, at least her back was no longer painfully arched. She heard a sound, and her heart lurched. Peter? She listened carefully. Not Peter. Not the ocean. It was a machine hum from far away. Motorboat?

She stared down the smoky coast and located the machine making the sound. An approaching helicopter. She wondered if it was going to drop water on the fire. Watching the blinking lights of the aircraft, she gathered her courage. At last, she worked to get her upper body out of the trap. She pushed and squeezed her breasts under the bar and twisted her neck as far as she could, and pulled herself free. She now stood on the ground, shaking, dazed. Her right ear and breasts throbbed, chafed by unforgiving metal.

She pulled her panties back, and smoothed down her skirt. But she still felt the dreadful sensation of Peter's fingers flicking over her. Where was he? She ran into the house and grabbed his gun. If Peter was still alive, she'd shoot him in the nuts, and give *him* a sensation. Looking down at the ornate weapon, she hoped it had bullets in it.

The helicopter seemed to be right on top of her now. Loud, like a thunderstorm. She recalled that the house had a heliport on the roof. Had Marc come? She couldn't wait around to find out. Not with Frances still in the climbing room. Maybe she was still alive.

Suddenly, someone burst in from the balcony. She squeaked.

Peter had come to finish the job. Terrified, she raised the gun at the advancing figure.

"Stay where you are," she rasped over the sound of the helicopter. She couldn't see Peter's expression, because of the smoke and the blazing light on the balcony.

"Terra." His voice was firm. Commanding.

Marc. It was Marc!

He strode toward her and took the gun away. Her whole body rocked from his sudden appearance; she wished she could sag into his arms with relief.

"I almost shot you, Marc!" she cried. "Why did you have to sneak up on me like that?"

"I thought I saw someone tied to the rails. I wanted to save time. Once the helicopter landed, I jumped down to the balcony from the roof."

Time. Frances was running out of time and air.

"Frances is in the climbing room," she said. "Peter shut off the air vents."

He gave her arm a little squeeze, and raced away, toward the basement. She rubbed her arm where he'd touched her. Every part of her body seemed to be bruised.

Surely Frances would still be alive. Marc's ex-wife was so tiny; she didn't need as much oxygen. In that case, she told herself, every little bit of extra air could help. She ran back to the balcony. The heat of the fire surrounding the house now warmed her face, and made her eyes smart. She leaned over the rails, and spied the sloping roof of the climbing room. The roof was about three feet below her. She could see one vent, shut, near a cluster of other shadowy mechanical objects. But what if Peter was down there, waiting? Marc had taken the gun. Telling herself that the wounded Peter would be no threat to her anymore, she climbed over the metal bars, and eased herself down to the metal roof. She walked across the incline to the vent, and tugged the lever. It seemed to be stuck.

She changed her position, and pulled harder. The lever released abruptly, opening the vent with an echoing clang. Her body went sprawling back into the shadowy mechanical area. She landed against something relatively soft. She was lucky; she could have been skewered by a pipe or been slammed into a hard corner of some metal box. Scooting away on her butt, she turned to look.

Nausea washed over her.

She had landed on Peter.

He lay on his stomach, unmoving, the line of his body paralleling the slope of the roof. She wondered why he hadn't slid down to the beach below. Her eyes fixed to his neck. She knew now what had broken his fall. The knot of his tie had gotten caught up in a large bolt sticking up out of the roof. If getting stabbed hadn't already killed him, then his own tie would have choked the remaining life out of him. He'd probably suffocated like his victims.

She turned away from him and threw up. The vomit landed with a wet drippy thud on the metal roof. She retched twice more. Finally, after a few dry heaves, she picked herself up and made her way back to the balcony.

Marc waited for her, cradling Frances tenderly in his arms. Terra climbed up the rails. The minute she got near him and saw his closed expression, she knew that Frances was dead. But there was no time to comfort him.

"We have to go," he shouted over the whirring of the helicopter.

She followed him through the central room, and up to the second story, and up another set of stairs to the helipad. It didn't take long for the three of them to crowd into the helicopter, and leave the beleaguered house. Marc's emotions were still hidden. Only when his eyes flicked over Terra's wrists, as they did again and again, did he betray his internal condition. He was wound up tight. Murderous.

She was glad it was too loud to have a conversation in the helicopter.

★

The minute Terra got to Marc's loft, she told him she had to use the bathroom. "I've got to take a shower," she said breathlessly, running past him.

Got to was an understatement. She was desperate. The entire time she'd given her highly edited version of the day's events to the police, she had been thinking about scrubbing off Peter's touch. She had imagined how clean she'd feel after a hot, soapy shower.

She locked the door. Now she could finally wash. Shedding her clothing quickly, she dropped her sweater set, pleated skirt, bra, and panties in a puddle on the marble-tiled floor. A spray of Peter's dried blood stood out on the white silk of her underwear. She moaned and clutched her stomach. The sound echoed off the walls in the large hard-surfaced bathroom. She was going to be sick again.

"Are you all right?" Marc called from outside the door.

"Yes!" she cried, unhappy he was skulking about, worried about her. "Please let me be by myself. Please."

She gathered the pile of clothing and stuffed them viciously into the miniature trashcan.

Now naked, she examined her arms, her legs, her torso. Fresh bruises crisscrossed her body. After the police had cut off the remains of the black Ethernet cable and scarf, they had advised her to go to the hospital and be examined. She'd refused.

She turned on the shower, making sure the water was scalding and sharp. Stepping in, the water felt like needles against her bruised shoulders. That would wash Peter away. She grabbed a bar of soap and washed her intimate parts. But she could still feel Peter picking and rubbing her there. When would that horrible sensation go away?

She dropped the soap and stroked herself with her fingers, trying to erase Peter's molestation. Faster. Harder. Yes. A big, fat orgasm would be just the ticket. She craved control of her body again. But the more intensely she masturbated, the more elusive pleasure became. Yet she kept at it, rubbing herself to pain. Tears rolled down her cheeks. She sobbed, abrading harder.

Finally, she gave up, and turned the water off. She forced herself to stop crying; she didn't want Marc to come and knock down the door. Not bothering to towel off, she pulled a silk foulard robe from a hook on the door, and put it on. The smooth material clung to her damp body. She tied it tight. At least the throbbing ache she felt was a sensation she'd given herself.

Opening the bathroom door, she found Marc standing in the bedroom, waiting for her, not looking a bit apologetic. She remembered he had stood guard at the bathroom door in the same way at the Vail lodge, after the avalanche. She had started to fall in love with him then. Sadness rippled through her.

Coming closer, he fingered a heavy strand of her wet hair. "How about a drink?" he asked. His eyes were watchful, observant.

"Yeah. That'd be nice."

He dropped her hair. She shuffled into the living room, and sank into one of the ultramodern leather chairs. Too late, she realized the bottom of the silk robe was glued to her wet skin, exposing her bruised inner thigh. She pulled the robe closed. But he had seen. His tension rose another notch.

He brought her a bourbon. She finished it in four gulping swallows.

Standing above her, he stared at the red indented stripes on her wrists. Her anxiety increased. Sooner or later he'd ask her point blank what had happened. And she didn't want to talk about it.

"Another?" he asked, taking the empty glass from her.

"Sure. The light is really hurting my eyes. Can you turn it off or something?"

After he made a drink for them both, he dimmed the light to a comfortable level. He sat down on the low couch across from her, alert, waiting.

"Feeling better?" he asked.

"Yeah," she said. He wouldn't be able to scrutinize her in the dark. "Tell me something, Marc. Frances said you were headed to San Simeon to find me after that phone call. She told me it would take a long time for you to drive down there. And that you'd tear San Simeon apart looking for me. But you came back to the house. You must have figured out it was a ruse."

"The closer to San Simeon I got, the more that phone call bothered me."

"I never made that call, you know."

"That's what kept nagging at me," he said. "According to caller ID you phoned me from Silicon Silk—and that wasn't possible."

"You were positive I couldn't have gained entry to any building on the SSI campus to make that call."

"Yes," he said.

She knew him well enough to realize he would never make excuses or apologize if he thought what he'd done was right at the time. It didn't matter. Her hurt and humiliation about being fired were gone. She'd come to grips with Marc's methods after trying to find Marina at the airport. And she understood him a lot better now that she'd spoken with Frances. He had something to prove about loving, and sometimes that meant running roughshod over her.

"After the funeral Peter stopped in at the company," she said. "He must have called you from there pretending to be me. Peter had no idea you had fired me. And of course I wasn't about to tell him, either. While he was inside SSI making his call, I was sulking in his car hoping the security guards wouldn't come out and take a good look at me."

Though she couldn't see Marc's facial expression in the weak light, his stiff posture told her he was tense, probably contemplating how he'd make up for that indignity without actually apologizing to her.

"Okay, so you figured out I hadn't called you. So what happened next?" she prodded.

"First, I stopped at a pay phone and called you at home. You weren't there, of course. And I couldn't get anything coherent out of Marina."

"Marina!?" So her sister wasn't surrounded by fire, or lying beaten in a hotel room somewhere! She felt profound relief. Marina must have come to her senses and left Jared. "You spoke to her? She was there, at the condo?"

"Yes. And hopping mad at Jared. The poor girl had expected a loving reunion with the father of her child when Jared arrived in Mountain View. Instead all she got was a cracker. His major concern was having her buy him another computer. In between Marina's curses, she warned me that the little shit was heading coastside, hell bent on getting back at me. I guess 'knight' Jared chickened out."

"I can't believe I forgot," she whispered, unnerved by her memory loss. "Marc, Jared was *there*. I think he started the grass fire. Peter shot him dead. I completely forgot to tell the police about Jared."

"It's all right Terra. We can tell the police later."

"I suppose." She took a gulp of her bourbon. Why couldn't she forget about *Peter*? "Um, so after you talked to Marina, you drove back?"

"No. I tried calling Frances at the house. No answer. *Then* I drove back, feeling like I'd been screwed, but I wasn't sure by whom or why. I was making good time until I discovered my land was on fire and I couldn't get to the house by car."

She took a deep, stabilizing breath. "All those people dead. Not that I really care about Jared, but Nancy Beck was someone I really liked and admired. And David Houle. And Steve Myatt. And especially Ray Iverson." She gazed at Marc in the feeble light. "You know, I don't think there ever was a cracker. It was Peter the whole time. An insider, just like I've always said. Peter 'cracked' just to provide a fake suspect and motive for Ray's murder. That's why everything Peter stole was nearly worthless. He didn't want to destroy the company, just kill the shareholders. And that's why he went through such great efforts to let you know the code was stolen. You know, with that message on that sticky note and those e-mails. I'll bet he expected you to inform the shareholders after that first incident. But you didn't."

Marc nodded in agreement.

"But I still don't understand why Peter killed Frances," she said.

"For her equity in the company."

"So SSI had seven shareholders?" she asked.

"Yes."

She sipped her bourbon. Was Frances was about to tell her that she was a shareholder right before they got diverted by a lack of oxygen? But even if Frances was a shareholder, how did killing her help Peter gain control of the company? Terra was still missing

271

something important.

"But that doesn't explain why he killed her," she said, shaking her head. "If I understand the way you set up the company, Peter would have had the right to buy Frances' shares, and so would you. You'd then each own 50% of the company. You'd be at an impasse."

"No. I would be minority shareholder."

With a small moan, she pulled her bare feet up under her. Putting his untouched Scotch down on the coffee table, he got to his feet, filled with restless energy.

"I'd be a lot happier if you'd get yourself looked at," he said. "Let's make sure you don't have any broken bones."

She ignored his request. "Why would you be minority shareholder?"

"My ownership of the company was split with Frances."

"Oh! She got the shares in the divorce settlement."

"No. That wouldn't have been possible. I gave Frances the shares before we got divorced. Our shared ownership of Silicon Silk was made part of the agreement when the company was incorporated."

So that's what Frances was talking about when she went through the "if-onlys" in the well. Frances regretted keeping the shares because she knew that's why Peter intended to kill her.

"Why did you give them to her?"

"Because SSI wouldn't have been possible without her, Terra." His voice was strained. He too, must have realized his role in Frances' death. "She was a loving, supportive woman. Unfortunately, by the time the company was a worthy gift, Frances thought our marriage was dead. She kept the equity in Silicon Silk, though."

"As payment for blood and tears," she mused.

"Frances said that to you?"

"Yeah. We talked when we were in the climbing well together. Of course at the time I didn't know…"

"You mean you were in the climbing room *with* her?" he interrupted. "How did you get out?"

272

"I didn't *get* out. Peter pulled me from the well unconscious, leaving Frances there."

"Unconscious?" he said, agitated. "That settles it, Terra. You're going to the doctor. I'll go get some sweats for you to wear."

"No," she said. "Sit down and talk to me. I... I got caught up in Peter's scheme, and I need to understand it. All of it."

He sat back down on the couch, stiff, coiled tight. "Okay, I'll tell you whatever you want to know. And then we go."

"So because you gave half ownership of the company to Frances at the very beginning, you owned fewer shares of the company than Peter did?"

"Yes."

"After Ray died, Peter owned half of the company. You and Frances together owned the other half. When Frances died, Peter would have had the right to buy out Frances' shares and so would you."

"That's true. But each in proportion to the percentage we already owned. And I owned less than Peter."

She did a quick calculation in her head. "In the end, if he'd succeeded, Peter would have owned two-thirds of the company. You would have owned only one-third."

"Yes."

She pulled her legs out from under her; the pressure of her body was making them sore. "You understand that Peter planned to take the company public when he got control."

"Yes. He had started to make rather bold preparations for that event after Steve died. Which annoyed the hell out me. We had a great many heated arguments."

"Talk about bold; Peter actually claimed that you'd never bolt SSI, even if he did take it public. I didn't believe him."

"Peter was right. I wouldn't have left the company. You don't abandon your child just because he's come under the influence of someone undesirable."

Then Peter's plan was nearly perfect. After killing off four of his partners, without a trace of suspicion on him, Peter would take the company public. The serene CFO would have had his millions, his prestige, his control. Marc would have stayed on as the pained figurehead, dedicated to nurturing his baby against all odds.

"Peter almost got away with it," she said.

"But he didn't."

"No."

Because he had wanted to experience the ultimate with Terra. *He experienced the ultimate all right,* she mused as she rubbed her wrists. She sensed Marc scrutinizing her again.

"I want to know what he did to you," he said. His tone hovered halfway between a demand and a plea.

"You were with me when I told the police," she said with a sigh. "Like I said before, Peter tried to push me off the rails, and I stabbed him with a stylus."

"Yeah," he said. "I heard you say that to the police. Now I want to know what really happened."

"That's what happened."

"Terra, when we approached the house by helicopter, I saw you outside on the balcony. You were tied to the railing. Immobile. Peter couldn't have been trying to push you off when you stabbed him."

She had forgotten Marc had seen her fixed to the rails. She shrugged weakly.

"Did he rape you?" he asked.

She didn't even have a name for what Peter had done. Was it rape? Worse than rape?

"No," she said shortly, pulling her robe tighter. "He didn't. And even if he *had*, Marc, there's nothing you can do to fix it. Peter is dead."

"But you're alive—and hurting," he said, his voice nearly cracking. "I'm worried about you, Sweetheart."

He *knew* Peter had done something terrible to her.

Tears now blinded her. Marc would never give up trying to find out what Peter had done. Not ever. Retreat or compromise just weren't in Marc's nature. He'd say his love made it right, and he'd push and push until she gave into his demands.

But she couldn't tell him. She needed to bury what happened, stamp it out, or it might destroy her. Pulling her hands into the sleeves of the robe, she sensed Marc's resolve.

"Let me get those sweats for you," he said, rising.

If he couldn't find out what happened from her, he'd try to get the information indirectly—from a doctor.

"I wasn't raped. Okay? So I don't need any more of your third degree. And you can stop trying to force me to get examined."

His eyes probed her in the near-darkness. She could feel his anguish, his love for her. He'd never give up.

He knelt in front of her. Very gently, he put his hands on her silk-covered knees. Lowering his voice to a near whisper, he did what she thought was impossible.

"I'm sorry," he said. "I'll stop."

Epilog

"I notice you aren't glued to CNBC like everybody else around here," Terra said to Marc. "So do you still feel like you've shoved your baby bird out of the nest?"

The president of Silicon Silk Inc. regarded her warmly. "It hurts less than I thought it would."

Glad he was taking the IPO so well, she glanced through the windows of his office at the cluster of black buildings that made up SSI. As of this morning, Silicon Silk was a public company. She turned her gaze back to Marc's orderly office. The space still reminded her of the inside of a computer: cold and gray. Today, though, in the middle of the CEO and Chairman's desk sat a brightly-dressed baby. Aurora, Marina's little girl, alternately shook and mouthed the bunch of keys Marc had given her.

"Are you sure Aurora won't cut her mouth with those keys?" she asked.

"Rori will be fine, Sweetheart."

Aurora shook the keys at him, cackling.

Just as on that first day, he had made her espresso. This time, however, the cup and saucer were on the floor, so Aurora wouldn't knock them over.

She stroked the infant's silky white-blonde curls. She'd offered to take care of Aurora while Marina went to take a look at the Child Development Program at San Jose State. Terra was nervous about taking care of Aurora. She just wasn't the mothering type. Luckily Marc was. He'd even been Marina's Lamaze coach.

"Well since you aren't watching CNBC, I guess I'll have to *tell* you," she said. "Last I looked, SSI's stock had gone up 265% since it hit the aftermarket. Impressive, huh? I stopped over at A & C, to see if Lyle was happy to see SLCN on a real ticker. He's ecstatic. We're both betting the stock goes up even higher."

"Don't tell me you bought stock, Terra!"

"Sure I did. Not being an employee of the company, though, I couldn't get on the underwriter's 'friends of SSI' list and so I had to buy the stock from a broker."

"I suspect nepotism would have been enough to get you in on that 'friends of SSI' deal," he teased.

This was the first time Marc had brought up marriage since all hell had broken lose. She'd let his proposal lie all these months, and so had he.

After finishing the interface for Personal Scout, she'd returned to her consulting business in New Orleans. Her business was solid. Personal Scout was going to be an incredible commercial product; she had the name in computational linguistics she always wanted.

Now she commuted back and forth to her office in New Orleans. Being away from Marc had become unbearable. This morning she and Aurora had taken a look at some business rental properties. She signed a contract for a little office in Sunnyvale, as Mountain View turned out to be too pricey. It was time to move her consulting practice to Silicon Valley. After all, the Valley was the lifeblood of her business.

"Speaking of nepotism," she said, "I bought those 200 shares for Aurora. It's her college fund. I've decided she's going to the University of Texas at Austin like I did, and major in computer science."

"Gorgeous cracker-girl, version two-point-oh," he said, laughing. "God help Apple Computer."

She harumphed, and then wagged her finger at him, mock serious. "I want a stock split every year. Minimum 30% yearly return."

"You bet, madam shareholder. I can't believe I'm hearing you say things like 'aftermarket' and 'split.' Or that you'd ever buy an

IPO. I always thought you considered the stock market too risky. And besides, I thought you were scrimping and saving for some bad-ass Cray."

"I am. But I've got this extra money coming in. I'm getting a finder's fee, you know. I've managed to convince Ted Newsom to come back to work for Silicon Silk again."

Aurora threw the keys to the floor, and he retrieved them.

"I'm glad you did," he said. "But even nepotism won't get you a finder's fee. You have to be an employee."

She snorted. "Sheesh, you SSI people sure are snotty bunch of elitists now that you've gone public."

After a good dosing of slobber, Aurora threw the keys down again, squealing. He picked them up, and handed them to the baby.

"You don't suppose that something has happened to gravity, do you, Aurora Justine Breaux?" he asked, cocking his head. "Better test it out."

The baby obliged.

She stood and lifted Aurora up off the desk. "We're going to meet Carolina in the cafeteria. She wants to hold a baby again. Emily is running a mile a minute, and can't be bothered with cuddles anymore. Hey, don't forget your keys are on the floor, and so is my espresso!"

He walked them to the door. He gave her a kiss with the baby sandwiched between them. She got little thrills up and down her body.

She never did tell Marc what Peter had done. But Marc had been patient and sensitive; his care had rewarded them both.

He opened the door. Aurora grinned at him. An expression of serenity and pleasure settled on his face. He was such a gorgeous, kind man. She wondered, as she had the first time she'd met him, why he looked so mean in his photographs.

The announcement of Silicon Silk's IPO had created a big stir; the offering was heavily over-subscribed. Marc became a Valley celebrity of sorts. During the SEC-mandated "quiet period" he even had a photographer or two stalking him. In every published photograph, he looked even meaner than he had before the IPO announcement. Unsmiling, with his black-hole eyes, he seemed to be staring down his competitors: Don't mess with me; I'm tougher than you are.

And he probably was.

But private snapshots were no better. Marina, in particular, loved to tease him about it. He'd shrug it off, claiming he just wasn't photogenic. Terra was secretly embarrassed about Marc's bad pictures. Sally kept asking to see a photo of the man she lived with in California. Terra kept on forgetting. On purpose.

She reached out to caress his cheek. "See you tonight."

When they were alone, she'd tell him she was moving her consulting business to Silicon Valley. She broke into a smile, imagining the tender and creative ways he'd show her his joy. And not one of them photogenic.

We hope you enjoyed this book.

Other titles from Metropolis Ink

METROPOLIS INK

Printed in the United States
5920

9 780958 054348